Copyright © 2025 Keira Montclair

All rights reserved under International and Pan-American Copyright Conventions

By payment of required fees, you have been granted the *non*-exclusive, *non*-transferable right to access and read the text of this book. No part of this text may be reproduced, transmitted, downloaded, decompiled, reverse engineered, or stored in or introduced into any information storage and retrieval system, in any form or by any means, whether electronic or mechanical, now known or hereinafter invented without the express written permission of copyright owner.

**Please Note**

The reverse engineering, uploading, and/or distributing of this book via the internet or via any other means without the permission of the copyright owner is illegal and punishable by law. Please purchase only authorized electronic editions, and do not participate in or encourage electronic piracy of copyrighted materials. Your support of the author's rights is appreciated.

No part of this book may be reproduced or transmitted in any form or by any electronic or mechanical means, including photocopying, recording or by any information storage and retrieval system, without the written permission of the publisher, except where permitted by law.

Cover Design and Interior format by The Killion Group
http://thekilliongroupinc.com

Thank you.

# THE BURDEN OF A Scottish Chieftain

CLANS OF MULL • 2

# KEIRA MONTCLAIR

## Clan Grantham

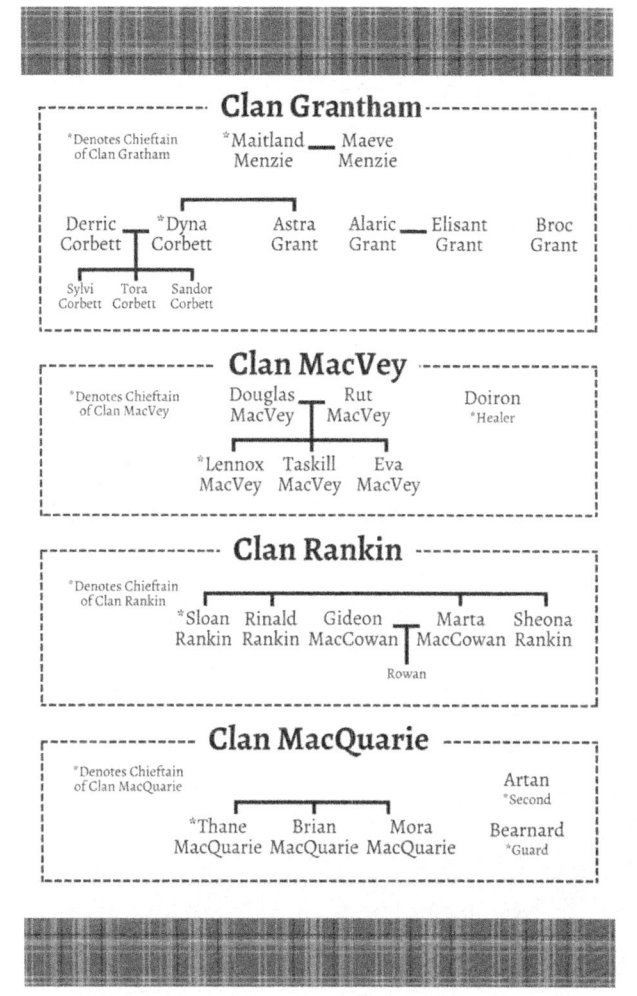

*Denotes Chieftain of Clan Gratham

*Maitland Menzie — Maeve Menzie

Derric Corbett — *Dyna Corbett    Astra Grant    Alaric Grant — Elisant Grant    Broc Grant

Sylvi Corbett    Tora Corbett    Sandor Corbett

## Clan MacVey

*Denotes Chieftain of Clan MacVey

Douglas MacVey — Rut MacVey            Doiron *Healer

*Lennox MacVey    Taskill MacVey    Eva MacVey

## Clan Rankin

*Denotes Chieftain of Clan Rankin

*Sloan Rankin    Rinald Rankin    Gideon MacCowan — Marta MacCowan    Sheona Rankin

Rowan

## Clan MacQuarie

*Denotes Chieftain of Clan MacQuarie

*Thane MacQuarie    Brian MacQuarie    Mora MacQuarie

Artan *Second

Bearnard *Guard

## PROLOGUE

THE MAN KNOWN as Egan strode across the courtyard to the small hut he'd been told to approach, grumbling under his breath. Why did they think he could handle bairns, of all things?

He knocked on the door and when it opened, he stepped inside, waiting for his eyes to adjust to the darkness before he spoke. There were three men inside, two he didn't know and the one he was accustomed to dealing with—the same man he'd dealt with since he left home.

The man was a cruel bastard, but he paid well so Egan continued dealing with him, even after two decades. Egan wiggled his shoulders, a reaction he always had to him, the scars on his back reminding him to do what was necessary in order to prevent any more whippings.

Once in his life was enough.

The man in charge, the one he knew as Karl—not his real name but one he used to protect his true identity—sat in front of the hearth while the other two flanked him, standing at attention, prepared to protect him.

Karl said, "I have news."

"What news, my lord?"

"There's more than one. This time, you have to get more. I want the golden faery, and there's a lad too. And since none of us were prepared for the female archers, I won't hold your failure at Duart against you. I'm giving you one more chance now that you know what you're up against."

"A lad?" Egan asked, doing his best to hide his frustration. This was getting more and more complicated.

"Aye. The lass with the golden hair is the faery, and they say there's a lad with special powers who will be guarded by the fae. That's why you have to take the faery and the lad. She is to protect him and won't leave his side."

"How old is he? What is his name?"

"How the hell would I know? That's why I hire you. Now get out there, get the lass, find out which one is the lad, and I'll handle everything else. If you see the golden-haired lass with a lad, he has to be the gifted one. Find him."

"No names?"

"Nay. Go. You have a sennight to bring them both to me."

Egan nodded, took the coin he was offered as partial payment, their usual arrangement, then took his leave.

Karl called out after him, "Garvie is gone. I'm depending on you."

"Aye, my lord." He gave the answer Karl expected and left.

How he wished he could be done with this.

The truth was that he loved this job. He'd done it for Karl for many years and been paid well. He'd kidnapped young lads and lasses wherever he could find them, turned them over for coin, and didn't care where they went. Oh, there had been a few who had surprised him, some even pissed him off, but none he couldn't handle.

But these young ones he didn't like. When he'd gone to Duart Castle, he'd seen too many, and quite a few of them had golden hair. How was he to know which lass was the right one? And they'd all been under ten summers old. He preferred them to be over ten.

The older ones he could slap, tie them up, even starve them, and they wouldn't be a bother. But these wee ones? The more you hit, the louder they got. If they got hungry, they cried nonstop. He knew there were two golden-haired ones at Duart Castle. He'd seen them both with his own eyes, but he had no idea which one was the faery or which lad to take. There had been several.

He climbed into his boat and rowed toward Mull. He'd find them. As long as he got one of them right, they'd lead him to the others.

Then he'd have the last laugh over those daft bitches at Duart who fired the arrows like they were men. When had women ever been taught to battle like that?

If he were smart, when he finished with the bairns, he'd take a couple of those bitches out, just for daring to fire an arrow at him.

But first, he had to hire more men and scout for some golden-haired lasses.

# Chapter One

*Lennox MacVey*

*Late summer, 1316, the Isle of Mull*

THE TIME HAD come.

Time for Lennox MacVey to go after the villain who had terrorized him years ago or continue to suffer the consequences. Why his conscience sought to haunt him now, he didn't know, but he could no longer ignore it.

His brother Taskill came along to join him at the hearth, his favorite place in the great hall of Dounarwyse Castle to pace. As chieftain of Clan MacVey, Lennox preferred to pace where others wouldn't see him, though it was difficult to do outside of his bedchamber.

The swish of a long gown on the staircase alerted him that his mother, Rut, was near. "What's wrong, Lennox? You're pacing. After all these years, I recognize your habits."

He did not wish to grumble at his mother so he held it in, instead stopping to plant a kiss on her cheek. She was still a vibrant, beautiful woman, her gray hair held in a bun at the back of her head, her gowns specially made in Edinburgh. She was a wealth of information, and Lennox had depended on her vast knowledge ever since his father Douglas's passing two years ago.

"How are you this morn, Lennox, truly?" she repeated. She expected a reply, including a full explanation. His mother would not allow him to escape with anything less.

His sister Eva joined them, and since the servants were busy cleaning up in the kitchens after the midday meal, readying the evening supper, the family were now the only ones in the hall.

But then Taskill smiled and said, "I think I'm needed at the gates." He disappeared, something he did well. Taskill never liked confrontation, especially when it involved their mother. His brother preferred to spend his time flirting with the clan's various lasses. He was a favorite among the girls, his light brown hair falling in waves to his collar, his green eyes sparkling whenever a lass came close. Lennox was accustomed to his mother's interference and didn't mind confrontation at all.

His sister was a quiet beauty with hair the color of the finest chestnut. She kept her emotions well hidden but liked to keep up on the clan events, something his brother wasn't always interested in. "Are you pacing again, Lennox? Why?" Eva asked, stopping to whirl her skirts first. A smile erupted as she watched the fabric fly about her heels, the rippling effect making her giggle.

"I have no reason," Lennox replied. "I just

needed to move my legs. I'm about to patrol our lands and the path for a bit. I was trying to decide which neighbor I would prefer to visit. It is a fine day for a ride. Mayhap I'll visit our neighbors at Clan Grantham."

His mother crossed her arms and said, "And I know that for the bull that it is. You need to face the situation and make a choice. Either accept the fact that your kidnapping happened a long time ago, so it is not worthy of your concern, or go after the feeble-minded bastard. You've ignored it for too long."

"Mother, as mistress of the clan, your language could be better." He didn't wish to admit that for so many years, he'd blocked out the memory of the trauma he'd suffered as a child. Only recently had it all come back to him, though why now, he had no idea.

"And you are the chieftain of this clan. Do you not agree that it is time you stop allowing that villainous soul to monopolize your mind? How often do you think about it? Answer honestly, please."

He would never admit to anyone how often he thought of the long-ago debacle. But the most difficult memory of the entire event was nearly nonexistent. It wasn't that he didn't recall it happening. The fear that coursed through him at the mention of it was something that riddled him frequently, but the details had mostly disappeared, as if his mind didn't want him to recall all that happened. And for some odd reason, as of late, it had crept into his mind more often than it had in the past. But at least now, he had a good idea of the villain's identity instead of just an inkling, one that haunted him repeatedly.

Each year of his life since then had added a piece of the mystery back. This year had brought the villain's face back to him. He knew the vehicle—a boat—and now the guilty party. How he wished he could recall all of it.

Why now? That was the question that forced him to pace.

Rut's slipper tapped on the stone floor. "Never mind. There is a more important matter at stake. I'm giving you one year to find a bride, or I'll find one for you," she stated, her fists now settled on her thin hips, her chin lifted defiantly.

Lennox laughed, shocked that she would construct such a ridiculous premise. "Mother, please. How can you say such a thing? And what would make you even suggest such an odious plan? I'll not marry your choice. I'll choose my own bride." He was aware that time was wasting. It was time for him to find a wife, but he had never met anyone he was remotely interested in.

Fortunately, the door opened, and his brother saved him from having to answer her question.

Taskill, pausing just inside the door to catch his breath, said, "Messenger from Clan Rankin. You'll wish to hear this."

Four serving lasses had already entered from the kitchens, one letting out a giggle when Taskill winked at her. He was the lasses' favorite, by far, and they had the odd ability to sense when he was around. It was as if he whistled to call them to his attention.

People considered Lennox to be too cold, too harsh, too whatever.

"Go on," Lennox said, giving Taskill his complete attention.

"Marta's son Rowan has been stolen. He was hunting with his uncle, they shot a deer, and as they went to retrieve it, another horse broke out, spooking the horse and sending Rowan into the air. He fell a distance away, and a strange rider flew out and took him. They've searched everywhere but cannot find him."

"Why did the messenger tell us about this?" Rut asked.

Taskill shrugged. "He's asking for our help. Wants us to send a patrol toward Ben More while they search their area."

"Taskill, the men, and do not stray after a light skirt. Eva, pull all the mothers and bairns inside the castle walls until I find out more. We cannot risk having any of our bairns stolen away."

Taskill left with a quick nod.

Lennox turned to his sister and said, "Eva, go to the village first and get them inside immediately. Then you may need to help some mothers with young bairns inside. Open the hall for them. Mother will have Cook make extra pottage for the evening meal."

"And we'll need more goat's milk. I'll take care of it," Rut said.

His mother gave him that look he knew well,

the one that told him she had much to say, but she would wait until they were alone.

And he knew exactly what she would say. Something about his past, something about taking care of unfinished business. She always told him so. The same thing she'd started their conversation with a short while ago.

Once they were alone, she didn't wait long. "Lennox MacVey, you need to settle this. Find him and put an end to this. You do realize the person who stole Rowan away could be the man you met so long ago. In fact, the more I think on it, the more I'm convinced it must be the same man. You need to set your mind to remembering everything."

"Mother, that was years ago. What makes you think it would be him?"

"Because it's the same time of the year. Late summer. It happens every year, or have you not noticed? A few older bairns go missing and no one knows where. You need to tell someone. And figure it out. You are an intelligent man, Lennox, yet you allow this event to control your life. It has for years. Do not try to deny it."

He paused, then admitted, "You are not wrong. I've had more nightmares than ever about that man. In fact, I searched for him not long ago, only to learn he's on the move, though I'm not sure where."

"Why did you not tell me this before?"

"Because I was unsuccessful in my search. I don't know where he is."

"At least you have tried. Now you must go

deeper. This pain will not leave you. Trust me that as you grow older, it will only haunt you more." She then used her perfect spin to lead herself back to the kitchens. "I'm going to the goatherd."

Good.

He hated it whenever he had to tell his mother she was right. Which was probably why he never did, but she was right.

It was time to find out who liked to terrorize the people on the Isle of Mull every summer.

## Chapter Two

*Meg*

---

MEG BEATON HID behind the door in her bedchamber, her ear to the rough wood surface. Ever since her sister Tamsin had been sent off to marry someone on the Isle of Ulva, Meg had hated her life. She worked all day, her nails sometimes bleeding from washing clothes and pulling garden weeds. Then her father would come home at night and check her work, decide if she deserved to be punished or not. Too often, he felt she deserved a slap or a paddle from the board, whatever struck him at the moment.

A small knife stuck in her belly whenever a vision of her sister Tamsin popped into her head. At this point, Meg should be used to her being gone, but she was not. Without her sister to hold her hand when she cried or to listen to her fears in the dead of night, she had become a shell of her former self.

Alone and unloved.

Ever since their mother died when Meg was seven, life had become miserable simply because their father was miserable. If she had any idea how to find her dear sister, she'd run away, but her father had threatened her, saying he'd call the sheriff to lock her up if she ever tried to escape. She didn't think her life could be any worse.

She had the oddest feeling that it was about to turn worse because her father had a visitor, something she hadn't seen since Tamsin left.

The worst part? It was a man. An older man.

Her heart pounded so in her chest that it interfered with her ability to hear the conversation in the main room.

"How long will it take you to have her ready, Henry?"

"My lord, I can have her ready to travel with you on the morrow. She's young, so I must prepare her for this event." Meg's father cleared his throat twice.

What event? Meg thought hard but couldn't recall any mention of a change in their usual daily chores.

"I've been searching for a suitable young bride for a while, so do not disappoint me. I need her with child within two moons. I want at least three heirs. I'll allow her one female, so perhaps four. It would behoove me to think of her duties, and a daughter could assist her. I would prefer my wife to only spend her time taking care of my needs. You understand, of course."

*Wife?*

The pounding of her heart became a thunderstorm in an instant.

*Wife?*

Meg flopped onto her bed before her knees buckled. Had she heard him right? A baron wished to take her as a bride?

She hurried back to the door, opening it a bit to peek out at the man. If he was handsome and kind and loving, perhaps her life was about to improve immensely.

He was none of those things.

The baron stood half a head taller than her father, his hair gray and balding, with a thick neck. As she was unable to see his eyes directly, she had to pray they would be kind. His nose resembled a bird's beak, and his belly protruded enough that his hands could rest there comfortably, though he had a habit of swinging them oddly when he spoke, as though the motion gave his words a semblance of importance.

Her father turned toward her bedchamber, and she jumped back from the door just before it sprung open. "Margret, come meet your betrothed. He will come for you on the morrow and take you to the church in England, where you will become his wife."

Church in England? Where was England? She had no idea since she'd never traveled more than a quarter day from their home.

*One, two, three...* Her fingers ticked by her side.

"Stop it," her father hissed quietly, his gaze dropping to her hands. "Do not act foolish."

How could she explain to her father that counting calmed her? It was something she did whenever she was uncertain of the outcome of a situation. Her father knew this about her. He'd heard her count whenever he hit her with the paddle.

When she stood in front of the man, her father said, "This is Baron Neville de Wilton. You should refer to him as 'my lord.' He has chosen you to be his wife. His baroness."

"Come over here, lass. I'd like to see you up close. See exactly what I'm purchasing." He took two steps toward her and waited for her to come to him.

She glanced at her father, who propelled her forward then said, "I shall return in a moment." He stepped out the back door, leaving the two alone.

"Greetings, my lord," she said, counting under her breath, her fingers kneading her gown to match the count.

"My, but your sire was not lying. You are a comely lass. Your hair is a bit red for my liking, but you have pretty green eyes. Forgive my intrusion, but I wish to learn more about you." He stepped closer and palmed her breasts through her gown.

Meg pushed his hands away, incensed that he dared to touch her there. He grabbed her wrists and squeezed.

"Do not ever push me away. Once we are married, you will do everything I say, when I want and what I want. Do you understand me?"

She nodded, just so he'd release her arms. *Twenty, twenty-one, twenty-two.*

He squeezed her breasts again and then walked around her. "Stay there. Do not move." His hands went to the globes of her bottom, squeezing there as well. "Very nice. You will suit me nicely."

She wished to put her fist in his face.

He came around to the front again and stood too close, so close that she could smell something rancid. She brushed her finger against the bottom of her nose as if to protect her from the odor, but it did little to help her. He leaned forward, pulled her hand down and kissed her, his tongue pushing against the seam of her lips until she opened them. He tasted of sour ale and rabbit, something that nearly made her heave, but she was afraid to push away.

She was eternally grateful for her father's entrance again. The baron stepped away at the sound of the door opening.

Her father stared at her, then at the baron. "Well?"

"She'll suit me fine. I'll return on the morrow for her," he said, taking a small bow to her and saying, "Until then, my dear."

He exited while she froze in her spot, but her sire followed him out. The baron bellowed at his men, ordering them about to assist him onto his horse.

Meg could only think of one truth.

She'd never marry that pig.

Given no other option, she'd have to run away. Soon.

## Chapter Three

*Dyna*

Dyna rushed her mount up the hill, though the beast wasn't as excited as she was. She had to see the view from the top, looking for the ship Maitland had just boarded. It was the last month of summer, and Maitland's wife Maeve would be having their bairn any day now. She smiled, happy for Maitland after losing his first wife when the two had been imprisoned by the English in a dungeon years ago.

It was time for Maitland to have some happiness in his life. She'd learned a few months ago that Maitland's son was to be under her wing. Dyna had been a protector of her grandfather from the very beginning.

Then she'd learned a while ago that she had three others to protect: Alaric, Eli, and Maitland's unborn son. She hadn't told anyone but Derric and Maitland, but she was pleased that she would meet the new laddie in another moon, probably. He wouldn't travel with the bairn until Maeve and the child were ready.

"Derric, I cannot wait to see Maitland with his son, can you?"

He nodded, then pointed. "Over there, Sandor. See the boat?"

Sandor giggled and pointed while Dyna turned to her sister behind her. "Astra, over there. Can you see it, Tora?"

Tora rode with Astra while Sylvi rode in front of Dyna. They had four guards along with them.

The ship moved on, and they reached the section of the path that traveled alongside the forest. "I hate this part, Derric. We need more men. I sent a message to my father to send more."

"I know. I was disappointed we only gained ten from the villages. Said many of the men had taken on working for someone else. We do what we can."

"After that issue in the beginning of summer when we were attacked, and I heard one man say they wanted the lass, I don't trust anyone or anything. I wish to be inside those thick curtain walls."

"We're nearly there." He pointed at the juncture ahead where the path split, one route going on toward the far coastline, and the other section going toward the point and Duart Castle.

Derric grabbed the reins and unsheathed his sword in one swift movement, yelling, "Diamond! Get to the castle!"

The four guards went after the five men who had come out of the forest on horseback, galloping straight for them. One voice carried over the others, something Dyna hated to hear. "The lasses! Get them!"

"Astra, go to the castle! Hurry!"

Astra did her best to lead the mare in that direction, but one man grabbed the reins of her horse and led the beast into the forest.

"Astra! Jump off!" Dyna had never felt such panic. She pulled out her bow and aimed, knocking one man off his mount, but not the one taking Astra's horse. She couldn't get a clear shot. Chaos surrounded them—swords clashing, grunts of pain, and men swinging weapons with a fury. They had taken two of the men off their horses quickly, but when the one led Astra into the woods, two others replaced him, swinging their weapons.

Derric handed Sandor to Dyna and said, "Take Sylvi and Sandor to the castle. We have to protect them. The guards will come with me to go after Astra and Tora."

She nodded and grabbed Sandor, her eyes checking him over for any blood but seeing none. "Bad men, Mama."

"Aye," she said, rushing toward the gates, yelling at Alaric when she neared the wall. "Astra and Tora were taken, Alaric. In the woods!"

The gates opened immediately, and she rode straight to the keep while Alaric and Broc mounted up and headed out. Alaric called to her in passing, "We'll get them, Dyna."

The door to the keep opened, and Eli ran down the steps. "What happened?"

"Take Sandor and Sylvi inside and lock the

doors. Attack by half a dozen men. They took Astra's horse into the woods. Tora is with her."

"Go, Dyna!" Eli said, lifting the two bairns down and following them into the keep. "I've got them. Go!"

Dyna turned her horse back around, pausing for a moment to close her eyes, hoping her skills as a seer would help her find her sister and daughter. All she saw was Astra on the ground. "Open the gate!" she shouted as soon as she got close enough for them to hear her.

She charged out again, yelling, "Close it now!" to the men behind her. Galloping toward the forest, she headed into the woods. The thick pines and bushes could hide anyone. Crashing through the brush, Midnight Moon flew across the path until she caught up with the others.

They were coming toward her, and without a child.

"Nay…" Her belly dropped with such a dread that she nearly gagged with fear.

"Diamond, we've looked everywhere." Derric shook his head. "They disappeared. We've got to make a plan and search the entire area. Did you get the others inside? Are the gates locked?"

"Aye, Eli has them, but Astra and Tora—we have to find them." Sick with worry, she scanned the area.

Alaric said, "Close your eyes, see what you see, Dyna. We'll wait."

Dyna had the reputation as a seer among the people she knew, but it was difficult when her emotions overpowered her. The connection didn't work then, but she stopped her horse, her gaze again searching the area, looking for any sign of the lasses. Then she closed her eyes, overcome by a shadow. She opened her eyes and shouted, "Over there!"

Derric headed in that direction and Dyna followed. A flash of green caught her eye in the bushes. She jumped off her horse and moved over to the spot, squealing, "It's Astra. Astra, are you all right?" She knelt next to her sister, feeling the inside of her wrist for the blood in her body.

But she was not awake.

"Derric, she's alive, but I don't see Tora. Find her, please, Derric."

Alaric said, "Her horse. I see him." He pointed and headed that way, Derric behind him.

Broc dismounted and said, "Allow me, Dyna. I'll get her."

He lifted Astra, and they managed to get back on their horses, Astra leaning against Dyna. "Astra, wake up. Please."

Derric returned with Astra's mount, shaking his head.

"Nay, nay…"

Astra opened her eyes and lifted her head.

"Astra?" Dyna asked. "Are you all right?"

"They took her! They knocked me off the horse and took Tora. Oh, my Lord in heaven, please help us. Tora! Tora!"

Tora had disappeared.

## Chapter Four

### *Meg*

MEG HADN'T SAID much to her father because she knew it would be a waste of time. She'd asked only one question: "Why?"

"Because it's time. You need to marry. Have a life away from here. Like your sister. She's probably living a happy life with two bairns by now. You could be in the same situation in two years, if you give it a chance."

*Away from you* is how she interpreted his reply.

There would be no arguing, so she had only one alternative. She would have to run away in the middle of the night. Grateful that her father said he had much to do outside, she spent time in her bedchamber, packing a small sack to take with her, hiding it under the pile of clothes she had yet to wash.

There were only three horses, but one was supposed to belong to her, so she would take that one. Big Blue wasn't the fastest horse, but she would get Meg to her destination.

That was her biggest question.

Finished with her packing, she stepped back into the main chamber, wondering where exactly she would go. She didn't know anyone other than the few neighbors in the small nearby village. And no one there would help her.

Many years ago, when her mother was still alive, they attended a church about an hour away, but that would be too close now. Her father would search for her and discover if she were nearby. It had to be farther away. She glanced into a small bowl on the side table, then reached for the one thing she would add to her travels.

Her sister's bracelet. Tamsin had made it for Meg years ago from a fine yarn she'd found, winding it into a circle of tiny, light-blue loops. She'd made herself a matching one and they'd vowed to wear them whenever they were together. Meg hadn't worn it since Tamsin left. Since Tamsin's departure, the bracelet had sat here in the bowl of collectibles, attracting dust with the other pieces. Meg picked it up and moved back into her bedchamber to tuck it into her bag.

Her father came in and stood just inside the door, staring at her. "Look, lass. It may not be the best match, but he'll not live long. Once he goes, you'll be a baroness and will be able to do whatever you wish. You'll have a couple of bairns, and you'll be happy then. Your mother adored you two girls. I'm sorry I couldn't do more for you. Just be a good girl and all will be fine."

She nodded, not knowing what else to say. "I'm tired. May I go to my chamber, Papa?"

"You'll need a good night's sleep, I'm guessing."

He waved her on, so she moved into her chamber, closing the door softly behind her. There was one other thing she had to get before she left.

Her axes. She had two of different sizes.

She and Tamsin had practiced using an axe long ago. Tamsin had been a total failure at it, but Meg had learned to use it well. If she hadn't learned, they'd not have eaten as well over the years. Her skill had branched from rabbits to deer, to her father's delight, though they had little ability to smoke much meat here. He'd taken it to the village smoker, though they had to share with the other villagers, but deer meat was the best of all.

In fact, that was the time they'd met the wee lass named Alana. She'd been seven summers and had cute blond curls. When they left, Tamsin had whispered to her, "Someday when I marry, I'm going to have a wee lass and I'll call her Alana, just like that girl. Was she not precious?"

Meg had never given any thought to having bairns or getting married.

She listened to her father fiddle in the main chamber. She knew he would then sit, read the Bible by candlelight, then go in to find his bed.

She planned to give herself another hour before she dared sneak away.

Resting on the bed, she counted in her mind the same way she always did. Numbers calmed her. Ever since her mother had taught them numbers, she'd loved them. In fact, long ago, she and Tamsin would play adding games. If one had twenty and you gained thirty, then how many would one have? After a bit of help, Meg taught

Tamsin how to do it easily in her head. Adding was fun.

*One and twenty mixed with seven would give you...*

Much later, Meg bolted up in bed, shocked that she'd fallen asleep. It was still dark out. She moved the fur back from her window after climbing off the bed, shivering as she stared up at the moon.

It was time to go.

She crept out, not making a sound with the door because it had never latched, then tiptoed across the floor, her bag in hand. She grabbed her mantle and a scarf, one of the lap furs by the hearth, then crept outside. She'd donned a pair of trews she often used when gardening, tucking two gowns into her bag along with her underclothing and a comb with a few slivers of soap. Lifting her axes from the rock outside, she wrapped both in the sheath, then in a heavy fabric, and hung them from the saddle along with her bag. She took some food for her mare, then a deep breath, and set off down the path.

While she questioned which direction to head, she knew only one thing about Tamsin. Her husband lived on the Isle of Ulva.

Meg had no choice. She headed toward the sea with the few coins she'd saved tucked away for a ferry to get her to Ulva.

Wherever that was.

She had no idea.

## Chapter Five

*Thane*

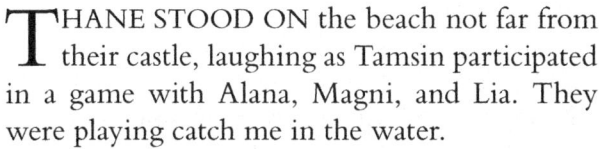

THANE STOOD ON the beach not far from their castle, laughing as Tamsin participated in a game with Alana, Magni, and Lia. They were playing catch me in the water.

"My do it? Pweez?" asked wee Alana, already soaked from head to toe.

"We'll move in, Magni. Give her a chance." She turned to her daughter, bending down to her level. "All you have to do is touch us and you will win, lassie. That's the game," her mother said, chuckling as her daughter headed straight for her.

"I get you, Mama."

Tamsin ran away from her, but slowly, so her daughter could catch her, if Thane were to guess. He'd never known such happiness as the day Tamsin entered his life. Well, once she'd gotten away from that cruel husband of hers. Alana was as sweet as could be, and watching Tamsin with the three bairns warmed his heart.

He'd once wondered if he even had a heart to warm. No more. She'd warmed every part of him until he'd fallen in love with her. Something that had pleased his sister as much as anyone. Mora had whispered to him, "I knew it. You are perfect together, Thane."

Brian had drawled, "Good. Now mayhap we can allow some lasses around once in a while. I'd like to marry someday." Thane had hated their mother so much that he refused to allow women in the keep, except for them to share in a meal. Things changed after he met Tamsin, to his siblings' delight.

Mora came flying down the beach and shouted, "Get me, Alana! Come catch me!"

Tamsin whirled around to see Mora, then tripped and fell into deeper water, going under with a sputter. Thane nearly got his boots wet to chase after her, but her confidence in the water had grown much, thanks to his help. Instead, she popped her head above the surface and said, "I'm fine, Thane!"

She giggled as Alana launched herself at her mother with a squeal. "Got you, Mama."

"You did get me, sweetum. Now go for Magni."

Lia made her way back toward Thane, saying, "I have a chill. The water is a wee bit cool."

Thane said, "I'll stay out with you, Lia. They can have their fun. I still don't trust the area." He glanced over his shoulder, pleased to see Brian talking with another guard, Bearnard. Thane wouldn't go anywhere outside the walls without guards.

Lia said, "We are all happy now, and I thank you for that, my lord."

"You are a large part of that happiness, little lady."

"Aye, but please understand that some things must happen. In order for everything to work the way the heavens wish, things often go awry. Fear not—all will be well, eventually."

He scowled, wishing to ask for more of an explanation for such an odd comment, but he sensed something behind him. A sudden chill ran up his spine because he knew it was more than the slight rustle of a squirrel scampering in the leaves. The vibration in the ground of large animals was too heavy and came from far away.

"Tamsin, get Alana and come here, please." He wasn't going to wait to see what it was.

A wee puppy ran straight toward them, drawing Alana's attention. Her chubby legs churned toward the animal, and her giggles carried everywhere, even over her mother's shouts for her daughter not to chase after the small dog. Thane was about to go after her when he heard shouts from Brian. Several mysterious horsemen came at them from three different directions and they wore no plaids, an indication of someone not of the isle. Who they were and what they were doing near his land he didn't know, but he wouldn't wait to find out. He had to get the wee ones to safety first.

"Go to the keep, Magni. Grab Lia and get on the horse and go!"

Tamsin screamed but was caught in her gowns. "Alana, nay!"

Thane went after Alana, reaching her just before one of the horsemen did, scooping her up with one arm. His weapon was at the ready, and he swung his sword so hard he nearly took off the man's arm, causing him to drop his weapon.

"Mora, run!"

Mora had her bow at the ready, firing as she hurried toward the castle while Brian and the other guard went after two men.

Thane grabbed Alana out of the path of the next intruder, then turned to Tamsin and pulled her close to him. He turned around to look for the others, though he only had two hands. "Magni, hurry!" But his warning was too late, and he was too far away to stop the bastards.

Two men grabbed Magni and Lia, then took off into the woods.

"I'll protect her, Thane. Do not worry!" Magni shouted after them.

Brian and Bearnard headed after the two men with the bairns.

Thane tossed Tamsin and Alana on one horse, slapping the animal's flank to send them toward the castle gates, then mounted his own steed. He set off toward the castle and leaned over to grab his sister just before another charging horse reached for her. He swung her up roughly, but he caught her, and she hung on tightly. Once she was behind him, the other man turned tail and left.

"Brian, I'll be right behind you."

He had to get Mora, Tamsin, and Alana safely inside the curtain wall before he could leave. Who were the men? He'd just begun to feel safe again after the failed attack on Duart Castle.

Killing MacDougall and Raghnall Garvie hadn't put an end to their terror.

What the hell did they want with the bairns?

Once they were inside the gates, he spoke to Artan, "Let no one in. I'm going after the men who stole Lia and Magni. Do not leave here, Artan. You are in charge."

Mora hugged him. "Please save them, Thane. We need Magni and Lia. They are such an important part of our clan."

He helped Tamsin down and she cupped his cheeks. "Many thanks to you for Alana. Now go save those wee ones." She gave him a quick kiss and he left, glad to hear the gates close behind his departure.

Where the hell would they be taking the two?

He found the path where Brian and Bearnard had gone. It took nearly half the hour to catch up with them, but they had both stopped in a clearing, scanning the area.

Bearnard was shaking his head. "Chief, they disappeared. I have no idea where they are. We saw one horse, but they split, and we must have followed the wrong one."

Brian rubbed his chin. "What do we do now?"

Thane searched the area briefly, then said, "We go back. I'm leaving you all at the castle to protect what is ours. To protect Mora and Alana. Get all the guards' families out of their homes and bring all the women and bairns inside the keep. There's room. We must warn the others that the men looking for lasses are back. I'll go to Clan

Grantham to see if anyone else has had trouble. We need more men than we have."

On the way back to the keep, all he could think of were Lia's last words to him.

*Fear not—all will be well, eventually.*

How he prayed she was right.

## Chapter Six

*Lennox*

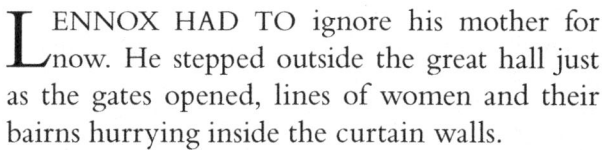

---

LENNOX HAD TO ignore his mother for now. He stepped outside the great hall just as the gates opened, lines of women and their bairns hurrying inside the curtain walls.

"Many thanks to you, Chief," one said, and then another and another.

He nodded to each one and said, "Come in where it's warm. We'll have pottage and bread for you. Be careful as you go up the steps."

Lennox neared the gates, and Taskill yelled down, "Outside. The Granthams are here."

This could not be good. He couldn't recall the last time they had come along for a friendly visit other than after they'd moved in.

Eva's voice carried to him. "I'm coming too. I wish to be aware of all that is happening. I have a bad feeling, Lennox. Don't tell Mama."

He ushered Eva through the crowd of villagers coming inside the curtain wall, the curiosity on each face as clear as could be. They had no idea what had transpired.

Dyna Grant was off to the side, trying to stay a distance away. "Please, we need your help."

"I'd say to come in, but I just invited all the women and bairns inside."

"No time for sitting, anyway. My daughter was kidnapped. Please help me find her." Dyna's face was so fear-stricken that Lennox wished to bring her inside, but she wouldn't be getting off her horse.

"Come, I have an empty cottage out here. We can chat there. It's starting to rain." He helped Dyna dismount, and two men also dismounted, motioning for the others to stay where they were. They had brought another ten guards. Too many for a visit.

Dyna said, "This is Alaric, in charge of our guards, and Broc, his second. We left my husband and Alaric's wife home with the other bairns. They'll not step outside the gates."

Lennox led the way, saying, "You are not alone. It happened to Sloan's sister. Her son of six winters is missing."

Dyna said, "Bloody hell! What is wrong with these bastards?"

They were about to go into the cottage when they heard another group of horses approach. Lennox guessed it to be Sloan and his men, but he was wrong. Thane MacQuarie appeared, his brother behind him, along with a few guards, and he had the same look on his face.

"We need your help."

Lennox waved to Thane in the rain. "Come

inside. Send your guards into the stables to keep dry."

Thane approached, Brian accompanying him.

Once inside, Lennox pulled out stools from a storage closet. The house was larger than most. Eva had followed and said under her breath, "Whose cottage is this, Lennox?"

He gave her a small smile and said, "Mine. When I need quiet." He knew his way around and sent Taskill to build the fire while he opened a bottle of wine and offered it or mead to everyone.

Eva arched a brow but said nothing. Once they'd all settled, Lennox said, "Marta Rankin's son was stolen early this morning." He nodded to Dyna, giving her the next chance to speak.

"Someone stole my daughter too. They tried to grab all of them, but we kept Sylvi and Sandor away. They grabbed my sister's horse, led it into the woods. We found Astra later on the ground with her horse nearby, but Tora, the middle one, is missing. I've never felt so powerless. What do you suggest?"

Lennox put up his hand, motioning her to hold her tongue so Thane could speak next.

Thane said, "Some men stole Magni and Lia too. We were on the beach. They tried for Tamsin's daughter and for Mora, but we saved them. We were too late for Magni and Lia. Five men survived to take them into the woods."

The door opened, and Sloan Rankin entered. "How many others are missing?"

"Three," Lennox replied. "Two from MacQuarie and one of Dyna's daughters."

"I'll kill them all when we find them." Dyna couldn't stop pacing.

Members of the group talked over one another, guessing who it could be, how to attack the problem, but there was no final agreement on who could be at fault.

Lennox held up his arms to quiet the group, then said, "We have to search the entire isle. I'll start by searching the ports. Find out who has been in and out. We need to determine if they are still on Mull or if they've left."

Thane said, "So we divide up the search? How many are we taking total, so we can divide evenly? Do you not agree? You have more men than I do."

Sloan said, "I have three score ready to go."

Lennox said, "I have two score."

Dyna said, "We have a score between us." She pointed to Thane. "We need more. I sent word to my sire."

"Who is your sire?" Sloan asked.

"Connor Grant."

"The chieftain?"

"The old chieftain. New co-lairds have started. So, trust me that my father will bring a powerful group too. I left my husband and Eli back to talk with them when they arrive. I sent a message a sennight ago that we needed more guards. I hope they're on their way soon."

Lennox pulled out a map from a cabinet in the chamber, then called Dyna, Sloan, and Thane over. "Let's divide this way." The chieftains made their plans, but then Lennox turned back to the group. "Any identifying plaids, marks, any horses you recognized? Does anyone have a clue who is doing this?"

Sloan said, "Small stallions with no identifying plaids. They were dressed in black. The only other thing I noticed was one was bald."

Lennox nodded, then pointed to Thane. "What did the men near you look like? Mayhap they sounded like the men near Dyna. We must learn how many we are fighting."

Dyna shouted, "Aye! Same men. Brown haired, brown beard, but the one was bald with a dark beard, and both dressed in all black. They must be the same men. Anyone familiar with a similar group?"

Lennox waited, but when there was no response, he said, "My guess is they were hired to do the deed. Once they deliver the bairns, they'll be gone. We have to approach this as a search for the bairns. If we look for certain men, we will surely fail."

Dyna said, "At least Tora is not alone. If she's with Magni and Lia, they'll find a way out."

"How can you be so certain?" Sloan asked. "My nephew, Rowan, was kidnapped, and he's six winters. How old are yours?"

"Magni is ten, Lia five, and Tora is nearly four."

"How can you possibly believe four bairns that age will escape their captors?"

Dyna said, "Because Tora is a seer."

Thane said, "Allow me to share what Lia said to me moments before their capture. She said, 'Please understand that some things must happen.

In order for everything to work the way the heavens wish, things often go awry. Fear not—all will be well, eventually.'"

"What the hell does that mean coming from a child?" Sloan asked in nearly a shout. "Are you daft?"

Dyna said, "Lia is more than a child."

Lennox gave her a quizzical look because he had no idea what that meant. "Explain, please."

Dyna cleared her throat. "I think Lia is a faery in disguise. She's the one they're after. I think they believe she is the green maiden of the forest. The one who can grant wishes."

Sloan threw his hands up in the air. "Now you are all sounding daft. A seer? A faery? A maiden of the forest who grants wishes? You've all lost your minds."

"Why do you say that?" Eva asked, her hands going to her hips. "You never believe anything other than what's in front of you, Sloan."

"Because there are no faeries or seers. This discussion has come up among my clan members for years, but I've yet to see any evidence of it."

Dyna paced in a circle, then sat again. "Tora once came and told me a 'bad man' was coming for me moments before he showed up. I'm a seer, and she's my daughter. It makes sense that she has the same abilities."

"Anyone can be a bad man," Sloan declared.

Eva crossed her arms and said, "Stop being so divisive and ignorant. There are seers. Many of them."

"Name one."

Five people shouted and pointed at the same time. "Dyna!"

"What have you ever done because of that ability?"

"I saw where my sister was lying in the grass after being thrown from a horse. I saw it in my mind and pointed in that direction. We found her exactly where I said she would be, unable to speak."

"Sounds like luck to me," Sloan said, grumbling under his breath.

Eva gave his arm a shove. "Stop it and believe her. It wouldn't hurt you to believe in someone for a change, someone other than yourself."

Sloan glared, but Lennox stepped in. "Leave her be. She's trying to help everyone. We have three paths. Which one do you want?"

They divvied up the paths nearby, hoping they'd cover the entire area. Lennox was sending Taskill to his assigned area with ten guards. He also assigned ten guards to go with Thane and ten to go with Dyna. That left thirty to protect the castle.

He was headed across the sound with a creeping suspicion who was causing all the problems. A man named Egan who was still haunting him, even in his sleep.

## Chapter Seven

*Magni*

---

Magni glanced from Rowan to Lia, wondering how they were going to get out of this locked chamber. He had no idea where they were, and neither did the others.

The door opened, and another bairn was tossed inside before the door closed behind her. Now who?

"Tora? Is that you?" Lia asked.

"It is Tora!" Magni had never been so happy to see someone.

Tora ran straight to Lia and hugged her. "Gweetings, Lia. Why are you hewe?" Then she hugged Magni before turning to Rowan and said, "I'm sowwy you were taken away when you were hunting with your uncle."

Rowan cast a suspicious look at her. "How did you know I was hunting? I don't even know you."

"Because I saw you hewe." She pointed to her forehead.

Magni grabbed Tora and pulled on her hands. "Will we get away?"

She shook her head and answered, "I'm not suwe."

"Why not?" Magni asked.

"We go away."

"What? Where are they taking us?" Rowan's eyes misted.

"I not suwe, but I know we will leave hewe," Tora said, making a spot to sit down. She pulled out a chunk of dried meat and shared it with the others. "Fiwst, we go to the chuwch."

"What church?" Rowan asked. "I want to go home now." His lips puckered as if he were about to cry.

Lia said, "I have faith that we will be saved in a short time. Not right away, but in a wee bit."

"Are you certain?" Magni asked. "If they come eventually, I'll be able to handle this." He chewed on the dried meat. "Even if I am scared."

Tora said, "When I see it, I will let you know. Do not wowwy, Magni." She tipped her head down and gave him a kiss on the cheek. "I think someone will save us."

"Eww," Magni whined, dragging the back of his hand across his cheek. "No kisses."

Tora giggled.

Lia said, "Magni, think about it. Where are we from?"

"Clan MacQuarie," he replied, giving her a puzzled look. He had no idea where she was going with this.

"Rowan, where are you from?"

"Clan Rankin." He stood up with a bit of

excitement and said, "I get it. Tora, where are you from?"

"Clan Gwantham and Clan Gwant."

Rowan shook his head. "You can't be from two clans."

"Aye, I am."

"Is she?" Rowan looked to Magni and Lia for confirmation and frowned when they both nodded. "Cannot be," he mumbled.

Lia clarified. "Rowan, she is loved by two different clans. One on the mainland and one on Mull. We are from one clan, and you are from one, and Tora is from two."

Tora peered up at the ceiling. "Gwandda is coming too. And Gwandmama."

Rowan and Magni jumped up at the same time, both looking to Lia for guidance. Magni declared, "There are four clans looking for us?"

"That's wight, so please be patient. Be nice to everyone."

Magni wrinkled his nose and made a fist. "Not to those mean men, I won't."

The door opened, and two men came inside. "We heard your conversation. Guess what? You are correct. There will be too many looking for you, so we're moving you now."

"Where are we going?" Magni asked, his fist opening instantly as he stared up at the first man.

"Across the water. We must get off the isle."

## Chapter Eight

*Meg*

---

MEG KNELT ON the bank and dipped the linen square into the burn, wiping her face and neck with the cool water, finding it so refreshing that she nearly cried. She'd been traveling for three days and had no idea where she was going.

She'd found a cave to sleep in last night, which had been a massive improvement over the last two nights, but her situation was becoming tenuous at best.

She had no food left, and while she'd found some berries along the way, it was hardly enough to fill her belly. To say she was starving was an understatement. There was no alternative. She'd have to use her axe and kill a rabbit or something.

But then she'd have to skin it, something she hated with such a passion that she'd often done it without looking. Tamsin had done it for her for many years, but Meg had been forced to do it a few times after her sister left.

Meg had taken care with her axes, separating them so she could grab one quickly if she were attacked. Last eve, she'd lain in the cave thinking about her dear sister, wondering how she would go about finding Tamsin when she had no idea where she lived other than on an isle with a man named Raghnall Garvie.

Tamsin had been upset when her sire had announced her betrothal in nearly the same way he'd done with Meg. He entered their hut at the end of the day and announced that Tamsin's husband would come for her the next day. Poor Tamsin had been up most of the night going back and forth between fearful and hopeful. Having never met the man, she knew it could be the beginning of a wonderful life for her. Meg hoped that her sister was happily married and would be easy to find.

She'd pulled out the bracelet made of the thick blue yarn that she'd loved, but she hadn't worn it in a long time. They'd vowed only to wear it when they were together. It sat tucked inside the small sack attached to the belt on her tunic, but she'd peeked at it often to make sure it hadn't fallen away. The bracelet was her most prized possession.

Once she was finished refreshing herself, she headed back to the path, but hearing a few horses coming toward her, she chose to hide in the trees until they passed. Dressing as a lad helped her be inconspicuous, a plan she'd hoped to protect her from the wandering eyes of passing men. Her hair was tied in a plait and pinned up inside the hood of her mantle, completing the image, or so she hoped.

The horses on the path carried a family of six. They spoke of the market near the kirk, not far from where they were.

That gave her hope, and the first plan she'd ever felt confident about popped into her mind. She'd go to the market, buy herself a hunk of bread, then travel on to the kirk, hoping that there would be a kind soul inside who would help her find the way to Ulva. Perhaps they'd allow her to sleep on a pallet in the stable for one night. Priests and nuns would surely help her, would they not? She prayed they would.

Filled with hope, she waited until the group was out of view, then headed down the path toward town. Sure enough, in less than an hour, she found herself at the edge of a market where multiple vendors sold their wares.

She walked amid the busy area in the village center, looking at all the goods: ribbons, fabrics, weaponry, bread, chicken legs, jewelry, boots, and beans. She'd never seen such a selection. Years ago, their parents had taken her and Tamsin to market, but it hadn't been this large. They'd bought ribbons, thread, and fabric, among other items, but they enjoyed the crowd.

Moving over to the baker's stand, Meg chose a quarter of a loaf and paid the vendor, then bumped into a man standing directly behind her.

"Where's your father?"

Not trusting the man, she said, "Over there."

The baker called out to her. "Stay away from him."

Once the man took his leave, she stepped back to the booth and leaned over to the baker, doing her best to drop the tone of her voice. "Which way to the kirk?"

The baker said, "Down that way. I'll warn you, lass, if you are alone, speak to no one and go there quickly. I see that you have tried to disguise yourself, but you are the kind of lass that cannot hide it, so you must make wise decisions to protect yourself. The kirk is the best choice for the night. They'll allow you to stay the night. There are some who love to steal a bride on market day. They'll be gone on the morrow."

Appalled at such a possibility, she mumbled, "Many thanks."

Moving down the path, she stayed to the edge, as far away from groping hands as possible. Nearly to the kirk, she passed the last stand, but then stopped, noticing that the vendor appeared to be selling maps.

Their mother had taught Tamsin and Meg how to read, something Meg loved, but she'd died before the two girls had become experts at it. Forming words and writing had been difficult, but her father had once shown them how to read a map.

Stepping over to the vendor, she said, "Do you have a map that could show me how to get to Ulva?"

The man chuckled and said, "Ulva? You have a way to go, lass." He opened the map and said,

"Here we are in the land of the Scots, not far from the Highlands."

She peered over his shoulder, picking out the wide mass of land, then a strip of something with upside-down *V*s on it. "What is that?"

"Water. That's the Firth of Lorn and the Sound of Mull. This is how you'll have to do this. You'll have to go to Oban, hire a spot on the ferry to Craignure, then somehow get yourself to the other side of the Isle of Mull." He paused to show her exactly where he meant, waiting to see if she understood.

She did. And it frightened her.

"Do you have coin for the ferry?"

"I do."

"Why are you going to Ulva, if you don't mind my asking?"

"I wish to visit my sister. She lives on Ulva."

"Then you need to take the ferry to Craignure. I would advise you to go to Clan MacVey or to Duart Castle once on the Isle of Mull and ask for an escort to the ferry that will take you to Ulva. You'll need to get a horse."

"But I have one. I hid her in the trees over there."

"Aye, but you probably will not have enough to pay for your horse on the ship." He told her the amount, and she scowled because he was correct. She could pay for herself, but not her sweet mare. What would she do with her?

"When you find your escort, they'll take you to the other side of the isle for the ferry. But you'll have to go around Ben More."

"Ben More?"

"The mountain. That's why I would go to Clan MacVey. They are a good clan, and they'll help you."

"How long to get to Oban from here?"

"Half a day, lass. Go to the kirk. It is too late for you to be out alone. Go quickly before it's dark. There are too many unsavory characters waiting for young lasses to get lost."

"Many thanks to you," she said, moving through the crowd to grab her mare and head in the direction of the street that held the kirk. Along the way, one man tried to grab her horse, so she pulled out her axe and held it over her head, ready to bring it down on his hand. "My horse, you thief."

The man ran away.

That was enough of an experience to set her heart to racing, so she hurried out of the crowd to find a spot where she could mount the animal, then galloped toward the kirk, reaching it a quarter of an hour later. Grateful to see a stable in the back, she led her horse around, willing to sleep inside on a mound of hay just to stay out of the rain. Drizzle started right as she stepped inside.

A man with kind eyes came over and asked, "May I be of assistance, lass?"

"Will they allow me to stay one night?"

He looked at her trews and then brought his eyes back up to hers. "They will if you are willing to help in the kitchens. One eve's work for one night's stay."

"I consider that fair. Will you take good care of my horse?"

"Aye. If you work, I'll feed her. If not, I'll put her in the meadow behind here in the morn."

"Fair enough." Meg stepped away, nearly ready to fall over from exhaustion and the intensity of her pounding heart.

"Use that back door and ask for the cook. Her name is Mabel."

"My thanks to ye." After kissing her horse on its head, she headed into the back of the large kirk. It was much bigger than the one she'd attended with her mother.

Mabel welcomed her into the kitchen, passing her a basket of vegetables to cut, so she set to her work. Mabel was one of those who would talk, no matter if anyone listened. "These are for the pottage on the morrow. We have a wee bit of lamb to add some flavor. Once you have finished, you can take the chamber down the stairs and to the right."

"In the cellar?" Meg thought that odd, but what did she know about what took place within a kirk this size? "How many chambers in this building? I've not seen one this large before."

That question gave Mabel enough to talk about for the next hour as she explained every chamber and its use, along with who lived inside. Meg did her best to pay attention, but she was so tired, she cut her finger with the knife. Fortunately, she was nearly done.

Mabel rushed to her side and peered at the cut. "Och, well. You've done a fine job, so you may take to your chamber. There's a well where you can gather a basin of water. I'll get your food ready once you return."

Meg filled the basin outside, wishing she could wash her dirty hands with her soap, but it was in her sack that she'd left in the kitchen. She rinsed them, but it didn't stop the blood from flowing. Once back in the kitchen, Mabel directed her to a chamber, so she took the basin first with her bag. When she returned, Mabel gave her a linen square and a bowl of vegetable soup with a small piece of bread and a glass of mead. She thanked the woman and did her best to make it down the staircase without spilling anything.

Fortunately, a torch illuminated the way at the base of the staircase, so Meg turned to the right and stepped inside a chamber that held four cots. No one else was inside, and it was cool, but it would suit better than the wet ground. The rain came harder as she settled herself and did her best to wash her hands and face. The rhythmic beats hitting the door at the top of the stairs soothed her, reminding her of counting her numbers. Her mother had taught her daughters of the importance of being clean, so she used the soap liberally, finding the aroma more calming than the patter of raindrops. When she finished with her ablutions, wrapping her finger, she foraged and found blankets in a chest, something that made her sigh. Sleeping in a cave was cold, and she'd honestly had enough of it.

Once she'd cleaned up to her satisfaction and returned everything she could to her bag, she found a candle to light from the torch, then closed the door. She'd cleaned her undergarments at the burn, but found they were still damp, so she hung them on a couple of pegs on the wall. Curling up on one of the beds, she covered herself with a blanket and fell fast asleep.

Running away was exhausting, but far better than marrying an ugly old baron.

## Chapter Nine

*Magni*

---

TWO MEN SHOVED the four bairns toward a small dock, a boat tied to it. Magni had no idea where they were, other than the water.

Tora grinned as she climbed onto the ship, exclaiming her delight. "I love widing in boats. I'm going to wave to my mama when we go by."

"Shut up, lass, unless ye wish to swim to the other side. I would wager ye don't know how to swim. Do ye?" He laughed, his beady eyes staring at her.

She stared back and said, "But you canno' swim either."

He jumped as if burned, then turned away, hollering over his shoulder, "Just sit down. Don't be causing trouble, wee one."

Magni said, "He looks like a pirate with that patch over his eye. Do you think he is one?"

Rowan observed the man carefully. "Nay. There are no pirates around here, or I'd have seen a pirate ship pass by my castle."

The ship wasn't as big as the usual ferry that went between Oban and Craignure, but Magni hadn't seen many ships, anyway. What did he know?

Rowan whispered to Magni, "Does Tora know that man?"

Magni shook his head.

"How did she know he can't swim?"

From the opposite side of the boat, Tora looked at him and pointed to her forehead. "I see it hewe."

"She's a seer," Lia explained. "The heavens gave her a special talent."

"What's a seer?" Rowan asked.

"She can tell what's going to happen, or sometimes she knows things that are only in your mind."

"Tora, what am I thinking?" Rowan asked.

"That you think I'm stupid, but I'm not. I'm wiser than you."

Rowan stomped his foot, but he jerked to face front because Pirate Man was back with someone else.

"He's hairy," Magni whispered. "He has hair everywhere. Even coming out of his ears and his nose." He made a face and looked at Rowan.

"Aye, he is. I'm calling him Hairy." Rowan nearly giggled but kept it in, staring at both men.

Magni did giggle, his hand covering his mouth. "Hairy and Pirate Man."

Pirate Man said, "Anyone who doesn't do what I tell them will have to clean my feet." He guffawed at his own jest.

Lia said, "I would do it, if you needed it, Master Pirate Man."

The man grabbed Lia by the neck and lifted her into the air. "What did you call me?"

Tora, Magni, and Rowan all yelled in unison, "Nay!"

"What did you call me?" he repeated, squeezing her neck.

Tora got up and moved in front of him, her hands on her hips. "Put hew down."

Pirate Man let go of Lia, dropping her onto Magni's and Rowan's laps. Then he picked up Tora by her shoulders and shook her.

"Put me down, or I'll tell him about the thing you have in youw pocket."

Pirate Man stopped shaking her, but still held her over his head. "What thing?"

"That thing you took fwom him," she whispered.

He tossed her down and crossed himself. "You're a witch! Stay away from me."

A group of men came aboard and went below deck to handle the oars if the sails didn't work. Pirate Man came back and said, "We're shoving off. All the bairns below deck and stay there."

Magni led the group, Rowan huddling with Tora and Lia strolling behind. Once they reached the bottom, they each took a hard look at the oarsmen, who said nothing to them. Magni moved to the back and put his arm around his sister. "I'll protect you, Lia."

"I'm sure I will not need protection here. But

many thanks to you. I know I can always depend on you, Magni."

Rowan turned to Magni and said, "Mayhap they will tell us where we're going. I bet they're taking us to Oban."

"But then where?"

Rowan stepped closer to one man and whispered, "Where are they taking us?"

The man grinned, revealing his two missing front teeth, and leaned toward Rowan. "To the land of daft ogres. You'll never get away."

Then he leaned his head back and laughed. The other men joined him, laughing and laughing.

Magni whispered, "But I don't like ogres."

Tora said, "I do."

The first man stopped and leaned down to Tora. "What did you say, wee one?"

"I said I like ogwes."

The man's eyes danced with delight, then he broke out in guffaws.

Magni couldn't help but wonder what kind of land they were headed toward.

## Chapter Ten

*Lennox*

Lennox stepped inside the keep and closed the door behind him, then headed to his chamber above stairs. For some odd reason, more and more of the event in his past continued to haunt him. More visions, more memories.

More truths and explanations of what had happened that day, though it was still unclear.

His mother proceeded toward him before he made it to the staircase. He knew better than to talk to her here because all the women were inside for the midday meal. Women, bairns—there were too many people inside.

He strode past her and moved up the stairs, disappointed to hear the click of his mother's boot heels on the steps below him. "Slow down, Lennox. I need to speak with you."

"Then speak to me while I pack my bag," he replied over his shoulder.

"Why are you packing a bag? Are you not going on patrol? You do not need a bag to look for those bairns. Listen to me, please."

He waited until he was inside his chamber, then waved for her to enter behind him, and she sat in the chair near the hearth. The look on her face told him she had much to say, but he didn't have time to listen. With four bairns missing, time was of the essence. "Tell me quickly, if you please. I have things to do."

"What have you planned? I can tell by the look on your face that you have sent Taskill to do the patrol. Then what exactly are you doing? Are you shirking your duty?"

He spun around and faced his mother. "Why are you pushing me so? What have I done wrong? I've kept the clan together ever since Da passed. I've run the clan just like he did. We grow our own food, train our guards, and help our neighbors whenever they call upon us. Our clan numbers are growing, not shrinking. What more do you want?"

"I push you because I don't understand you. I want you to stop lying to yourself and to me. Tell me the truth. Why are you running away from patrol? Your father would have taken control and led all the guards, but you run in the opposite direction. Why?"

"Because I have something I have to do. Why do you care?"

"Because you should act like the leader you are. You are not a happy man, Lennox MacVey. I care not what you say. You need a woman in your life, you need bairns in your life, a son who will pull on your plaid and say, 'Uppie, Papa.' You need the love of a good heart for your soul, to fire you up to want to do more."

His mother continued, "If you did, you would do more. If you married, more of our guards would marry. If you went to court to meet King Robert, you would gain his favor. Who knows what you could do with that quick mind of yours? Don't you want more from your life?"

He did want more, but he had no idea what it was. Why the hell she was bringing it up now, he was clueless. But what exactly did he want? He didn't know. Did he want wealth? To be the king's favorite? To have a wife? To be father to ten bairns? He could have any woman he wished for.

But he couldn't think of one worth wasting his wishes on.

The golden-haired lass had asked him a simple question when they'd met. "What do you wish for, my lord?"

How the hell did he know?

"Mother, this is not the time for this conversation, but I'll say this much. I am happy being chieftain of the clan. I am happy that you and my siblings have a fine home and good food. What more do I need?"

"You asked me about Logan Ramsay once. You said you would love to be a spy like he was. Do you know what he would tell you was the happiest day of his life? The day he married Gwyneth. Together, they bore children, trained archers, and built a kingdom within Clan Ramsay that many wish for. You should ask him sometime. See what he thinks is of value now that he is an old man."

"I have no interest in being a spy now."

"Then stop running and choose a wife. Stay here if you don't wish to go on patrol. But running away does not suit you."

"I am not running away!"

"Then what the hell are you doing, Lennox? Your allies have been struck with tragedy and you choose to send someone else on patrol. Why? Where the hell are you going?"

Lennox closed his eyes, then strode over to stand in front of his mother. "You are the only one to know this. If I find out you reveal the truth to anyone, I'll send you to Clan Rankin. Understood?"

"Fine. But I know you are going alone, and someone should know where and why. You are the chieftain of the clan who should never go anywhere alone. You know that."

He couldn't argue with her reasoning, but he hated to tell her in case he failed. "I'm going after him."

"Him?"

"The man who nearly ruined my life."

His mother's eyes misted, something he hadn't expected to see. Then she said, "You think he is the one involved in this heinous crime?"

"Aye, I do. I've given your words much thought, and since he did it years ago, he is probably involved somehow. I cannot deny that you could be right. But I cannot waste my time going on patrol if he is involved. He is undoubtedly guilty of hiring someone to bring the bairns to him, so he's unlikely to be on Mull. I believe he is in

Oban. It makes sense that he would be near the coast somewhere."

She stood in front of him, her face paling. "You are going to the mainland, then."

"I am. Please handle what you can while I'm gone. Taskill can take care of everything else."

His mother turned her back for a second to manage her emotions. He'd seen her do it numerous times in his life. She'd not shed a tear around the others. While she turned away, he finished packing his small bag and changed out of his identifying dark green plaid into black trews and a tunic.

She whirled back around, the picture of control reinstated, her chin lifted. "I bid you Godspeed, my dear son. I pray you do find him, even if he is not guilty in this instance."

He kissed her cheek and said, "Remember your promise, Mama."

"I would never betray you, Lennox." Then she gave him that look that frightened many of the serving lasses. "Find that bastard and put your sword in his wicked heart."

Lennox left, silently vowing to do as she said.

Before he descended the staircase, he stopped, turning back to her. There were so many conversing in the great hall that no one could overhear his words. He took two steps back and did the one thing he'd vowed never to do. He leaned over and whispered in her ear, "You're right, Mama. You've always been right about this."

A single tear slid down his mother's cheek.

## Chapter Eleven

*Meg*

---

Meg awakened the next morning, hoping she hadn't slept too late. She sat up, rubbing the sleep from her eyes. It took her a few moments to orient herself to where she was, but no sooner had it all come back to her than she overheard male voices outside her chamber. Rather than open the door to see who was there, she decided to listen and moved closer.

"You will keep her here."

"She is heading to Oban, so the stable master said. She'll not wish to stay."

"You must find a way to keep her here."

"Why? I know that shipment arrived, but they'll not bother her. They are all sleeping. What can she do?"

"True, but unless you wish to control those four bairns, I'd say keep her. They'll be picked up in a day or two. Offer her coin. Women are much better at handling bairns than we are, and you know it. And I'll not ask Mabel to do it. She's got to cook for them on top of her other duties."

"Agreed."

Meg stepped back from the door, aware of movement. A knock rapped against the wood, so she opened it and peeked around the corner. A man stood there with a bowl of porridge and a pitcher of fresh water. Grateful, she thanked him, closed the door, then sat on the cot, eating the porridge while it was still warm. No matter what happened today, she would need her strength.

Once she finished breaking her fast, she used the pitcher to wash up then donned her trews again. She still had one gown she hadn't worn, but she decided to save it to put on if she needed to obtain passage on the ship.

For now, she wished to depart before it was too late. She had no idea what the men had been discussing about bairns and shipments and such, but it was time to take her leave. Even though this was a kirk, she also recognized that much of this building was hidden. She was certain very few were aware that the cellars featured sleeping chambers.

She hadn't seen any nuns or heard any priests, though she supposed the two she'd heard this morning could've been priests; she just couldn't be sure. It was time to get on her way. Packing her things carefully, her axes hidden, she moved out of the chamber, looking both ways before creeping up the stairs to the back entrance as quietly as she could.

She opened the door carefully, then hurried to the stables, but that was as far as she got. Two large men approached her.

"Come with us," one said, taking her by the elbow and turning her toward the building they'd just exited.

"Nay, I must be leaving now." She shoved against his chest, though it was rock hard—her effort did nothing to sway the man. She'd hoped to push away from him, but he wasn't about to allow it.

"You're staying with us."

"Nay, I'm leaving." She kicked him in the shin.

"Ow, you wee bitch."

She shoved him harder, so he put his hand over her mouth and lifted her up, carrying her toward the building, a good distance away from the kirk. Knowing she had to get away before it was too late, she fought and kicked and even tried biting the man, but she couldn't fight him off. She still clutched her bag, but her axe was at the bottom of it sheathed where she couldn't reach it.

"Open the door, Herbert."

"Stop using my name."

"Open the door, eejit."

Meg squirmed and fought, but to no avail. Herbert opened the door and the man who held her tossed her inside, then slammed it shut behind her. The sound of the key turning in the lock set her insides to boiling, so she swung around and grabbed at the doorknob.

It didn't give.

She banged on the rough surface, but a small voice called to her, "It will not help you to do that. We've tried since we arrived."

Turning around slowly, she noticed what had

evaded her before—four bairns huddling together in the corner of one cot. Feeling the cold, she rubbed her arms and tugged her mantle tighter. The chamber was just large enough to hold one cot, one barrel on the wall next to the door, and a couple of stools. Bags of seed and other contents covered shelves on the walls.

"Please help us," a boy of around ten winters said.

Just like that, her objective changed. How could she deny the lad? Picking up a stool close to the wall, she set it directly in front of the group. "All right. If you wish for my help, you must tell me who you are and why you are here."

All four voices began at once, so she held up her hands to silence them. "One at a time. You decide."

Three of them pointed at the boy. "You tell her, if you please, Magni." The older blond-haired lass nodded to him, speaking as if she were an adult rather than a bairn. Meg wished she had the ability to guess their ages, but she could not.

"Go ahead, Magni."

The lad was the tallest of the group, and he beamed at being selected as their representative.

Meg folded her hands in her lap so the boy wouldn't consider her a threat. "Go ahead."

"I'm Magni, and I'm ten. This is my sister Lia, who is five summers. Rowan is six winters, and Tora is four. We were stolen from our different clans on the Isle of Mull. They put us on a ship, but we have no idea where we are going. Where are we? Will you help us? We wish to go home."

Of the four, three were filled with fear while the fourth, Lia, was calm as could be, something Meg found oddly disconcerting. She wore an oddly-colored green gown that was covered with dust, while Tora wore a fine pair of wool trews with a dark red tunic top. The boys wore identical trews and tunics, both as dirty as any she'd seen. The state of their clothing showed how bad their journey had been.

"I will help you, if I can. I don't know where we are, other than on the mainland about half a day from Oban. If we return to Oban, we can catch a ferry back to the isle, which is where I am headed. That should be our goal. Does that make sense to the four of you?"

The children nodded.

"Do you know who the kidnappers are? Or where you are headed?"

Magni said, "Nay. Pirate Man and Hairy left us here last eve. Said we'll be leaving on the morrow. We have to get away quickly."

"Harry has a name, but not the Pirate Man?"

"Nay." Magni giggled. "We call him Hairy because he has so much hair." Then he leaned forward and whispered, "Even in his ears."

"I think his name is Herbert. His true name, but I'm not sure. I heard him called that just now."

"Who awe you?" Tora asked.

"My name is Meg, and I am going to visit my sister on an isle."

"Mull?"

She shook her head. "But she can wait. I'll help you first."

"I want my mama," Tora said, her lower lip quivering. "I don't like dis woom."

Rowan said, "Now you are upset, Tora. You didn't care before."

"I wish to go home now. I've changed my mind."

"Let me take a look around and see if we can figure out a way to open that locked door." Meg took out her axe from her bag and did her best to break it, but it wasn't to be. She glanced over at the four disappointed faces. "Mayhap it would be best to try again in the middle of the night. If we managed to open it now, it would be in vain because the men are just outside the door. I can hear them talking not far away. And the cook would see us leave. We need to wait. I think it would be better to leave in the dark."

She moved over onto the pallet, and they made room for her. Leaning her back against the wall, the four huddled around her, two on each side. "I thought it was morn when I woke up, but the sun was high when they brought me here."

"You'll not leave us, will you?" Magni asked.

"Nay. I promise to stay. We'll find a way out this eve."

"Good," Magni said. "Because the men will be here after the late meal on the morrow. They gave us something awful to eat earlier, and we pished outside one at a time, but they have not been back. We'll have to leave before high noon on the morrow to be safely away."

"We'll get out. Don't worry. I know it's not dark yet, but you all look exhausted. Now close your eyes." Meg hummed a song her mother used to sing until the four bairns calmed in her arms, finally closing their eyes. Being captive was indeed exhausting.

She closed her eyes, saying a quick prayer to the Lord to find a way to unlock the door when she awakened next.

---

When she woke up, it was dark, but she had no idea how long she'd slept. The lads were still asleep, but Lia and Tora were awake.

Lia said, "They're coming at high sun. I heard them talking about it."

"Then we must act now," Meg said, though she wasn't certain what exactly to do.

Tora gave Magni a kiss on his cheek. He woke instantly with a loud "Yuck," then swiped his cheek and glared at Tora, who put her finger up to her mouth.

"Shush." She pointed to the door. Rowan sat up, wiping the sleep from his eyes.

Meg had formulated a plan. Now she had to get four bairns to do as she said. She still had two axes in her bag, so that would help. "Here's what we're going to do. Lia, I want you to cry so they'll come in to check on you. Rowan, you'll be on one side of the door, and Magni, you on the other. When the two step inside, you put your foot out to trip them and push them to the floor. Then we all rush out over them, close the door, and lock it. That will give us enough time to run away. And we need to run deep into the forest, not on the main path. Stay together so no one gets lost. Understand?"

"How do you know the key will be in the lock?" Magni asked.

"Because when they brought the food in last eve, that's what they did. They left the key in the door and retrieved it after they locked it again. I'm sure that's the only way they can open it."

Rowan said, "What if only one comes in?"

"Good question." She had to think about it for a moment. "If both girls cry, then I think the other will enter. We'll start with one crying and if we need to, we'll have Tora cry too."

"Now?" Lia asked.

Meg took one last look around the building before making the first move. The room comprised about half the building, but she didn't know what was in the other half. Various bags and containers lined the walls, but she had no idea what they held. The door was in the middle of the wall, easy enough for the two lads to trip them with one on each side. There were two windows, but both were too high to look out. They'd have to judge everything by sound.

She moved the two stools in front of the door with the hopes that their falls would be a bit harder. If she hid in the corner, once the men fell, she'd easily get to the door and be able to lock it from the other side. She held her bag close to her chest, ready to grab one of her axes if necessary.

She'd never used one on a person before, but if she had to, she would.

"Aye. Wait for the lads to get in position. We'll

have to walk. I had a horse, but it won't hold five of us, so I'll have to leave the mare behind. But we can hide better without her."

She glanced from one dirty face to the next, their trust humbling her. She'd certainly lived a life different from any of them. "Lads, take your positions. I'll hide next to Magni so they can't see me."

They took their spots by the door, then Meg nodded to Lia, who broke out in a wail until the door opened. One man stood there and said, "Shut your mouth."

Then Tora screamed and the other man pushed in behind the first one. "I'll shut them up."

Both men tripped over Magni's and Rowan's feet—one fell on the other with the loudest bellows, and the other hit his head on one of the stools, cursing. All four bairns stepped on the fools while Meg grabbed the key and shouted, "Hurry!"

The four clamored out the door, waiting for her, and she slammed it, locking it just in time as Pirate Man grabbed the handle.

"Run!" she said.

Meg took off behind the children with her saddlebag over her shoulder, surprised when the lad from the stable tossed her a bag of something. Whatever it was, she'd check later.

They ran and ran down a path headed deep into the forest, away from the main path.

Though Meg had no idea where they were headed.

## Chapter Twelve

*Lennox*

Lennox made his way toward Craignure, Taskill following him. He had some essentials already packed and attached to his saddlebag.

"Where the hell are you going, Lennox? I thought you would be joining our patrol with us. We're leaving in a quarter hour."

"Listen, there's something I must attend to, Taskill. You can handle the patrol. I'll be back on the morrow. I'm just following a hunch, but I do not wish to pull any men away from the patrol."

"You are the chieftain. You should not be going anywhere alone. You know that, especially off the isle." Taskill crossed his arms, looking serious now, something Lennox rarely saw. "If Mama finds out, she'll never let you forget it."

"I would only travel alone off the isle. No one on the mainland knows of me. I'll be unrecognizable." He waited, knowing that Taskill would not argue. He never did. It was simply not in his character to do so. "How would anyone know me without my plaid?"

Taskill glanced at his attire, then shrugged and said, "True. All in black with black trews. Looks the same color as your hair, Lennox. No one will recognize you. Tell me on the morrow all about it and Godspeed."

"Of course. You'll be first to know." His brother turned around to head back toward Dounarwyse Castle, and he wondered how two brothers could be so different coming from the same two people. Taskill was fair while Lennox was dark-haired like their sister. He ran his hand through his hair, thinking he should probably trim the long locks soon, but he hated to fuss over something as shallow as his looks. While many lasses had begged for a proposal from him over the years, most had given up at this point.

Finally.

A few had blamed it on his blue eyes, one telling him they were as cold as ice. That comment had hurt because sometimes he feared she was right. It took a great deal for him to become invested in anything. He blamed the man he knew as Egan. Since that horrible time during and after Lennox's abduction, he'd locked up his heart, and he knew it wouldn't be unlocked until he freed the world from men like Egan.

Pushing his thoughts down deep, he had to focus on his present task: where exactly to look for the fool.

He was nearly at Craignure when he was approached by Dyna and her husband, Derric.

"MacVey!" Dyna shouted.

"What is it?" He turned around, surprised to see the two alone. "Are you not going on patrol?"

"We are, but I wished to speak with you. Rankin is too upset to discuss anything, and Thane recommended I have a conversation with you about my visions. He says you know the isle best."

Dyna's aura was something he wasn't accustomed to. What would it be like to have a child who was much like you were? And how would it feel to lose that wee person? Tora was the image of her mother, hair nearly white and haunting blue eyes.

"I'll help in any way I can."

"Where are you going? You're a chieftain traveling alone?" Derric asked.

"I have to take care of something. Taskill is handling our assigned patrol. Worry not. I'll be back on the morrow. I need to see to a situation on the mainland." Then he waited for Dyna's question.

"I've had some visions and because I don't know the area, I have no idea where they are. And I've had more than one, so it confuses me. I need help sorting through the pictures in my head."

"Go ahead. Tell me what you've seen." He had his doubts whether Dyna was indeed a seer, but it was worth hearing her out. He respected Dyna and Eli for all they'd accomplished in their lives—Dyna was a chieftain of Clan Grantham with Maitland Menzie, and both were powerful archers.

"One scene is the four huddled on a cot in a strange building and the other one is three of them in a small boat. They wouldn't be going from Craignure in a boat that size, would they?"

"Nay. It would be too rough for a small boat, though if they have at least six oars and a sail and the sea was mild, they could do it on a good day. Mayhap to Ulva? I'm not sure. It could be on a loch. The cot could be anywhere. I wish I could help you, Dyna."

"The boat was dark. They dragged it out of some brush."

The skin on his neck raised, but he didn't let on. "If I think of anywhere like that, I'll have my patrol check, and I'll definitely let you know. It's a bit too vague."

Dyna looked devastated, but what could he tell her? That the boat sounded like the one he'd been on fifteen years ago when he'd been stolen away?

"Dyna, fear not. The plan we created will cover the Isle of Mull. If they're here, we will find them."

"And if they're not?"

"Then we'll create a new plan on the morrow. I'll be here to assist with that. I'll be aware of everything I see on the mainland."

Memories washed over him and nearly made him shiver, but he held the emotion inside. The mention of the small boat in the brush had set his mind churning.

Derric said, "Diamond, we must move along. Godspeed on your journey, wherever you go, MacVey."

He waved to them and led his horse to the small port, glad to see few people around, because he needed time to think on what Dyna had said. As much as he'd tried to forget everything that happened to him, perhaps it was time to allow the memories to return. More and more memories resurfaced, and the puzzle of all that happened was finally making sense to him. It was time to put the pieces of the puzzle together.

Once he settled on the ship headed toward Oban, toward the fool who stole him away, he allowed the memories in.

This had to stop.

*Fifteen years ago*

*Lennox woke with a pounding ache in his head. He was being dragged across the path in a forest, one he'd never seen before. He had to get away. He kicked and fought, doing his best to be free of two fools, one who held his arms and the other his legs, but they held tight.*

*"Stop fighting, lad. We are not going to hurt you. You're going to work, that's all. You get a pallet to sleep on this eve, then on the morrow, we'll take you to the new castle far away. They need big, strapping lads to muck their stalls and carry stones to make their curtain wall. You'll see. It's not so bad."*

*"When my sire finds you, he'll kill you."*

*"I might worry, but your father will never find me. Will he, Egan?"*

*The other man laughed and said, "We're making good coin for the big lads, but tell him the next one must be smaller. I cannot carry them up the hill."*

"Where am I? Where are you taking me?"

"Nowhere that matters. The lord wants a new castle and a new wall. So, you'll be building it."

Lennox fought for all he was worth. He finally freed one foot and kicked up, catching the man who'd been talking right in his jaw. He let out a screeching bellow, dropped Lennox for a second, but then grabbed him and landed a punch square to his jaw.

Lennox punched him back.

"The blow to your head wasn't enough for you? Well, I know exactly how to fix you, laddie. Fingal, you know where we're putting him, do you not?"

"Aye, in the cottage."

"Nay. This one is going in the cellars."

He grabbed Lennox's legs and tied them together, then laughed when he picked him up again. "You'll not be kicking me anymore, you spoiled brat."

"In the cellar? That's not nice, Egan."

"It's where he goes."

The two didn't say anything, as dark was nearly upon them and the trees were thinning. They entered through a back gate, then carried Lennox over to the rear door of a dilapidated building. Lennox stared at everything, doing his best to memorize his surroundings in case he was able to break free.

If he had the chance, he'd run, but he had to know where to go.

Once inside, they carried him down the stairs into the castle cellars, into a dark room where they tossed him on an old cot.

"See how you like this. You can sleep with the rats. When you wake up, they'll be nibbling on your toes and your nose."

*The two men left, and the mean one named Egan laughed through the small window in the door. "I can't wait to see how hungry you are on the morrow. See how many places the rats have nibbled you."*

*Lennox said nothing, looking around the chamber for any means to escape, but he found naught useful. The door was locked and solid, and the cot was filthy, but the floor was worse. A dim torch far down the passageway provided the only light through the small window, and an urn sat in the corner, probably one to pish in.*

*He'd never been so frightened and angry in his life.*

*He stood at the door and screamed until his voice was raw. He remembered something his father had told him about being captured, that the most important thing was to maintain your strength. If you had your strength, you could wait for the right moment to escape, but the best way was to outmaneuver the bastards.*

*When Lennox had no voice left, he moved over and sat on the cot, the smell horrible, but it was better than the floor. He didn't see any rats, so he put his head down and cried, eventually falling asleep.*

*Something awakened him in the middle of the night. He opened his eyes and peered into the darkness, and when his eyes adjusted, he found himself staring into the eyes of a mouse. He screamed and screamed. In his desperation, he finally came up with his solution.*

*He would give them what they wanted.*

*When Egan and Fingal came in to get him in the morning, he didn't move. He had no voice left, no strength, no will to live. He'd lost all hope. He stared straight ahead, not answering any of their questions, not responding to any of the pinches, punches, or cuts on his body.*

*They could do whatever they wanted to him. He would not respond, saving his strength for what he would need to do.*

*Another man came in behind Egan and moved over to where Lennox sat on the cot, leaning against the wall. The man spoke to him, poked him, slapped him, yelled in his face, and finally spit on him, but Lennox didn't react. Not once did he flinch.*

*The man spun around and said, "He's no good. Take him and toss him overboard."*

*They carried him back to the coastline, pulled a boat out of the bushes, then set him inside. He still didn't react. He had no idea where he was, but having lived his whole life on an island, he was a strong swimmer.*

*They moved across the water, waited until they were near the middle, and dropped him over the side of the boat. He fell in with hardly a splash.*

*He went under, held his breath, and swam as hard as he could. He pushed himself as far as possible, not coming up for air until he had to. To his surprise, it had started to rain and the two in the boat were busy yelling at each other to row faster. They were rowing away from him.*

*He closed his eyes and swam harder, keeping his strokes calm until he came up for air again. He looked both ways, satisfied that the boat had nearly gone ashore. They weren't even looking at him because they didn't care.*

*He turned to the opposite bank, glad to see it was visible, but he'd have to swim. So, he paced himself, starting on his back and opening his mouth to drink the fresh water coming from the sky rather than the loch water. He'd been sickened by it once and would never drink from the lochs or oceans again.*

*He swam and swam, alternating from his back to his belly, pleased he didn't encounter any creatures along the way. When he was nearly there, he worried that he had weakened enough that he wouldn't be able to climb up the bank.*

*But he did. He climbed across the rocks and found a grassy section, falling into it with relief.*

*He'd made it.*

*He didn't recall anything else until he woke up in his chamber at home, his mother sobbing by his bedside.*

*But he never told her all the details. He'd told her he couldn't remember anything that happened—not the men, the mice, nor the beating he'd been forced to endure from Egan after the other man had left.*

## Chapter Thirteen

*Meg*

---

THE FIVE ESCAPEES had been running for two days, and Meg had no idea where they were. The first day, the man they called Hairy had caught up with them, but she threw one of her axes square in his forehead, dropping him instantly. It had been unsightly, so she forced the bairns to run in the opposite direction before they got a good look at all the blood. That meant one less man to chase them.

The first night, they'd slept huddled in a clearing together, but last evening, she'd noticed a cave, a much more appealing prospect since it had rained again. They slept hard, all of them hungry, yet hopeful as they huddled together to keep warm.

This morn when Meg awakened, she was pleased to see the sea, though it still lay a distance away.

She made her way back into the cave to see if the others had woken up yet.

Magni sat up and said, "We're still free. Can we find a boat this day? I'm going outside."

"I hope to make it to the ferry soon. Go ahead, but please remember to be quiet and do not venture too far away, Magni. There could be men still looking for us," Meg advised, giving a little squeal when she looked down at her finger. It had hurt just to touch it, something she noticed two evenings ago. Now it was swollen and red, which she knew was bad. She reached into her small sac attached to her belt, feeling for her sister's bracelet for good luck.

But it wasn't there.

"I'll be right back," Magni said as he skipped outside into the cool morning.

She searched the floor around her but didn't find her missing bracelet. There was no way she could have lost it.

Magni came back inside and grabbed her by the hand. "Meg, what's wrong?"

"My bracelet. I can't find it. It was in my bag on my belt. It's gone." She couldn't stop the misting in her eyes, but then took three deep breaths to stop because she had to be strong for the bairns. "It's blue. I've looked everywhere. Please help me find it."

She dropped Magni's hand and went over to one corner in the cave, then raced to another, her vision blurring. "I must find it."

Lia pointed for Magni. "Over there. I see something."

Magni raced over and bent down. "Is this it? It's blue yarn." He held it up for her examination.

Meg took one look at it and let out a sigh of relief. "Aye. That's it. Many thanks to you, Magni." She tucked it away, then yelped when her finger caught on her belt. "Ow." She felt her finger and her hand, surprised at how warm the area was to her touch. She had no ointments or potions, so she didn't know how to fix her wound. If they could get to the ferry quickly, then perhaps she could find a healer on the Isle of Mull.

Magni came closer and looked at her finger. "You were as warm as a hearth last night, Meg. I didn't even feel the cold stone next to you."

Lia explained, "She has a fever, Magni."

Meg replied quickly, "Nay, I am fine. It is only a wee cut I made while slicing vegetables the other day." She couldn't slow this trip down. Now that she could see the firth, she hoped the ferry was just a brief journey ahead so they could board a boat by midday. If she had some of that water to wash her finger, it would surely heal. The waterskin she carried was empty.

She needed water—water would surely fix it, fix everything, clean the pus from her wound. But where would she find it? Near the ferry! Surely she could wash it before they boarded. "We must hurry to get to Oban."

Even though she was quite certain she didn't have enough coin for all of them to go across, she'd arrange for them to go in two trips. She'd let Rowan go first because his uncle could send a boat back, or so she thought. It all depended on how much the fare was.

Lia looked up at her when the others went

outside and said, "You do have a fever. You must get home. You may go ahead of me. I have one task I must do, so I'll gladly stay for the second boat."

"Where are you going, Lia? I could not leave a young lass alone, but surely you know that. I'll stay back with you. But what kind of visit have you planned?"

"I must go to Loch Aline. I will share a secret with you, Meg, but please do not tell the others. I am a faery so I can go off on my own and not get hurt. I am here for a reason, though that must stay a secret."

Now Meg was certain she had a fever. A wee lass expected her to believe that she was truly a faery. She must have a fever because no person would ever confess to such a thing. Surely she was hallucinating.

Tora sat up, rubbing her eyes, while Rowan stood and ran outside, chattering over his shoulder, "I have to pish."

Tora looked at Meg and said, "You awe sickly. We must get you home. Gwandpapa is down neaw the watew. We'll get thewe soon." She got up and went out with the two lads.

Meg didn't feel well. Now that she'd gotten to know them better, she had to admit that the four bairns were all a bit odd. Lia acted as if she were four decades old and thought she was a faery. Tora claimed to be a seer. Magni said he was Lia's brother, but she saw no resemblance between the two. And Rowan claimed his uncle was a chieftain. She prayed he wasn't lying because they could use the help of a chieftain. Hopefully, he could also help locate her sister once she was on the Isle of Mull. After all, she was told Ulva was on the far side of Mull, so he might know exactly where she lived.

Lia touched her hand and said, "Do not worry. You will find your sister. She is in love with a chieftain, and she is verra happy."

"How do you know my sister? I haven't even told you her name."

Lia smiled and opened her mouth to speak, but the three came running inside, cutting her off, all whispering with sheer fright. Magni said, "Someone is coming. I heard him in the brush!"

"I heard him too! It's a man." Rowan ran to Meg and knelt in front of her, grabbing her hand, but she winced, yanking back. "What's wrong?"

"Naught. Tora, did you see him?"

"Aye. You must see who it is. I don't know him," Tora said.

"I'll go," Meg said, retrieving the axe from her sack, then turning to the four sets of eyes locked on her. "Do not come out under any circumstances until I tell you it's safe. If he takes me away because I cannot fight him off, then stay here until we're gone. Then run to Oban and the ferry. They'll come back for me, but you must go for help. Do not follow me."

"But—"

"No buts! Promise me now." She whirled to face the four. "All of you."

"I pwomise. Gwandda will help us. I'll find him." Tora gave an emphatic nod.

Rowan and Magni looked at each other, then both agreed.

Lia said, "I'll do whatever you ask of me, dear Meg."

"Stay here in the back of the cave." She waited until they were well hidden behind a rock, then stepped outside. Listening for footsteps, she was pleased that it was only one man.

The crackle of the brush continued, strong, steady steps that came directly toward them. Her heart pounded because she feared she'd fail protecting these poor bairns. They were all in need of food and water. If she weren't sickly, she'd launch her axe with her usual accuracy, but her hand shook a wee bit, even though the wound was on the other hand.

The crunch of boots on dirt came closer, making her wonder why he hadn't stayed on the path.

She took out her axe and stood, though she found her legs too weak, so she had to find a rock to sit on.

The man appeared in front of her.

He wasn't any of the men she'd seen at the kirk, and she'd not seen him at the market either. Hesitant, she waited until he saw her, and she held the axe over her head. "Come any closer and I'll fire this."

The man stopped as soon as he saw the axe. "I will not come closer, then. But I have a question. I promise I'm not here to hurt you."

"Go ahead, but if you come any closer, I will throw. I'm verra good with it." Her lower lip trembled so she bit down to stop it, but she was certain he'd noticed. He was a handsome man. Tall, broad-shouldered, hair as dark as the night and eyes the color of a cloudless sky in summer. He had a sword sheathed over his shoulder. "Do not go for your weapon."

He held up both hands. "I thought I saw a couple of lads. We are missing some bairns from the Isle of Mull. I've come to take them home."

"Sure you are. For certes, you are lying. You're from the kirk. I'm sure your plan is to steal them away and take them back, but I will not allow it. You'll have to kill me first." She lifted her chin to let him know she was not jesting.

He knelt on one knee. "Lass, you are sick. I can see from your flushed cheeks and the dullness in your eyes that you have a fever. Probably from that swollen cut on your hand. I can see the scab and the redness from here. I need to get you to a healer if you wish to live."

He rose and took two steps forward, so she stood and swung the axe back in an arch over her head.

His arms flew up over his head quickly. "Nay, not yet. I'll stop."

"You're not taking me to a healer."

"How about this? There are four bairns. Two boys about six and ten. Two lasses around five, both fair-haired."

"If you are the one who stole them away, then you would know that, wouldn't you? That proves naught to me."

"The younger lad knows me. Allow him out

and he'll attest to me. Then I'll take us all to Oban, about two hours west of here. I have one horse, and you may ride it with the lassies. I'll pay for your fare. I'm the chieftain of Clan MacVey. We have two wonderful healers on the Isle of Mull. I wish to get the bairns home and get you to a healer."

She listened, hoping that this handsome man was telling the truth. He gave her enough reasons that she thought to trust him until Rowan could vouch for him. Tears rolled down Meg's cheeks and she whispered, "Will you help me get to Ulva after? I need to find my sister."

"I promise to get you to Ulva. I'll help you in any way I can." His blue eyes bore into hers, and though there was a touch of coldness there, she believed what he said. He'd offered a perfect way to prove whether he was lying. All she had to do was ask Rowan if he knew this man.

Right now, she needed help. Could he be her savior?

She had to trust him, not because of his looks or his words, but because she *was* getting sick. Her mind was no longer working the same as it should. She was unsure of whether she could make it to the ferry, and it was more important that someone take care of the bairns.

"Magni! Bring your friend here."

A moment later, Magni stuck his head out, then Rowan came up behind him, launching into a squeal as soon as he saw the man. "Uncle Lennox!"

The big chieftain opened his arms and Rowan jumped into them with a shout. "We're safe! He's my uncle's closest friend. He'll take us home."

Meg fainted and tumbled from the rock.

## Chapter Fourteen

*Connor*

---

CONNOR GRANT STOOD by the port of Oban, barking orders at everyone he saw. Alasdair, his nephew, reached his side and said, "Chief, please allow me to handle this."

Connor and his brother Jamie had been co-chieftains of Clan Grant, but they'd passed the lairdship on to Alasdair and Alick, their nephews. Even though Alasdair was now chieftain of the clan, he referred to Connor as chieftain out of respect.

Connor sighed, his hands settling on his hips as he stared at the ground. "You are correct, Alasdair. I have no sense of reason when I know my grandbairns are involved."

"We don't know that for sure yet. Dyna may have found Tora by now." Alasdair moved over to the captain of the ship onto which they were boarding the warhorses. Numerous Grant guards assisted with the task as the sound of the waves unsettled the animals.

Sela, Connor's wife, joined him and said, "Let

Alasdair handle it all. We'll go on the first ship. He can go on the last one."

Alasdair returned to them and said, "Nay, I'll not be on the last one. Alick will."

Connor grinned. Everything about Alasdair reminded him of his deceased father Alexander, and his deceased brother Jake, Alasdair's sire.

"Chief, we already had a score of guards ready after we received the first message from Dyna. We'll get this group over quickly. The wind is in our favor. More will follow."

The birlinn they'd hired to cross was the largest and most expensive ship to be found in the area. There would be oarsmen not far from the horses while the others rode the upper deck.

"I need to see our daughters and granddaughters," Sela whispered. "I can't wait to board that ship."

"And Sandor," he finished, kissing his wife's forehead. "You won't mind the ride, will you, love?"

Sela grinned, her multiple braids in her nearly white hair perfect for the wind they were experiencing. "Nay. I used to love sailing." Sela's heritage was Norse, and she hadn't been on a birlinn in years. "I'm excited to see Mull too." Her skin carried a golden bronze from the summer sun, and the fine lines around her eyes made her more beautiful in Connor's view.

"If Dyna hasn't found the bastard who stole my Tora away, I'll find him." Connor let out a bellow at Alasdair, who was now moving among the Grant guards, giving instructions. "Alasdair! Don't forget."

His nephew cast a small grin back at him. "I know, Chief. You have rights."

It was part of the Highlander code of honor and the principle of just due. Whoever is harmed the most by a villain gets the rights to inflict the killing blow.

Damn right he had the right of due justice to the fool who dared to touch a Grant bairn.

Alasdair chuckled. "Poor bastard."

## Chapter Fifteen

*Logan*

---

"WHO TOOK THE bairns?" Logan asked, approaching the fool he pretended to agree with. He was getting too old to play games with men like this, but if this bastard had anything to do with the bairns, he would deeply regret it.

Logan adored bairns. They were much easier to deal with than idiot adults.

"I don't know."

Logan took two steps closer. "Surely you do. I can see it in your eyes."

"Nay, I have no use for the bairns. I wish to control the Isle of Mull, not bairns." The man spit off to the side and set his hand on his weapon's hilt. "I asked to see you because there are scores of horses trying to get on the ferry. And there's a giant birlinn unlike I've ever seen. Why?"

"What you are seeing is the response from Clan Grant to having one of the chieftain's granddaughters taken."

"Someone stole a Grant bairn? Now that is foolishness I'd never commit."

By the look on the man's face, Logan guessed he was telling the truth. That didn't mean he was about to let the man off easily. Bairns were a sore spot with him. "Connor Grant and his nephew Alasdair are on their way. The two finest swordsmen in all the land. You better be forthright because they will find you if you are guilty."

The man let out a slow whistle, then Logan caught the slight smirk.

Logan stepped forward and grabbed the fool by the throat. "If I find out you had anything to do with stealing the bairns, I'll cut off your bollocks and make you eat them for dinner. Then I'll give you to Connor to do as he wishes. You better tell me now what you know."

The man was about to turn green, so Logan let go of him, mostly because he didn't wish to be heaved on. The fool rubbed his neck and looked as guilty as anyone he'd ever seen, so Logan took another step closer.

The fool held up his hands. "All right. I had naught to do with it, but I know why they stole the bairns away."

"I'm listening."

"There's a man on Ardnamurchan who wants the faery."

"What faery?"

"The green maiden. She has the ability to grant wishes. They say she appears in the middle of the forest when she finds someone she can trust, and she can take any form she wishes. They say she's a bairn this time." The man rubbed his neck.

Logan hoped he'd left a bruise, but he had to pursue this a wee bit further. "Out with all of it. I can see it in your eyes."

"They say there's a child who is also a seer, so they stole her too. They have plans on how to use the green maiden, but that I don't know."

"Mayhap to be rid of you."

"I've done naught to anyone." His voice rose a pitch.

"Who? I want names."

"I don't have any. I am not familiar with Ardnamurchan."

"Names!"

The man let out a deep sigh. "I truly do not know who ordered the stealing, but I know the men who stole them. They were to take the bairns to the mainland and hide them for a sennight, then take them to Ardnamurchan."

"Names, I said." Logan whipped out his sword and had it at the man's neck before the fool could even move his hand.

"Hell, but you are fast for an auld man." He hitched his breath, then said, "Herbert and Ellis. That's all I know. They're from the mainland in Oban."

Logan sheathed his sword and mounted his horse. "I hope, for your sake, that you told me the truth."

## Chapter Sixteen

*Lennox*

LENNOX SET ROWAN down and rushed to the girl's side. Shocked to have finally found the bairns after he'd been searching for two days, he thanked the Lord above that they all seemed hale. He removed the axe from her hand and gave it to Magni, who said, "I know where she keeps it, but you have to help her! Her name is Meg and she saved us from those awful men who were going to sell us to work for someone. I'm not going without her."

Lennox had to smile. He lifted Meg into his arms and sat on the boulder, settling her on his lap. "Rowan, my horse is back a bit. Please go with Magni and fetch it here. But it's not far from a wee burn. I have a skin on the horse for water. Fill it for me and bring both back. Once I can awaken her, we'll head to Oban."

Magni jumped and said, "Aye, Chief. We'll get the horse and the water!"

Once they left, Lennox called out, "Tora! Are you here?"

The white-haired lass came out of the cave holding the hand of a golden-haired lass who was as serene as any he'd ever seen. "Greetings, Lia."

"Aye, that is my name. I think we have met before. And you are the chieftain of Clan MacVey, my lord?"

"Aye, true. Tora, your mother is verra worried about you. I promise to get you back to her before nightfall."

Tora pointed toward the sea. "Gwandpapa is nearly at the fewwy. They're going over to help Mama. I can wide with him. He has his howse, Midnight Star, with him."

"I'm sure he'll be pleased to see you, but the horse will ride in the bottom of the boat. They won't wish to risk him falling overboard. Do you have anything to gather? Will you get Meg's things together so we can leave once my horse is here? We need to get her to our healer."

"Orw ouw healer. Eli is vewwa good."

"She is, and if Doiron cannot help her, then we'll get Eli. But first, please gather everyone's things."

The two lasses rushed back into the cave.

That gave Lennox the time to do what he wished—stare at the most beautiful face he'd ever seen on a brave soul. She had stood strong against him to protect four bairns—with a fever. Who was this lass? He placed his hand to her forehead, not surprised to feel the fire burning there as strongly as in the rest of her body. He cupped her cheek and turned her face so he could look at her directly.

Her skin carried a bit of the sun with a dash of freckles across her nose, though he would wager that in winter it would be as clear as ivory. She had high, delicate cheekbones and rosy-red lips that begged to be kissed, though it didn't interest him in her present condition.

Her hair was the color of his favorite chestnut horse, with just a hint of red in it. Her plaits were quite messy, something he found oddly appealing. She had the longest legs he'd ever seen, visible since she was dressed in a pair of men's trews. He'd have to wonder more about that, but not at the moment. Other than the women at Clan Grantham, he'd never seen a lass in trews.

The lads returned. Magni rushed to Lennox's side with the waterskin while Rowan led the horse, who nickered sweetly upon finding his master again, his long tail swishing in greeting. "Rowan, grab a linen square from my saddlebag, if you would."

Rowan found the towel, and Lennox wet the cloth before setting it across Meg's forehead. He moved it to her cheeks at the same time the lasses exited the cave and Lia announced, "We have everything, my lord."

Lennox glanced at the lasses and said, "Rowan and Magni, will you attach the bags to the horse, please? I was hoping to allow Meg to ride along with Tora and Lia, but I think I'm going to have to hold her up. Her fever is too high."

Tora said, "I will walk and pwotect you with my bow." She pulled a weapon from the inside of her tunic. "I keep it hidden fwom the bad people."

He couldn't help but smile. If no one had told him, he would have known her to be Dyna's daughter.

"Then I'll ride with Meg and, Lia, you may ride in front of Meg to help keep her steady. You lads will walk with Tora, please."

"We will," Magni said, his expression growing serious as he stepped closer to Lennox. "Do you promise not to let the bad men take us back?"

"I do, Magni. Fear not. I'll have you back at Duart Castle by dark. I'll send a messenger to your uncle, Rowan. I think perhaps it will be best to have Eli treat Meg."

Meg lifted her head, stared into his eyes, and asked, "Who the hell are you?"

Tora ran over and put her hand on Meg's forehead to soothe her, and said, "He's bwinging us to Oban and my gwandsire. Do not wowry."

Lennox said, "I'm Lennox MacVey, chieftain of Clan MacVey. I came here looking for four bairns, so I promise to get you all to the Isle of Mull safely. Then their parents will come for them after I send messengers. You will see our healer."

Her eyes misted and she clutched his arm. "Promise? I'm too tired to go any farther. Please get them safely home."

"I promise." Her eyes were a shade of the forest in early spring when the buds were just beginning to break out. "Meg, I'm going to help you get on the horse, and I'll mount behind you. You can lean against me. You're not strong enough to ride on your own."

She grabbed his hand and said, "Nay, I'll walk. The bairns can ride."

Three voices shouted, "Nay. We wish to walk."

Lennox smiled and said, "They are anxious to get to Oban. It's not far, and better to release their wiggles before we get on the ship. They'll be fine. Lia will ride in front of you, so if you must grab on to anyone, grab her."

"Magni, please get my axe."

"I have it, my lady." He grinned and held up her carrying case.

Lennox managed to get the two on the horse and mounted behind them. It wasn't the best arrangement, but he thought it would work. "That way on the path, lads. If you hear anything unusual, you will get behind the horse. Understood? You too, Tora?"

The three nodded and they were off.

Lennox had to admit that he was drawn to this lass. He couldn't think of one other female he'd like to ride a horse with, but she fit against him quite well. He'd noticed that she was quite tall, her head nearly even with his. Long legs that went on forever made him envision things he shouldn't be considering with a sick lass and four bairns in his present company, so he had to chastise himself.

He had four important people counting on him to get them home. He'd better be more attentive.

They'd traveled for about two hours when Magni let out a whoop. "There it is! I see it! There's the sea. We're going home. Really going home."

Lia said, "Thane and Tamsin will be verra glad to see us."

Meg sat up and said, "Tamsin? That's my sister's name. But she's not married to anyone named Thane."

Lennox had to admit that thought gave him a jolt. Could Thane's new friend be Meg's sister? He'd have to find out later.

She fell asleep again, occasionally moaning from bad dreams or the fever, he wasn't sure which. "Stay close, Magni. Please do not run ahead."

They continued for another hour before the dock and multiple boats became visible. In fact, there were more birlinns and large galley ships than he'd ever seen. Lines of men in red plaids with their horses stood around, making an unusual crowd for the wharf area. What was taking place at the ferry to cause such crowding? He couldn't help but wonder why there were so many men needing to ferry to the isle.

And now he was worried they'd not get boarded before it shut down for the evening. But the heavens were watching over their wee group, because Tora came over to him and said, "Up, Chief, pwease?"

"I can't lift you, Tora. Not with Meg here."

Lia said, "I'd like to get down, if you please, to move my legs. Tora may come up."

With Magni's help, they switched the lasses, giving Tora the chance to peer into the crowd. Moments later, she yelled out, "Gwandpapa! I'm ovew hewe!"

Within seconds, every horse around Lennox

moved enough to turn toward them while each guard in red plaid unsheathed their swords in unison to point at him. He froze, unsure of what was happening. "Lads, Lia, stay close to me. Do not move." The bairns backed up, holding hands on one side of the horse.

The sea of animals parted before him, and a large black warhorse came toward them, the rider dark-haired with broad shoulders. The intensity of his gaze was one that could intimidate many, but not Lennox. Whoever the hell this man was, he was not going to take any of the bairns away.

When the man neared them, he called out, "Tora? Is that you, sweeting?" He set his horse to a gallop until he was next to them, his hand on the hilt of his sword.

Magni and Rowan started to cry, but Tora grinned, leaning over to the lads. "Don't be fwightened. This is my gwandpapa. He won't huwt you." Then she sat up. "Gweetings, Gwandda."

"Tora, did this man hurt you? Did he steal you away?" the man in red plaid asked.

"Nay, Gwandpapa. He saved us. And Meg saved us too." Tora whirled around to pat Meg's cheek, but she didn't respond. "Will you take us home? I want Mama."

The man removed his hand from his weapon and reached for his granddaughter, lifting her onto his horse and hugging her tight, and if Lennox was correct, he shed a few tears as well. When he was back in control, the man said, "Connor Grant. I am indebted to both of you. The lass is injured?"

"Lennox MacVey, chieftain of Clan MacVey of Mull. The lady is feverish from a wound," Lennox answered. "She needs a healer. She saved the four and got them to a cave three hours back where I discovered them."

Tora looked up at her grandsire. "Meg got a cut from the kirk where they hid us. They locked hew up with us too. Gwandda, take hew to Eli, please. She must go with us. She saved us."

Connor nodded toward the three bairns. "And the others were taken with you, Tora?"

"Aye," Magni said, tears erupting. "Please take us back to Mull. I don't want to be here anymore."

"Grant," Lennox said. "If we have to wait until you are all ferried across, Meg may not survive. I respectfully request to cross ahead of some of your men."

"She'll go on the first boat with me. I can take her once we are near the ferry."

"Nay, I'll see her to Mull. I promised her."

"You know her?"

"Nay, but I have spoken to her, so she is familiar with me. She may think you to be another trying to steal her away."

Connor arched a brow but didn't argue. "I'll see that you all travel on the next voyage. If we have all the missing bairns, I'll send half my force back to Grant land."

"Dyna will welcome your guards. I spoke with her this morn before I left Mull. We sent patrols across the isle searching for the bairns."

"Anything for my daughter." Connor motioned to two of his men. "Take the lads and the lass to the boat. Tell Alasdair to leave room for six more." The two headed down toward the boat. The crowd opened for the group as soon as Connor whistled.

The guards around them put their weapons away. One of them took Magni and another took Rowan and Lia. The men waved to Tora along the way, and she giggled, waving back at them. Lennox followed, making sure to keep up with the massive warhorse so he'd not be left behind. Once they made it to the loading area, things became a bit chaotic.

Grant asked, "Your horse going?"

"Aye, if you please."

A female voice squealed, "Tora? Is that you?" A woman with the whitest hair Lennox had ever seen approached and reached up for Tora, pulling her into her embrace, tears flowing down her cheeks.

"Gweetings, Gwandmama. I am fine because Meg saved us, and then the chieftain saved us too."

Connor dismounted, handling his animal while he leaned over and kissed the woman and Tora. "My wife, Sela, Chief MacVey."

"I'll take her on the ferry, Connor. It is too crowded out here," Sela said. "I don't like it."

"Wait, Sela. These two saved them, so they will travel on the first ferry along with the other three bairns." He motioned for his guards to let the bairns down and they moved over to Tora's side. "The woman is feverish, so we must get her to Eli. But please, take the two lads and the other girl with you. Go right to the front while I help MacVey with the lass."

Sela said, "Many thanks to you, Chief. My husband will repay your kindness when we arrive at Duart Castle. Know you our daughter, Dyna?"

Lennox handed Meg to Connor, then climbed down before taking her back into his arms. "Aye, we arranged a patrol with the other clans to search for the missing bairns. Now I see why Dyna's visions were confusing. She saw the boat and the place where they were hidden. It's an amazing skill your daughter has."

They moved among the crowd, and another man who looked like Tora's grandfather approached. "Tora? Is that you?"

"Aye, Uncle Alasdaiw. I'm going home now."

Connor said, "We'll only take four score since the bairns have been located. Send the others back to Grant land. Clear them out. We're leaving quickly."

"I'll tell Alick and join you."

"Their savior is sickly, and I wish to move along. Once you speak with Alick, please help Sela get the bairns situated safely on the ship. I'll take care of Midnight and MacVey's horse."

Alasdair glanced over at Meg and Lennox, then directed his question to Lennox. "Do you know who abducted them?"

Connor turned to Lennox, who shook his head. "We don't. I haven't questioned the bairns yet. They were too upset. My goal was to get them back first. The five slept in a cave last eve and have traveled for three days, so the men are surely looking for them. Meg was about to collapse when I found them. I did what I thought was best."

Alasdair said, "Wise move. Get the bairns to safety first. We'll find the bastards."

Connor said, "They had better start running."

Leaving his horse with Grant, Lennox found a spot on the upper deck and sat, laying Meg down with her head in his lap. He'd protect her from the bouncing of the birlinn the best he could. The waves were not bad, but there were enough horses on the lower deck to move things if they got upset. He noticed Alasdair chose the men who were to go below deck to keep the animals calm. *A wise move*, he thought.

The ship was crowded when they finally shoved away from the dock, but he noticed Magni and Rowan stuck close to Connor while Tora held on to her grandmother's hand, sitting on her lap.

"Magni, where's Lia?"

Magni didn't look him in the eye when he answered. "She had somewhere to go."

Lennox glanced back at the disappearing shoreline searching for a wee lass running about. "Who took her?"

Sela teared up. "I was so excited to have Tora back that I neglected to pay attention to Lia. I thought the lads had her."

Connor looked confused. "Where did the other lass go, Tora?" Connor asked.

"Lia said she would be busy. She told us all last night not to fwet about hew."

Rowan nodded. "She said she was going for

a brief journey, then she'd return. She made us promise not to tell anyone until she was gone."

Lennox didn't want to yell, though he felt the need to, but this was ridiculous. A young lass like Lia didn't just make plans to go off on her own.

Tora got up from her grandmother's lap and moved over to pat Lennox's hand. "Do not wowwy. She's not twuly a lass."

"What?" Connor and Lennox said in unison.

"She's a faewy. She'll weturn soon."

## Chapter Seventeen

*Lennox*

Once they arrived at Craignure, Lennox found his horse, Meg sleeping comfortably in his arms, then led the beast up the hill while he waited for Connor and his wife with the bairns. No one was there to greet them, but it was nearly dark, so the patrols should all be ending. It wouldn't take long for any at his castle and Duart Castle to notice the arrival of the recent visitors.

Sela approached him and said, "You know, Eli was trained by the two finest healers on the mainland. I know naught of your healers here, but please consider that it might be best to take her to Duart Castle. I'd be honored to watch over her. She's an angel sent to save these four."

"Many thanks to you, but I'll take her to Eli if she is receptive. I don't know Meg, but I have spoken with her, so she knows me enough to trust me. It has been a long day. I'll see what Dyna says about the other patrols and have her send messengers to Clan Rankin." He nodded toward Rowan. "His uncle is the chieftain."

Connor helped Lennox situate Meg in front of him in the saddle, then they led the first group up the hill to the main path just as two riders approached.

"Da!" Dyna squealed with excitement. "Is that Tora with Mama? Tora?"

Tora said, "I'm fine, Mama."

Dyna nearly dismounted but her father stopped her. "Tora's fine, but I ask that you wait until we are at the castle to greet her. We need to get the lass who saved them to a healer. She and MacVey brought them to safety. Is Eli at the castle?"

"Aye. Of course. Lennox, I'll need to hear everything." She led the way, and Connor fell back while Lennox moved abreast of Dyna.

"You have them all?" she asked.

Lennox said, "The two lads are coming with Alasdair."

"And Lia?"

"We had her, but she disappeared in the crowd. She gave some odd tales to the other three. We will send someone back for her. As for their abduction, I searched the area half a day east of Oban when I thought I saw Magni running about, so I followed him. This lass threatened to throw an axe in my chest if I approached Magni. She had them well hidden in a cave, but she's feverish from a wound. Tora said she saved them from a kirk, someplace they were locked up. That's all we know at the moment, but she is very sickly. We'll ask the bairns once they are inside and settled.

They are exhausted, hungry, and skittish. Tora seems unharmed."

Dyna glanced over at Meg. "Who is she?"

"I thought you might know her."

She shook her head. "I've never seen her. You didn't ask?"

"Once I got the axe from her and found the four bairns, she fell off the boulder in a faint and has only come to when she heard the name *Tamsin*. Said her sister's name is Tamsin and she's going to visit with her."

They arrived at the promontory and Dyna led them to the castle walls, calling ahead to open the gates and let them all in. Once they dismounted, Dyna said to Derric as he approached, "Take them to Eli. I'll get Tora. She's with my mother."

Derric said, "You found them? Is that not Magni with the Rankin lad?"

"Aye, I'll explain inside."

Derric led Lennox, Meg in his arms, into the keep just as Alaric and Eli opened the doors to greet the guests, with Broc behind them.

Derric said, "Eli, she needs you."

"Who is she? I've never seen her. Was that Tora's voice I heard?" Eli asked, peering over their heads. "Please tell me you have them with you, Lennox."

Lennox said, "Three of the bairns are safely with us. Lia is still missing. This is the lass who saved the bairns. Helped them escape from a locked chamber in a kirk."

"By all means, bring her in. Alaric, why don't you go with Broc? There are lots of horses still coming up the hill to be settled in the stables. See Murreal first for a light repast for all. Dyna will be too upset to think clearly."

Eli led Lennox into the healing chamber and pointed to a large bed. "Set her there. You can tell me what you know, then I'll ask you to leave so I can wash her and get her out of that filthy set of trews she has on. Start with her name."

Lennox did as she said, then found a stool and fell onto it. He had to admit that he didn't like letting the lass go. "Her name is Meg, that's all I know. Once they escaped the kirk, she kept them safe, I think two or three days before I found them. They slept in a cave a half day east of Oban. She had an axe and was ready to kill me if I stepped any closer."

Eli said, "An axe? I am impressed. I'll have to take some lessons. So, she found the four of them, and they are all here?"

"Aye. Well, almost. Lia stayed behind at Oban because she tricked everyone. She rode with me until we arrived at the ferry. She managed to get lost in the crowd of horses. Told the others she had something to do."

"A lass that young?"

"Ask Tora. She'll tell you things I question."

"I'll trust Dyna to take care of that. The three bairns are all hale to your eyes?"

"Aye. All happily jaunting toward Oban. Afraid, hungry, dirty, but anxious to get away. And they trust the lass completely. They're verra worried about her."

"I'm not worried. We'll go back for Lia. Back to this lass. Why is Meg feverish? A wound?"

"Aye. The bairns said she cut her hand chopping vegetables at the kirk two or three days ago. She held up until Rowan ran into my arms, then she fell off the boulder she was sitting on."

"Strong woman."

"Aye. One of the strongest, and I fear that axe could have landed in my chest."

There was a knock on the door and Eli said, "Enter."

Lennox's mother came in.

"Mother, how did you get here so fast?"

"The boats, the horses. We heard all. Rowan is fine. Sloan is on his way. Come home, Lennox. You said you'd be gone for a day, but it's been a few."

"Nay, I'm not leaving her." He nodded toward Meg on the bed. "Look, Mama. This woman is the one who saved the bairns. I will see her to her destination and explain everything to you in the hall. Please allow me to finish with Eli first before I answer your questions."

He could have sworn his mother smirked, but the look vanished and she said, "I'll wait for you."

He turned back to Eli, not willing to argue because he was too exhausted. "Check her finger under the dirt. I could see the swelling on her left hand."

Eli sat next to Meg and lifted her hand, moving the finger a touch.

Meg bolted up in the bed and said, "Don't you touch those bairns or I'll kill you." Her right hand swung out and punched Eli in the cheek, though the strike was not powerful enough to hurt. "Leave them alone. Leave me alone."

Lennox moved Eli out of the way and wrapped his arms around Meg so she couldn't move. "They're fine, Meg."

She stared at him and tried to wriggle away. "I wish to see them. I have to get them home."

"They are home," he said in his most calming voice. "Remember me? I'm Lennox MacVey. I found you in front of the cave where you threatened me with an axe to my chest if I moved. You're at Duart Castle on the Isle of Mull. Tora is with her mother, and Rowan's uncle is on his way. Magni's sire will be here soon."

"Lia? She left, did she not? She told me she was going to leave the others in Oban."

"We'll get Lia. This is Eli. She's a healer, and she's going to fix your finger. Once you've changed, the bairns will come in to see you, but we'll feed them first. You have my word that the three are safe, and we will go back for Lia."

Meg's head fell on his shoulder, and she clung to him. "Please don't let anyone harm them, Lennox. Promise me you'll find Lia."

"We will. I promise." He rubbed her back and glanced over at his mother, who was as wide-eyed as he'd ever seen her.

Meg closed her eyes and said, "Save them. The men will come back for them. They've already tried to follow us. Cruel bastards."

He peered over at Eli, who motioned for him to lay her back down. Once they had her settled, she said, "I'll wash her up and change her, then I'll have to lance her finger. I could probably use your help with that, so I don't take a fist to my other cheek. Give me a quarter hour and I'll call you in. Rut, mayhap you could ask Murreal for some vegetable broth? Meg needs food."

"Of course. I'll bring it back in for you, Eli. I can help feed her."

"Nay, I'll feed her, Mother. She doesn't know you." Lennox would not argue with her, so he stepped out.

He swore his mother looked at Eli and said, "Finally."

## Chapter Eighteen

*Connor*

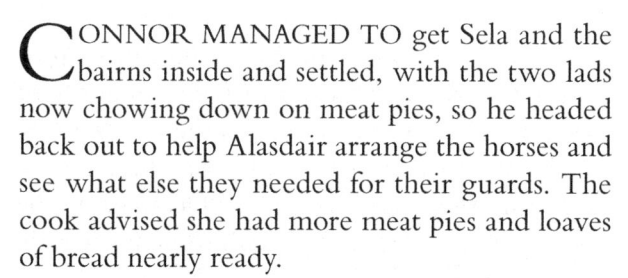

---

CONNOR MANAGED TO get Sela and the bairns inside and settled, with the two lads now chowing down on meat pies, so he headed back out to help Alasdair arrange the horses and see what else they needed for their guards. The cook advised she had more meat pies and loaves of bread nearly ready.

The men could wait, and they knew it.

Alasdair approached. "The stable buildings are beautiful. One made of wood with plenty of stalls with a wee bit of fire damage that we can fix, and a stone building with stalls and plenty of pallets and stools for our men."

"It's a fine night to sleep under the stars. Tell them to take care of the horses and we'll feed them in about an hour." Connor's gaze traveled to the castle entrance. "Alasdair, is that Logan?"

Alasdair spun around and asked, "Truly? No one has seen him since Alaric's wedding, or so I thought. Mayhap he's living here?"

Connor strode toward the entrance, pleased

to greet his old friend. He came in with two women on horses, and he swore one was Logan's wife, Gwyneth, the woman they thought to be dead from an infection in her leg. He approached to help one woman down, one he didn't know. "May I be of assistance, my lady?"

"Why, you surely could. I happily accept your help."

Connor smiled and lifted her down. "Connor Grant, father to Dyna, grandfather to the three wee hellions."

"A pleasure to meet you, Connor Grant. I am Eva, sister to Lennox MacVey. Is he here?"

"He is. I met him and he's a fine man. Your brother is part of the reason the bairns are here. He found the lass who'd moved them secretively nearly to Oban, and he's with our healer now, not for himself but for the lass. Please go inside and you'll hear the story. I wish to help this lady. Broc?" He waved over to his nephew.

Broc ran over to assist. Connor said, "Please escort Lady MacVey inside. I'll help Gwyneth."

As the two left, Connor grinned. "Hellfire, but you two are a pleasant sight to see, Logan and Gwyneth Ramsay. What are you doing here?"

Logan dismounted and moved over to his wife. "I'll get her, Connor. She's got issues now."

Connor waited but noticed right away that Gwyneth had lost her leg. "Sorry to learn you have issues, Gwyneth." He leaned over and kissed her cheek. "But I'm more pleased to see you are well. You are healed?"

"Aye, and my niece is working on some fancy

contraption to help me walk so I don't break Logan's back. It's lovely to see you, Connor. Glad you are here. There are some evil people on this isle. It's a lovely place with some fine clans, but there are always a few. You can help them, I am sure."

"There are evil people everywhere, Gwyneth, but you know that. I'm glad to be here to see my daughter and family. They are all inside. Are you staying here?"

Logan replied, "We stayed with Clan MacVey for a bit, but we're moving here now. I'll go let Alaric know, and then I'll return once I find myself an ale, Grant. We need to talk."

Connor nodded. "I'll be waiting."

"See if you can find a private place for a discussion."

"I'll find one. I believe I see a bench on the far side of the courtyard." He pointed to an area in the dark, but still inside the curtain wall. "Bring me an ale too, if you can, Logan. I'll be over there in a few minutes."

Connor hadn't expected to see Logan here, but it was a great surprise. He trusted Logan to assess the situation on the isle and update him on anything he needed to know. Logan had more experience than Derric and Dyna, and with Maitland on the mainland, they must be busy learning the area.

A few moments later, Connor found the bench and took a seat, loving the night air and scanning the new castle where his grandbairns would grow up. The smell of the salt air was unique to him, and he found it pleasing. He couldn't wait to explore the area on the morrow. After a good night's sleep.

But first, he must find a way to get all his worries off his mind. Relax, enjoy his family, his friends, his clan, and their many allies. Tora was home with her mother. That was the best part of his day.

Logan returned promptly carrying two goblets. "Fresh just for us, so the serving lass said. It tastes fine to me."

Connor took a sip and smiled. "Just what I needed. The meat pie can wait. I wish to hear your thoughts on the isle. I've talked with Maitland extensively, and he seemed pleased thus far. He didn't detect any true threats. Your concerns suggest otherwise."

"One that I know of. I'll update you with all I've learned." Logan took a seat next to Connor on the bench, but he barely had time to get his thoughts arranged when a lad came barreling out of the keep straight for him. "Chief Ramsay, you must do something. Please help her."

Connor looked to Logan and said, "You know this lad? He was one who was captured?"

"I do. Magni, calm down and tell me what has you in such a state." He moved to the edge of the bench, leaving a space for the lad between Connor and Logan. "Sit right here. You'll have the two strongest men to protect you."

"You have to go back for Lia. Please."

"Why didn't she come with you? I was

informed all the bairns were found." Logan looked at Connor for confirmation.

"All were found by Meg and Lennox. Lia didn't return on the ship. She remained in Oban."

Magni added, "Rowan and Tora came back, but Lia didn't. She made us all promise not to tell. So, we couldn't. She said she had to go somewhere to take care of some things."

Connor could see the lad was riled up over the issue, but he didn't know Lia or the lad, so he had to let Logan handle the situation.

"Magni, why are you telling me if she made you promise to keep her secret?"

"Because she said we couldn't tell Meg or the chief, but she didn't say we couldn't tell someone else. And besides, you already know she's not truly my sister." He leaned in to whisper, "You already guessed the truth, Chief Ramsay. They all think she's my sister because that's what she told me to say and I had to promise not to tell anyone where I found her and then she said to tell everyone we were brother and sister, but she never said I couldn't tell you the truth, but you already knew so…"

Logan held up his palms and said, "Magni, take a breath. Calm down. Do you see this man behind you?"

"Aye. Tora's grandsire."

"Aye, he's the chieftain of Clan Grant and they have nearly one thousand guards to help him. They'll do whatever he tells them to do. We will find Lia. I promise you."

Connor set his hand on the lad's shoulder. "I

swear to you, as one of the best swordsmen in all the land, along with my nephew, we will find the evil souls who dared to touch you and my granddaughter. They will be found, and they will pay."

"My thanks to you. But I don't know them."

Logan said, "Listen, Magni. We have many resources to help us, but I need you to tell me everything you know. Start at the beginning. Where did she find you? And where are your parents?"

Magni let out a deep sigh, but his shoulders relaxed, telling Connor he had calmed a wee bit. "Take your time, lad. Logan will wait."

"My parents were killed, and I was stolen away. The bad people brought me to Ulva, but I escaped."

"Good job, lad," Logan said.

"So, I hid in the forest on Mull and one night I was crying and that's when she came to me."

"She?"

"Lia. She was hiding under a leaf."

"A leaf?" Logan nodded but gave Connor one of his doubting looks. Connor motioned with his hand to let the boy continue.

"When I first saw her. You see, Lia is a faery of the woods, of the green meadow. And she can appear any way she wishes. She made herself bigger, but not quite my size."

"Why is Lia here? Faeries usually have special powers, special purposes."

"She does. She told me this in the cave after Meg saved us. She said that she had to take care of a few things, to help fix them, but she promised she'd come back to me. She said she can't change things herself, she has to push people to do things. I don't understand what that means, but she said people needed her. I begged her not to go. She promised not to leave me until we were safely on the boat. And when Lennox came, she said he would save us all, the five of us. So, she went to the docks with us, but then she said she had to leave for a bit. And then…" Magni peered up at Logan, then at Connor.

"Go ahead, Magni. Tell Logan everything."

Tears fell down the lad's cheeks and he said, "But you'll never believe me."

"We will. Tell us what you saw and what she said. Take your time." Logan set his hand on the boy's shoulder, and he nodded, then wiped his tears.

"She turned into a woman with a scarf and said, 'I've been waiting to do this for a long time. Now I must go, Magni.' Then she kissed my cheek and said, 'I'll be back.'"

He stared into space, transfixed. But then he broke into a wide grin. "Then she told me she would always be my sister. And I made her promise because I don't have anyone anymore. Just Thane."

Logan cleared his throat and looked up at the stars. "Lad, I'll be needing a grandson here. Connor, he's got a daughter, a grandson, and a granddaughter. And I have a granddaughter…"

"Who's that?"

"Eli is my granddaughter, but she spends all

her time with Alaric, her new husband. I have grandsons far away, but I miss them. I wish to adopt one here."

Magni looked up at Logan, the hope in his eyes nearly causing Connor to look away, but instead he broke into a wide grin. Logan had a way with bairns unlike anyone else he knew.

"Me? You'd pick me?"

Logan shrugged. "Only if you wish to be my grandson and if Thane agrees."

"Aye. I would. And Thane will agree. I told him I never had a grandda or a grandmama." Then he paused, scowling a bit before he lifted his head again. "But only if you promise to find Lia first."

Connor laughed and patted Magni on the back. "Ramsay, he must be yours. He's already conniving."

"I'm conni…con…what?"

"Never mind. I agree to your conditions."

"So how will we find Lia?"

"Did she tell you where she was going?"

"Nay, but she told Meg! She did. I heard her."

"What did she say?"

He shrugged and pouted. "I don't know. I never heard of the place, but Meg knows."

"Then I guess we'll be waiting until the morrow to go after Lia. Meg should improve by then."

"But what if we can't find her?"

Logan said, "Lad, if everything you told me about Lia is true, if she's truly a faerie, and I do believe you, then we won't find Lia until she wishes to be found. But if we don't find her, I'm sure of one thing."

"What?"

"She'll come back for you."

Magni threw himself at Logan, wrapping his arms around him in a big hug.

Logan glanced over at Connor.

Connor nodded, the silent pact made that they'd be going after the men who dared to kill this lad's parents and abduct him.

"Magni, I think the bread should be ready now. Go check. You must still be hungry."

"I am!"

Logan gave him a wee push toward the keep, the lad running so fast that it made Connor shake his head.

The two men stood at the same time, staring at the keep.

Connor asked, "You believe him?"

Logan ran his hand through his long gray locks. "Oddly enough, I do. Gwynie will. I'll be interested to hear what Meg has to say. I'll give instructions to Eli and Lennox that I am to be awakened when she comes around." He crossed his arms and asked, "You think he's telling the truth, Grant?"

"Aye, though I have no sound reason to believe in a faery. My daughter is a seer, and I believe my granddaughter is too. And sometimes I wonder about Astra. She is different, but Sela and I haven't quite figured out how."

"I'll ask a favor."

"Ask and I'll honor it."

"I can't quite handle my sword the way I used to. My shoulders are giving out on me somedays.

When we find the bastards who killed his parents, will you do me the honor?"

"I'll do better. I'll hold the sword, and you can plunge it into his heart."

Connor put his hand on Logan's shoulder and the two headed inside. "Glad to have you still here. You worried many."

Logan laughed and said, "Tell everyone at Clan Grant that we'll visit when we get this settled. But we have things to accomplish first. That's exactly what I told Brenna to tell all of Clan Ramsay." He stopped outside the door to the hall, staring up at the parapets. "Miss your sire, Grant."

"Every day."

"You leaving with me on the morrow, Grant?"

"First light."

# Chapter Nineteen

*Meg*

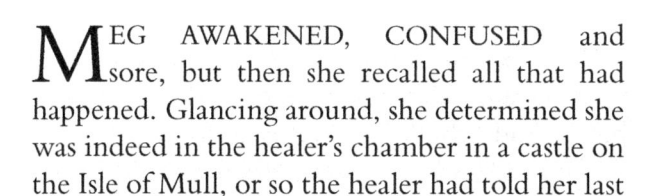

---

Meg awakened, confused and sore, but then she recalled all that had happened. Glancing around, she determined she was indeed in the healer's chamber in a castle on the Isle of Mull, or so the healer had told her last eve. Eli. That was it.

She recalled Eli's careful work, lancing the wound on her finger to drain the ugly green fluid from it, but then she soaked it in water before covering it with an ointment. She also gave her a potion to drink to help with the fever and added something for the soreness.

What she recalled more than Eli was Lennox.

Lennox held her while Eli sliced into her painful wound. She'd been leaning back against him, seated on his lap, and she'd turned her head into his chest, letting the tears flow as Eli did what needed to be done. It hurt worse than a tangle of bees when you tried to dig out the honey, or so her mother used to say.

He'd held her softly but tightly, his hands as

gentle as anyone's. Rough but gentle. His chest had felt like leaning against a stone wall, but the warmth of his arms around her had made her wish to never leave. It made her think on how long it had been since she'd been warmed by an embrace.

"You're awake?"

She had thought she was alone, so she searched in the dark for the speaker.

"Lennox? You're still here?" She scanned the area lit with a small torch by the door. It had to be the middle of the night.

"Of course. How is your finger?"

She picked it up, studying the bandage Eli had wrapped around it, moving it gingerly. "It is much better. And I think the fever is gone."

"You still look a wee bit flushed, but not as bad as you were earlier."

"And I'm hungry. Is that not a good sign?"

"Aye. I'll find something for you when you're ready. The castle has been busy this eve, so there's still bread available, and ale, even though most have taken to their beds. Mayhap some wine. Do you have a preference?"

"Nay, no ale or wine. The broth was fine. It felt good on my throat. None of us had much to drink while we were hidden away." She glanced up at him. The scruffy beard covering his face was now as dark as the starless sky, and it was oddly appealing to her.

Lennox was a handsome man.

Then something occurred to her. "Lennox, where are my things?" Frantically searching around the cot, she nearly stood up, swinging her legs out, but he stopped her.

"Lass, you have not eaten anything. I don't wish to see you fall. What exactly are you looking for? Your axe came with you. I saw that bag."

"My bracelet. The one my sister gave me. Please…" She swiped at the tears, trying to break free. "I must find it. Tamsin said…"

"I'll look. Was it in your sack?" Lennox moved over to a chest where her bag with the axe sat. "Is it in this bag?"

"Nay, I had a small bag attached to my belt. It's blue."

Lennox searched the area, then pulled something out of the larger bag. "Was it in this one?" he asked, bringing it to her.

"Aye," she said, taking the bag from him and opening the ties. She reached inside and felt the soft yarn. She let out a deep sigh. "It's here. I found it. Many thanks to you."

"Shall I put it back?" he asked.

"Nay," she replied, too sharply, but she kept it in her lap.

"Why don't you wear it? Naught will happen to it here. I'll help you tie it on. What is it made of?"

"I cannot wear it. I promised my sister I would only wear it when she was wearing hers. I'll keep it close." She returned it to the small bag and closed the ties, then glanced back up at him, suddenly lost in the blue of his eyes. Had she ever seen eyes that blue before? The torch gave them an odd glow.

"Look, Meg. I don't know how much you recall, but thanks to you, we have returned with Magni, Tora, and Rowan. Lia is still missing. Everyone is grateful for all you did for the bairns, but they are seeking answers."

"And they should be grateful for what you did, Lennox. You helped us all get to Oban. I couldn't have gone any farther." She meant that. Now that her mind was clearer, she could recall how sick she was, how her mind had begun to turn fuzzy. Could she have made it to Oban? Probably not without food and water first. This man was her hero.

"I think you would have if you had to. You've proven your strength to us all. But we still have many questions and are seeking your help in this. We need to know who stole them away and why."

"I don't know." She wasn't sure exactly what had happened, bits and pieces trying to connect in her mind. *Thirty-four, thirty-five, thirty-six, thirty-seven...* Her fingers clicked as she counted. She had to recall something.

He got up and sat on the bed next to her, taking her uninjured hand in his and cocooning it until his warmth suffused into her skin. This man did things to her that were unknown, confusing, but pleasant.

This close, his eyes entranced her even more, a most unusual shade of blue. His hair was nearly black, curling a wee bit at his neck, his entire aura so appealing that she had trouble paying attention to his words. Had she ever been this close to a man, other than her father?

The ugly baron did not count. She'd only wished to push him away, far away.

Lennox rubbed his thumb on the back of her hand. "Listen, mayhap if we talk about it, you may recall more than you think. It was also suggested that it might be better to speak with you when the bairns aren't around to hear your comments."

"But they could add some important parts that I don't know. I wasn't with them from the beginning."

"They have, but they're in bed now. It's late. Tora's parents and grandparents are here and would like to ask you questions, and Rowan's uncle is also here. I'll go with you when you are ready. I'll sit by the hearth next to you to keep you warm and promise to help where I can, but we can't have those men returning for the bairns. We think that is a possibility, don't you?"

She had worried of that happening, which was why she'd made them wait in the cave when Lennox had arrived. Of course, they'd all been frightened of exactly that situation. "Aye, it is surely possible." She gave his comments some thought and replied, "I will answer questions, if I can. Anything to help us find wee Lia. Mayhap they could help me determine where my sister is."

"I think they might be able to help with that too."

"But we must help the bairns first."

"Aye," he said with a smile, something that made him even more appealing. He stood and reached for her. "I'll help you stand, see how you feel. I can send Eli in, if you need her."

"All right. I'll try." Meg moved her legs to the side of the bed. "I'd like to wash my face, rinse my mouth. Is there water here?"

"I'll get a basin for you."

She stood, pleased that her strength was indeed returning. "I'll follow. See how well I do."

Lennox found a pitcher of water and filled a basin, setting it on a table in the middle of the chamber, then located two linen squares and a sliver of soap. "I wouldn't get that bandage wet, lass, until Eli takes it off. I'm sure she'll check it in the morn."

"Many thanks to you." Meg didn't know exactly how to speak to a man like Lennox. She'd never met a chieftain before, much less one who sent her heart racing and warmed her all the way to her toes with just one touch. Tall and broad-shouldered, his physique spoke of many hours working with his sword, if she were to guess. The man was made of sheer muscle, no chubby belly like she'd seen on the baron.

"I'll find Eli for you."

"Lennox, wait, please," she stuttered, flustered once he moved closer. *Sixteen, seventeen, eighteen...*

"Aye?"

"I just wish to thank you for your assistance. We were losing hope when you found us and... I'm sorry I nearly threw my axe at you. I was a bit muddled then, but without your help...and I don't recall much after that. I'm not sure how I even got here, but... Many thanks to you."

"It surely was my pleasure to find you and help you all return to the isle. Think naught of it. We all owe you for helping the bairns when you did. If not for your help, we may never have located them. We must move forward from here."

Then he smiled, his teeth so white that they lit up the dark chamber. And all she could do was stare. But then he surprised her more with what he did next.

He leaned over, kissed her cheek, and said, "I thank you for more than you know. You're forgiven about the axe. Someday, I'd be pleased if you would show me how you use it." He grinned and opened the door. "I'll return after Eli visits with you. We'll gather by the hearth so you can stay warm."

He left, and Eli entered a few moments later carrying a night rail for her. "Lennox said he asked you if you would speak with us. Do you feel up to it? We'd all appreciate it if you could do so now. We don't want to lose the ability to track the evil beasts who stole the bairns." Her words came out in such a rush that it gave Meg an inkling of how upset the parents of the bairns were.

"If you could help me with my ablutions and then find me another goblet of broth, I'd be in your debt, Eli. Many thanks for helping me with my wound. Then I'd be glad to answer all your questions."

Eli aided her in washing and then helped her don the robe. They were nearly finished when a knock on the door sounded.

"We'll be right there, Lennox."

Eli fussed with Meg's hair, trying to push the strays away from her face, but Meg said, "I don't mind. They don't bother me."

"And you're oddly as beautiful with or without the wild curls about your face."

Meg blushed, unused to hearing a compliment. "I'm ready." Never in her life had she considered herself beautiful.

Eli opened the door and Lennox stood outside, holding out his arm to assist her. "We're ready for you, Meg. I'll make introductions once I get you settled. We'll sit in the large chair in front of the fire. I'll make sure to keep you warm."

Meg had no idea what she was about to step into. Having never been around many adults other than in a kirk, this would be an unusual experience for her. *Eleven, twelve, thirteen…*

Lennox led her to a small grouping near the hearth, where several men and women were seated while one gray-haired man paced. She nodded to the group and the men bolted to their feet while Lennox settled her in a chair wide enough for two and gave her a fur for her lap.

"Allow me to make introductions, then we'll ask Meg to give us the story as she remembers it. After she finishes, then you may ask your questions. Meg, if you tire at any time, say so, and I'll escort you back to the healing chamber and the questions will end."

She nodded, swallowing as she took in the men and women around her. *Seven, eight, nine, ten…*

She squeezed her hands together so she wouldn't tick off the numbers with her fingers.

Eli offered her a goblet and placed a small table next to her to set it on. Meg, grateful, sipped the warm broth before putting it down.

Lennox motioned to one man. "Grant?" Two men and a woman came forward while another man stood with his arm around a white-haired woman's waist.

She guessed it to be Tora's mother and father.

"Meg, these are Tora's parents and grandparents. Connor Grant, retired chieftain of Clan Grant, with his wife Sela. His nephew Alasdair Grant, chieftain of the clan. Dyna Grant, Connor's daughter, and her husband, Derric."

Meg nodded to them, and Connor came forward with a brief word. "We are in your debt, lass. Let us know how we can repay this debt, and I will see it done."

Meg nodded and waited while Lennox moved to the next person. "My mother, Rut MacVey."

"My pleasure to meet you, Meg. May the Lord continue to shine His grace upon you."

Lennox's mother looked as though she were a queen seated in her court, the gown she wore unlike anything she'd ever seen. Meg's own mother had talked often of the beauty of the royal court, though Meg had never seen it.

Lennox pointed to another man who came forward, a bit too close for her comfort, but she had nowhere to go so she held still. "This is Rowan's uncle, Sloan, chieftain of Clan Rankin."

Also a handsome man, he reached for her hand, but as quickly as he reached, Lennox blocked him. "Do not touch her."

Sloan turned to Lennox and said, "I was going to kiss her hand as my thanks. The lass is unmarried, is she not?"

Lennox narrowed his gaze and said, "She's wounded. You will not touch her."

The two men stood chest to chest for several moments, though Meg didn't understand it. But she caught a few other movements while the two faced each other.

Rut's hand covered a wide smirk, Dyna wore a huge grin, and Alasdair came over and placed a hand on Sloan's shoulder. "Later. We have more important things to do."

Sloan stepped back, then gave a small bow. "I'm also in your debt, Meg."

The man with gray hair stopped his pacing and said, "Let's begin, MacVey. Time's a-wasting."

"And who are you, my lord? I did not hear your name." Meg waited, surprised when the man waved, dismissing her.

"You'll learn soon enough who I am." Then he turned away from her again.

Meg stood and said, "Excuse me."

## Chapter Twenty

*Meg*

---

THE GRAY-HAIRED MAN turned back to her, a shocked expression on his face, but the truth was that Meg had had enough of men and their rudeness.

"Were you speaking to me, Meg?" The man's face held a smirk she didn't like. Who was he and what was his relationship to the bairns?

She stood her ground, and Lennox moved beside her immediately, something she'd not soon forget. His support meant everything.

"I did, my lord. I spent most of my life being ordered about by my father, even to where he betrothed me to a baron who disgusted me. I left on my own and was insulted in many ways on my voyage, even in a kirk. Then I found men again deciding my fate without consulting me, trying to tell four innocent bairns and me what we were to do with our lives. Frankly, I've had enough insults, and I don't trust many at this point. So, I'll repeat myself. Who are you? Please be respectful and introduce yourself, or leave."

The old warrior strode over to stand in front of her, his alert eyes a dark green. Lennox took a step closer, but the man put a hand to his chest. "No need, MacVey. Please take a seat, my lady, and I will explain."

She did the best to quell the shaking in her legs before she sat again, arranging the fur across her lap. To her surprise, the man knelt and said, "The name is Logan Ramsay, and I am in your debt because I don't abide men treating women and children the way you were treated. I will avenge what happened to you. You have my word on it."

"My thanks, Logan Ramsay. It's a pleasure to make your acquaintance. Now, where shall I start? My journey or the bairns'? Though I just told you the major parts of my journey."

"The bairns' story, then, if you please," Connor said.

She cleared her throat just as Lennox settled himself in a chair across from her, his gaze locked on her face.

"I was told by a merchant in the village market that the kirk would allow me one night's stay in exchange for some kitchen work, which I was glad to provide, though that is how I injured my finger. I cut the vegetables, was given a warm meal and a small pallet for the night. When I awakened, I heard men discussing a shipment of bairns they'd received, and one man advised the other to keep me to care for them.

"I attempted to take my leave, but I was forced inside a small chamber in a different building where I met Lia, Magni, Rowan, and Tora. As soon as we were able to, we escaped and made our way toward the sea."

"What town was the market in?" Alasdair asked. "Or the name of the kirk?"

"I cannot tell you. I had only been away from home to a kirk and a small market when I was younger, so I am unfamiliar with the area. This was two days from my cottage. I'd never been to this kirk before. I followed a family to market, then was advised by a vendor to get to the kirk for my own safety, unsavory characters usually prowled the market, he warned me.

"I rode my horse to the kirk. I had to leave my mare behind when we escaped—but the kirk did have a large building for the altar, a smaller part in the back where the kitchens were found. I slept in the cellar. There was a stable behind it and two other outer buildings, the one we were held in, and another. I have no idea the purpose of the other building."

"The men," Logan said. "Names? Did you hear any?"

"One was named Herbert."

Logan said, "The other must have been Ellis."

Meg said, "Then I'll refer to him that way. The lads called Ellis *Pirate Man* because he had a patch over one eye." She did her best to describe both men. "Herbert was verra hairy, so the lads gave him that name, but I heard him called Herbert. Drab brown hair sticking up, a long brown beard, hair coming out of both ears and his nose, and he was thin. Ellis was tall and stronger as he was the one who lifted me when I fought, but I couldn't fight both of them."

"How many days did it take you to get to Oban from the kirk?" Sloan asked.

She thought for a moment, then replied, "We ran and walked for much of a day, spent one night on the ground, then found a cave for the second night. I don't recall how long it took to travel to Oban from that cave where Lennox found us."

"Half a day, so a two-and-a-half-day journey from Oban."

"Did no one follow you?" Dyna asked.

Meg blushed, a sudden memory in her head. "Aye." She paused, kneading her hands in her lap, taking a sip of the warm broth before confessing. She hated to do it, but she guessed she might need their help. Her hands shook at the horrid memory, something she'd forgotten.

To her surprise, Lennox moved over and set his hand on hers. "We will protect you from anyone, lass. We are all in your debt. And when they all take their leave," he said as his gaze scanned the group, "I pledge to protect you and see you to your sister. No one will harm you." He took two steps back but remained standing.

"You may not feel the same when I tell all." She looked up at Lennox, grateful he was there, but she had to be truthful. "I killed a man. He tried to steal Lia and Tora, so I threw my axe and hit him in the forehead. I did not think, I just reacted instinctively." She closed her eyes at the gore she recalled.

No one said a word, but she was suddenly lifted,

her eyes opening to find herself settled next to Lennox, his arms wrapped around her, warming her. "I suppose the sheriff will be coming for me for killing a man."

"Like hell. Do not worry on that," Logan said. "I'll give you a reward for killing a man and saving four innocent bairns. Did you recognize the man?"

She nodded. "Herbert. The one the bairns called Hairy."

"We need you to finish this story," Lennox prompted. "I'll keep you warm." His explanation suited her fine. "Now, how exactly did you escape from the chamber at the kirk?"

Taking a deep breath, she said, "Who is the parent of Lia and Magni?" She'd missed that introduction or forgotten.

Dyna said, "They are orphans. Brother and sister. Why do you ask?"

She wasn't quite sure what she wanted to say, but she finally asked, "Does Lia seem different to anyone else? We were locked in that chamber for a long time. I tried the door several times, tried using my dagger on it, even my axe to break the lock, but I couldn't do it. It was locked from the outside and there were no windows that we could reach. So, we made a plan to get the men inside, trip them, then escape and lock them in. It worked, but I think Lia helped a bit."

"Lia?" Sloan asked.

"Lia seems much older than her age. She managed to get the men inside without much work on our part. She's…different."

Logan glanced at Connor, but neither said anything.

"Where is Lia? I know she's missing, but I don't recall what happened."

Lennox explained, "She told Magni and the others she had something to do. She promised him she would return, but she intentionally lost herself in the crowd. We plan to return to find her at first light."

Connor said, "Once you've told us all you recall, we'll make our plans, but we will be breaking into groups. One group to look for the kirk, one to look for Lia, and one to attempt to find out who is running this collection of bastards. Who was in charge—Ellis or Herbert?"

"Neither. I heard them say they were paid to get the bairns from the kidnappers to the kirk where they were to be picked up the next day to go across the sea. All different men. Some to kidnap them and get them to the kirk, men to watch them until they were put on the boat. I don't know the destination."

Dyna spun and wrapped her arms around her husband, burying her face in his chest.

Sloan said, "I need to be the one to find the kidnappers who stole them away on the isle. The ones on horseback at Clan MacQuarie, the one who stole Rowan, and the ones who stole Tora. Those men are local or just came from Ulva or Iona or somewhere close. I want those bastards."

Connor said, "I want the head of the operation. I'll go to the kirk. Meg can describe the church for me. There cannot be that many two days from

Oban, near a market with outbuildings as she described."

Dyna said, "You mentioned being betrothed to a baron. I'm wondering if he could have anything to do with all of this?"

"I don't know how. He was to return the day after I left. He couldn't have followed me. And I don't think he would involve himself with this kind of situation. He wanted heirs. Three lads in two years."

Connor asked, "Meg, did the baron pay your sire any amount of coin for you?"

She thought back to the conversation she'd overheard and had to admit that Connor was probably correct. "I think so. I don't know how much. Why do you ask?"

"Because if he paid coin for a wife, he will want to find you. Please keep that in mind. While I'll agree with you that he's not likely to be the one to steal four bairns away when he was about to wed you, I do believe he might be searching for you. He may have hired some men to find his bride. I would not wander anywhere alone. Since you were a day ahead of him, he just hadn't found you yet. I would wager he will be seeking you out."

She had not considered this after she'd found the bairns. Her focus had been on saving the four innocents, not on her own situation. But there was much truth in his statement.

Neither her sire nor the baron would have been pleased to discover that she ran away.

They asked a few more questions, and Meg

answered what she could, but she had to admit, she was tiring quickly. However, she had her own questions too.

Logan stood and said, "Many thanks to you, Meg. I believe we'll get a few hours' rest, then we'll leave at first light. I suggest we meet at the stables and divide up the men as we choose then."

Everyone agreed and got up to take their leave. She wouldn't have it.

"Wait, please." Meg stood, stepping away from Lennox.

They all turned to look at her. Her voice cracked, but she wouldn't be ignored. "What about me? You all said you were in my debt, but you have not asked me at all what I want. I need your help. Please. I don't know where I am, who you all are, or where to go next."

Logan lifted his chin and crossed his arms. "Tell us and it will be done."

"I need to find my sister. She's supposed to be on the Isle of Ulva. Where is that? I have no idea. I have no ship. Little coin left. What do I do? I had a mare, but I had to leave her at the kirk. Please help me."

Eli came across the chamber while the others gathered around Meg. "What is your sister's name?"

"Tamsin. She married a man named Raghnall Garvie, but I never met him. Have you heard of him?"

Eli nodded, then smiled. "Spit and slime! Does your sister have one blue eye and one green?"

"Aye. She does. You know her?"

"Aye. It's a long story, but your sister is well. Her husband has passed on, but she lives on the Isle of Mull with Clan MacQuarie. She's verra happy, and you'll be pleased to learn that you have a beautiful niece named Alana. Their chieftain, Thane, is on his way here now. You may speak with him when he arrives."

Meg fell into the chair and sobbed. She knew immediately that this was her sister.

Tamsin had once said if she ever had a daughter, she would name her Alana.

She'd found her.

## Chapter Twenty-One

*Lennox*

LENNOX ESCORTED MEG back to the healing chamber while Eli followed. "I'll take it from here, Lennox. I wish to apply more ointment to her wound."

"Much thanks to you, Eli."

Meg moved to follow Eli into the chamber, but then she stopped, tugging on Lennox's arm. "Wait. I just recalled something that Lia told me when we were in the cave. She said she needed to go to a loch. Loch Aline, I think she said. Do you know where that is? Would that help you find her?"

"Nay," Lennox lied. "There is nowhere with that name that I am aware of. I think we have a good idea where to go from here. Don't worry about it."

Meg nodded and went inside the chamber, the door closing behind her.

Lennox hated lying to Meg, but he knew where Loch Aline was and that was exactly where he'd already planned to go. But this would be his search and his alone. He owed the bastard who had kidnapped him many years ago, and he swore the man lived in the castle overlooking Loch Aline. He'd received word that he had left, but now he wondered again. Perhaps Lennox needed to return to the site of the original crime against him.

Much as he tried to recall all the details, the memory had escaped him for years, preventing him from going after the fool. He'd been plagued with horrid dreams about a rowboat, but bits and pieces had still been missing about the entire event. When a nightmare brought the dreadful incident back to him, he'd gone to that site, only to learn the cruel bastard had moved on. He'd believed he'd done all he could, but he could no longer ignore it. He had to end this man's twisted ways. He'd tell no one, but he had to go back to his castle at first light. And Meg would go with him. He would not leave her behind. He didn't know why, but he was drawn to her and wasn't ready to leave her yet. He could leave her with his mother and Eva, then depart without telling anyone.

He just had to find a way to get there because he refused to use that vessel in his boathouse, the one that gave him the shivers whenever he approached it. Why, he wasn't sure.

But he had a feeling everything about the event was about to be uncovered.

He turned around and made his way back to the chamber where the group discussed the situation quietly. His mother hadn't moved, but her ears were taking in everything, Lennox was certain of that.

When he approached, he asked, "Your plan, gentlemen? And Dyna. My pardon."

Logan spun around and said, "Look, MacVey. I don't know if you and Rankin are aware of it, but someone is trying to gather enough men to take over the isle. Know you who that might be? Where they're working?"

That comment took him by surprise, so he peered at Sloan to see if it struck a chord with him. Sloan looked as confused as he was. "Nay, I know nothing of that. The eastern side of the isle is here—Grantham, MacVey, Rankin. MacQuarie on the west, and we're on fine terms with them. I know MacClane is trying to establish himself here, but he doesn't have enough men to take over the isle. Where did you learn of this, Ramsay?"

"I have my ways. I told him it was an impossible task now that Duart Castle was occupied by Grants and Ramsays. He isn't concerned. I made sure to let him know that any involvement with kidnapping bairns would involve an arrow to his bollocks, but he swore that he's not interested in the bairns."

Alasdair set his hands on his hips and paced in a small circle before stopping again. "So, we have a few possibilities—the baron who is to marry Meg, this fool who thinks he can take over the isle, and two twisted souls in a kirk back on the mainland about two days from Oban. Did I miss anyone? Preferences for pursuit? Who's going where?"

Sloan said, "I wish to search the isle. I want the bastard who stole Rowan, and I'm sure he's here. Hired from the outside."

Connor said, "Alasdair, we're going after the kirk. Dyna, I love you dearly, but I'd like you to stay back. There's no guarantee that the bastards won't be bold enough to return and attack. You need to be here to protect your bairns—you and Derric. I'm leaving half our forces to protect Duart Castle."

Derric said, "I agree, Connor. We'll stay here, and I thank you for your extra guards. But please find the bastards. I couldn't sleep thinking of all poor Tora could have been going through."

Logan said, "I'm traveling with you, Grant."

Then they all turned to Lennox.

"I'm going back to my clan, gathering some guards, and we're headed to Coll." Not exactly a lie, but not the truth either. "I've heard many times that there is some group in the Western Isles causing trouble. Suppose they are on Coll? We need to search farther out and not so close to home."

"Why?" Sloan asked, his hands on his hips. "We know the men who stole the kids are local."

"You all just patrolled Mull. Mayhap the first group are local, but someone is paying them coin to do it. I think the man Ramsay spoke with is from Coll or Tyree, mayhap Skye. We don't know. You heard Meg say it was different groups. Someone bringing them to the kirk, someone else caring for them until the third group arrives. How many more groups are involved? But it doesn't matter because the initial order is coming from someone bigger than a clan of Mull, and I want to know who. I've heard enough of foul deeds—Garvie, Thane's mother, Magni's parents being killed, Logan hearing someone who wishes to take over the isle. Something bigger is out there, and I intend to discover who is running it."

Logan said, "MacVey is right. Go to a different area and see what you can uncover. We need to explore farther. We'll be on the mainland learning what we can and will hopefully find Lia. Mull is Rankin's job. MacVey is going to Coll. Meet back here in a sennight and hope we all have some results to share. Gwynie will stay here with you, Dyna."

"Wonderful. Eli and I welcome another gifted archer."

Alasdair said, "I told Alick to hold four score men in the area, in case you changed your mind, Chief. They should still be not far from Oban."

"Wonderful thinking. I'll leave more here to protect the castle. MacVey, Rankin, if you need more men, I can send a score with each of you. Just say the word."

Sloan said, "I accept."

Lennox said, "Many thanks, but I have enough for now."

He wasn't telling them where he was going. Oh, he might end up on Coll, but he was starting right across the Sound of Mull to Loch Aline. Based on all he'd heard, he made the decision to leave Meg at Duart Castle until he returned. She'd be safer here because of all the Grant guards left behind. They would help protect Duart from any attackers.

He would find the bastard named Egan if it killed him.

## Chapter Twenty-Two

*Rut*

---

Rut paced outside the healing chamber, ignoring the conversation going on in the great hall. They could make their plans to find the bastards who stole the bairns, and she was sure they would, though she believed Lia to be in control of her own destiny. Faeries were real in her mind. She'd never met one, but she'd never mess with one either.

Time would tell in that respect.

She had more important duties to attend to.

She'd been waiting a long time for this. Her son was smitten, and with a lass who was as smart and feisty as they come. Rut had so many moments to tell Douglas about, the old goat, and he would enjoy every one of them, though she really believed that she needn't tell him anything. Her dead husband watched over them all the time.

She'd just witnessed the event she'd been waiting for, and how fortunate that it had taken place in front of her own eyes. When Sloan had attempted to touch Meg, and Lennox had stopped him, Rut nearly stood and cheered.

Lennox was falling for Meg.

Rut MacVey, as the wife of the past chief Douglas MacVey, had an obligation to see this through. She'd done her duty and produced two lads to take over Clan MacVey, but now she needed to ensure there were a couple of grandbairns before she could move on.

Lads or lassies, it didn't matter. The bairns that would come from Lennox and Meg's loins would be powerful. Of that much, she was certain.

Any lass who threatened her son with an axe deserved to be a MacVey.

Now she had to maneuver this just so. It was her duty.

She'd overheard Meg mention Loch Aline to Lennox, and she'd heard him lie through his teeth to tell her he didn't know of such a place, another event that nearly sent her to crowing. She'd never guessed that watching her son fall in love would be so damn entertaining. Now it was her turn to act.

She'd pull Meg aside and tell her that she had a way to find the exact location of Loch Aline, that she should come to their clan because it was closer to the loch, and that she'd send someone with her to look for Lia at Loch Aline.

Sure as the moon shone at night, that would be enough to piss Lennox off and force him into action.

Rut would not stand by and let this lovely lass get away. She needed a grandbairn, and she was about to get one in a year's time.

# Chapter Twenty-Three

*Meg*

---

Dawn arrived before she knew it. How was she certain?

Because of all the activity in the hall. Guards stuffed their faces with bread and porridge, their banter light and friendly, but there was something else.

The bairns were back and you could feel the happiness, the excitement, but also the tension. Magni bounced about, hugging people and giggling, but Meg could also tell when something stopped the poor lad in his excitement. Lia was not back yet. Tora didn't move far from her mother, and Rowan's parents had arrived, and he refused to leave his uncle's side.

Meg had awakened early and washed, dressing in a lovely pair of soft trews that Eli had called *leggings*. She'd never seen anything like them before for a lass, but Eli promised her that all the women in her clan wore them at some time. She'd also given Meg the finest tunic she'd ever worn, made of a deep blue that she adored, along with an extra tunic in a rich brown.

Eternally grateful for all they'd done for her, Meg thanked Eli many times, especially after changing her bandage and giving her an extra one along with a supply of ointment to put on her wound. Eli waved her away with a smile.

Meg hadn't spoken to anyone in the hall because the men were busy deciding who was going where, what horses, which ship, which guards. Listening to the strategics of such a big operation fascinated her, but even after she'd heard it all, she was still bothered.

Would they be able to find wee Lia?

She knew there were other issues—Ellis, the kirk, the men who wished to take over the isle—but her mind was on a sweet lass who'd never hurt the tiniest insect.

Meg had the urge to go after Lia on her own because she feared she might be forgotten amid the clan's worries. If she only knew where that loch was located—but if Lennox didn't know where it was, how would she?

She sat in a chair by the hearth, finishing her porridge, when Rut joined her. They were the only two by the fire, so she greeted Lennox's mother warmly. "Good day to you, my lady."

"Good morn to you. Are you going to return with us to our castle, Meg? You are more than welcome, and with all the Grant guards here, Eli and Dyna have more than they can handle, I fear. It would be much quieter where we are, and we have a lovely view of the sound."

"I'll consider it, surely, but I'd like to ask you a question, my lady. I'm not sure how to address your son."

Rut waved a hand at her. "He's not your chieftain, so just call him Lennox. He won't mind. Don't pay attention to anyone else."

"I did notice the trestle tables were full this morn at dawn. Are they not usually this busy?"

"Nay, Connor Grant brought all the guards to help find Tora. They're from the Highlands, and they will deliver just due for what was done to Tora. Connor and Alasdair will find the fools who dared to touch Connor's granddaughter." She leaned closer to Meg. "The villains should be running, if they have brains in their heads. Alasdair and Connor are both big, powerful warriors, if you ask me. How I'd love to be there when they find the fools."

Meg caught the glitter of appreciation in the older woman's eyes, something odd. She had much to learn about the world, having been hidden in her small village all her life. "Is Lennox on good terms with the clan where Eli thinks my sister is?"

"He is. He'll be glad to take you there, though I would bet Thane will bring your sister here once he learns of your arrival. I would wager he is on his way to check on things, probably with his men only, but I think he'll come to our clan first. Magni and Lia did stay with them for quite a while. Thane is the one who saved them from… Well, from the idiots who held him on Ulva. Anyway, our clan is closer, so he usually stops to visit with us before coming all the way to Duart Point."

Meg considered this, glancing around at the activity in the hall. "If Eli and Lennox agree, I will be pleased to come with you."

"You may have your own chamber up on the balcony next to Lennox's chamber. He'll protect you, fear not."

Meg had an idea that her own chamber would be larger than the one her parents had slept in forever. This was a different world on Mull.

Rut reached for her hand. "Besides. I overheard you talking with Lennox about some loch, but he didn't know of it. My Douglas loved maps. We have maps of all the isles and most of Scotland. If you wish to find that loch, I'm sure my daughter Eva could help you. She was here but she returned home. She was hoping to meet you."

A large group of guards rose from the trestle tables, some flirting with the serving lasses, some heading out the door, while Logan and the two Grant chieftains spoke near the hearth. Lennox came toward them. He greeted his mother, then said, "And how do you fare this morn, Meg?"

"Better, thank you, Lennox. Are you leaving this morn?"

"Aye, we will head out in about half the hour. I'm giving the Grants access to the stables first so they can make their way to the ferry. Sloan has taken his leave. We will go next. If you wish, you may stay here with Eli and Dyna. I'll return for you on the morrow."

"Oh," Meg said, unsure of how to make her

request. "Would it be acceptable for me to travel with you to Dounarwyse Castle? Duart Castle seems a bit crowded, and your mother thought Thane might stop on your land first. I would love to ask him questions about my sister. And—"

"And I told her Eva would love to meet her. Do you have any problems with that, Lennox?" His mother interrupted Meg, something she wasn't expecting.

Lennox appeared surprised, but then shook his head, though his expression was one of a calculating person, Meg thought.

"Nay, I don't mind, though I will be on patrol myself." He glanced from his mother back to Meg, his eyes narrowed.

Rut said, "I'll keep Meg busy, and Doiron can help with her bandages. Eli and Dyna have enough worries. That settles it. My saddlebag is by the door, Lennox. I'll help Meg gather her belongings."

Meg couldn't help but recognize that Lennox's mother had manipulated him rather well, making sure she got her way concerning where Meg was going next.

If she were being honest, she was happy to go to Lennox's home because she felt safe around him. Not that she didn't feel safe here with all the Grant guards milling about, but she knew Lennox. She trusted him. He'd helped her when she was lost. That had to mean something.

Not to mention that she wished to explore her feelings toward him a bit more. She'd never had a man's presence affect her so. Her heartbeat sped up, her palms sweated, and her mind moved slower than ever, her thoughts jumbled whenever he was near.

But those feelings switched to ones of worry soon enough. The urgency over Lia took over so she forced herself to listen to the groups in the hall again. Emotions were high, disagreements arose frequently, and everyone had strong opinions about what to do next, where to go. They spoke of the kirk, of the men who chased them, of the baron, of the man who planned to take over the isle.

There was one name she wasn't hearing, and it bothered her. She was so upset about it that she concluded that perhaps it was best to handle it herself.

Finding Lia.

The lass's name was not mentioned much, and Meg was worried. The lass did seem to be a different type, but regardless, she was only five summers old, and she was out there, and no one knew where. Lennox had said he was going on patrol, but where exactly?

Someone had to go after wee Lia. Meg had healed and rested enough. Perhaps it was time for her to go after the lass herself, if she just could determine exactly where Loch Aline was.

It seemed the place with the maps would be a great start.

And while a small part of her wished to rush to the other side of the isle to locate her sister, she knew that finding Lia had to come first. If she met Thane, mayhap she could convince him to go after Lia with her. Once Lia was found, Meg would run to Tamsin's side.

Lennox looked to Meg and asked, "Is this agreeable with you, lass?"

"Aye, I would like to see your home, and I could also—"

"Meet Eva and possibly Thane too." Rut cut her right off, of that much she was certain. So, the real question was, why didn't Rut wish to discuss the maps in front of her son?

What was the woman planning?

## Chapter Twenty-Four

*Lennox*

A FEW HOURS LATER, Lennox was standing not far from the stables on MacVey land, giving instructions to one of his most trusted guards, Jasper. "I'll be gone for about two days. Taskill will remain here, but I'll take five guards with me."

"Where are you headed, Chief?" The older man stood strong, his chin lifted because he prided himself in his hard work, having been a guard for both Douglas and Lennox.

"Eventually to Coll. I'm taking a short jaunt myself across the sound, then I will return to gather the men and go to Tobermory to cross there on the ferry. I want horses with us. You know my favorites." Giving Jasper this task would keep him from noticing that Lennox was headed out alone. This was something he needed to handle by himself.

"Aye, I'll see it done, Chief."

Lennox had spent his time in the stables while his mother quickly ushered Meg inside, though he had no idea why they were in such a hurry. Sometimes he recognized that getting involved in female matters was not the best idea, so he'd gone about his business. Undoubtedly, Rut probably took Meg straight to Doiron to discuss her wound. It would take days for the poor lass to recover completely.

"Where the hell is Taskill, Jasper?" He stepped outside the stables, surveying the area for his brother.

"Your mother requested his presence a short time ago, Chief," Jasper said, heading to a group of guards in their lists practicing their sword skills.

His mother had called for Taskill? What the hell was she up to now?

His sister came out the door, so he called to her. "Eva, is Taskill inside?"

"Aye, he's going over the maps with Meg. She's looking for Loch Aline. Mayhap you should join them, brother dearest? Your mother is at her finest." Then she gave him that warning grin the siblings shared when it came to their mother's antics.

"Hellfire," he grumbled. "My thanks, Eva." He strode into the keep, his boot falls echoing across the stone floor since the great hall was now empty. He loved the MacVey hall, beautiful tapestries of the castle and Mull decorating the walls, a hearth at each end to keep the area warm. He stopped, as he did whenever he found himself alone, just to admire the beauty of the dark carved wooden chairs on the dais, the carefully sewn cushioned chairs arranged in a semi-circle around each fireplace. Sometimes he was amazed that it belonged to him now that his sire was gone.

He had a sudden image of a hall full of bairns running around the tables, a beautiful lass with long legs staring up at him with a smile that affected him more than any other. How had meeting one lass altered his view of life so much? He shook the vision from his mind and headed toward the voices, not surprised to find the trio in his solar, studying maps.

"That's it," Taskill said. "It truly is nearly straight across from our dock area. We have a couple small boats and one ship we use. We keep them in a boathouse on the sound, though Lennox does not want one of them used. But there's no wind today. We could cross easily. Would you like me to take you?"

It was as if a small explosion erupted in his mind. What had he just heard? Taskill was taking who where? What the hell was happening?

Lennox flew around the corner into his solar, standing in the doorway. "Nay, you'll not be taking her anywhere." He knew he'd been a bit loud, but how had this turned into a trip across the sound in less than an hour? "Taskill, Jasper needs you outside. Go help him. We are going on a journey later, and I need your assistance."

Taskill did his usual, shrugging with a smile. "Sure, Chief. No reason to get upset. I was just trying to help. I'll take my leave now."

"Aye, go." He gave his brother's shoulder a shove when he reached the door, sending him out. If he were to guess, this was all part of his mother's careful planning, not Taskill's, so there was no reason to be upset with his brother.

He stepped back to get out of his way, but then Taskill leaned over to whisper in his ear, "If you don't claim her, I will. She's a beauty."

He grabbed his brother's tunic and said, "Nay, you willnae. Get out now."

Taskill chuckled and left, winking.

Lennox stepped inside, where his mother sat behind the desk wearing a smug look he'd wonder about later. He didn't have time for that now.

Meg glanced at him. "Lennox, Loch Aline is right across the sound. Taskill showed me on the map here."

"You can read a map?" His anger and annoyance vanished as soon as he locked eyes with Meg, her beauty stunning him. She was no longer disheveled and feverish. No wonder Taskill was interested in her. He couldn't stop himself from running a quick look down to her toes, surprised to see her wearing those tight trews the Grantham women wore. The kind that clung to every womanly curve she had. A soft groan left his lips, something he'd been powerless to stop. Those long legs called to him again.

His mother got up and strolled over to the doorway, looking into the hall.

"What?" Meg gave him a quizzical look just before she licked her lips. "Did you say something or are you upset with me?"

"I just asked if you could read a map. Most women cannot."

"I am not most women, Lennox. I understand that most are far more worldly than I am, but I am able to read a map."

The woman was going to embarrass him. His erection forced him to step behind his desk, turning slightly to hide it. "How?" That was the only word he could get out, anything to distract her.

She stopped to square her shoulders and stare at him, as if he were daft. "My mother taught me to read, and my sire taught me how to read a map."

"Still doesn't mean you can *interpret* a map, but well done. Most lasses do not possess that skill." He wiped a bead of sweat from his forehead. The lass was torturing him. He'd never had the desire to want someone so badly and be unable to touch her the way he wished.

Everywhere. He would touch every part of that tall, willowy body. First with his hand, then with his mouth. He'd taste every part of her if given the chance. What the hell was happening to him?

Her hand settled on her curvaceous hip. "Why didn't you tell me Loch Aline was over there?" She pointed to the Sound of Mull.

"I thought you said Loch Aleve. I misheard you." Damn it, but now he was in a twist. He hated lying, but sometimes there was no other recourse.

His mother coughed so loud, he cast a warning side-eye at her, but she still kept her gaze on the hall, peeking back occasionally.

Meg said, "I'd like to go over there. I am capable

of rowing on my own. Do you mind if I borrow a boat?"

"Aye, I do mind. You cannot go. You are sickly."

Meg glanced at Lennox's mother, who turned to shrug, then she looked back at him. "I'm not sickly, my lord. I'm fine. I'm verra worried about Lia. I see you have your own destination, so I'll go by myself."

"My name is Lennox. Not *my lord*." He would hear his name on her lips as often as he could. There was something about it that entranced him.

"Fine. Lennox, may I borrow your boat, if you please?"

"Nay, you may not. Women don't go on boats alone, Meg. I can see you don't understand how things are done, but I'll forgive your ignorance."

Meg looked as though he'd slapped her, and he caught the fury in her expression, her cheeks as red as the best apple in the orchard. Hell, but even angry she was gorgeous. Though for all that he'd said, he couldn't understand why she was so upset. He'd said nothing wrong. Had he?

"By the way," his mother interrupted, "Meg is worried about the baron. What shall we do if he comes for her?"

"Meg is not going anywhere. Not across the water and surely not with a baron, whichever idiot baron it is. When you recall his name, let me know and I'll send the fool a message."

"But Lennox, surely any baron could call upon the king to get his way…" His mother was persistent.

"King Edward mayhap would try, but King Robert would not allow him rights to a Scottish woman. I'll marry her, and that would surely put an end to this."

Meg gasped, then shoved at his chest. "You speak of me as if I'm a child, or not even here. As if I have no say in anything in my life. Get out of my way."

"Lennox," his mother said. "Be more considerate of her delicate constitution."

He spun around to speak with his mother. It was time to get her out of the solar. "Delicate constitution! She's about as delicate as Dyna Grant. Have you lost your senses, Mother? I don't have time for this." He turned toward Meg, but there was already a problem.

Meg had disappeared.

"Meg, get back here." Then he added, "If you *please,* come back here."

He was about to lose his mind.

## Chapter Twenty-Five

*Rut*

---

Rut NEARLY LAUGHED aloud, clapping her hands together with delight, but she held it inside. "Oh, Douglas. Our son is in for one hell of a night."

Glad that she'd had the foresight to give Meg a wee tour of the keep, she noticed that the lass had already grabbed her bag and headed out the back door.

Rut hurried over to the stairs, running up as fast as she could. As soon as she reached the landing, she nearly knocked over one of the housekeepers. "Your pardon. I'm going to take a rest for a wee bit. Please don't bother me, lass."

Then she raced to the end of the passageway, yanking the door open to the parapets to get up there before she missed anything. She grabbed her stool, the one she kept hidden in the small alcove for herself, then opened the door and tore around the corner to get to the back of the castle so she could watch the show.

"Douglas, we are going to enjoy this. Your son

is about to fall hard for this lass. My wager is he'll be bedding her before the night is over. But not until she's set him straight about her place as a woman."

Rut peeked through the crenellations, glad to see that Meg was nearly at the water's edge, trying to get inside the boathouse. Lennox was skipping steps to catch up to her, yelling as he did his best to keep up.

"See what I mean, Douglas? He's so upset that he can't calm down. He can only yell. And I have a feeling our Meg will put an end to his yelling in a quick moment. This will be fun to watch, I wager!" She giggled, covering her mouth.

"Don't you dare touch that boat or the oar, Meg!"

Rut tipped her head back and laughed, holding both hands over her mouth so her son wouldn't hear her. She was in luck because any sound made near the water carried beautifully. "Douglas, I believe we'll hear every word."

## Chapter Twenty-Six

*Meg*

---

MEG WAS SO angry with Lennox, she was ready to spit.

"Meg, wait. Please."

She stopped and whirled around. "Fine. I'll wait. What is it you wish to tell me now? How foolish I am? How weak I am? What now? I'm sorry I'm not a chieftain as you are, but that doesn't mean I don't have a brain."

"Forgive me, I did not mean to imply you are ignorant."

"You used those words, Lennox. I'll forgive your *ignorance*. Did you forget them already?" Her hands balled into fists on her hips. Oh, how tired she was with all these men telling her what to do.

"Your ignorance about women rowing their own boat. Naught else. Forgive me. Please calm down and allow us the time to talk about this."

"Oh, I think I know exactly what you wish to tell me. *Be kind, Meg. Don't get me upset, Meg. Do as I bid you, Meg. Do as I say, Meg.* What else do you have to say?"

"You're changing my words, lass. Do not twist this around to your favor."

"All right. Then let's start with this. Why did you lie to me about Loch Aline?"

"It wasn't intentional. It was—"

"It most certainly was intentional. Another lie."

He growled. "Meg, don't push me in a way you don't want. I can only tolerate so much insolence."

"You can only tolerate so much insolence? I'm not in your clan, Lennox. And guess what? I'm tired of men telling me what to do. Why do men think they should be deciding what's best for me? Mayhap I might know what's best and what I want. And by the way, I'll not be marrying you, you insufferable lout. How dare you assume something for me."

"Insufferable lout! You insult me on my own land, after how hospitable I've been to you?"

"Aye, I do. I'm taking that boat whether you like it or not. You may come with me if you prefer, but I'm going to cross that water if I have to find a log to climb on. There's a wee lass of five summers who needs me. All you wise men are worried about everything else. I'm worried about Lia!"

"You'll not be taking that boat. I haven't allowed anyone to touch it, so surely I'm not going to allow you to take it. Leave it be, Meg."

She spun around and opened the door to the boathouse, tugging out a boat and shoving it into the water.

"You can't do this."

She turned to glare at him. "Watch me." She grabbed the boat but he yanked it back.

"Not that one."

"Why not?"

"I don't need to give you a reason. Use the other one."

"It's dirty."

"Well you can't take either one. I won't allow it. You'll never make it on your own."

"Lennox, I am not a wee bairn. I can row."

"Mayhap on a different day, but you had a fever for the last two days. How could you possibly think you are strong enough to row across the water on your own?"

"Mayhap because I *am* strong? I can throw an axe. I killed a man by putting an axe in the middle of his forehead. I was intelligent enough to hide our tracks as we crossed the mainland toward Oban. I found my own way when I left my home. And I can verra well find a wee lass before someone steals her and insults her all. Day. Long." Tears misted Meg's vision, but she swiped them away. "Why must you continue to insult me? I'm not weak nor am I ignorant, Lennox. Please get out of my way." She reached for the first boat again.

"Not that one."

"I prefer this one." She glared at him, then grabbed her saddlebag and tossed it into the vessel. "The water is like the finest calm day of summer, nearly like the ice in winter. I will be fine. I promise to return your vessel by the morrow, Lennox. Now please step aside, and I'll not bother you again." Her voice dropped to a calmer tone. She was tired of arguing with the arrogant man. And she would not cry.

He grabbed two more oars and threw them in the boat, then grabbed a bag from within the boathouse and tossed that inside. He removed his sword and placed it in the bottom of the vessel that he hated so. He didn't know if he could get in it, but she wasn't changing her mind. He'd have to be the strong one in this pair.

"I'm going with you."

"No need. I'll be fine."

"It's my boat. I'm going with you." He sighed and said, "You want the truth? I was headed to Loch Aline on my own. The man who lived near that castle kidnapped me long ago, but I escaped by outsmarting him. And he did it in a boat that looks just like this one. They were to do the same to me—sell me to some fool who wished for me to build a curtain wall, never to return home. They dropped me over the side of the boat, hoping I would drown, but I swam underwater. I never told my mother or anyone all that happened. But I know. I know what he looks like, where he hides, and I'm going after him. I cannot allow you to go alone. You have no idea who you're dealing with."

Meg stopped, staring up at Lennox, his hands on his hips. His eyes had that shadow of deep pain, the blue as cold as the ice on a winter loch. Somehow, she had a sudden understanding of this handsome, strong man who'd been undone long ago as a lad, his world shattered in an instant by a soulless fool who'd stolen his innocence.

"I'm sorry, Lennox." What else was there to say? This powerful chieftain just confessed something he'd never told another. He deserved a hug, but it would be inappropriate. Words were all she could offer him.

"I'm going with you, Meg," he said in a small voice. "I have to. I'm a fool sometimes, but I know what's right and what's wrong, and those bastards are wrong."

She reached up and cupped his cheek. "Many thanks to you. I'd be pleased to have you along." She dropped her hands and turned back around, only to find herself tugged back into his arms.

Lennox's mouth descended on hers in a kiss that startled her, mostly because she'd never been kissed like this before.

But damn if she didn't like it. He let her go as quickly as he'd pulled her close, but then he kissed her forehead and said, "Let's go find Lia."

Lennox helped her into the boat and attached the oars, settling their few belongings. But the oddest thing happened. When he shoved the boat away from the coastline, Meg swore she heard someone clapping.

## Chapter Twenty-Seven

*Lennox*

―⚬―

Hellfire, THIS LASS was going to test him, but he hated to admit that he'd never felt more alive. Meg was gorgeous, smart, feisty, with legs that he hoped to have wrapped around his waist soon enough.

Still shocked that he'd volunteered to marry her to get her out of her betrothal, he found that marriage wasn't the abhorrent idea he would have called it in his past.

He could picture Meg as his wife, only being a touch away on the other side of his bed, managing the castle, even bearing their children. First, he wished to see her with her hair unplaited. How long was it? Would it go to her waist or was it long and thick enough to cover the round globes of her bottom?

He shook his head, vanquishing the thoughts from his mind.

They were halfway across the sound, no other boats in sight, fortunately.

"That is Loch Aline. And the castle I seek is at

the far end of the loch." He pointed ahead, the landscape beautiful, as it usually was in summer.

"I'm sorry you had to go through that, Lennox. I'm sure the memories don't leave you often," she said, turning back to him as she rowed. They rowed in unison, both facing the loch, and though his strokes were stronger, she kept an impressive rhythm.

He had to stop thinking about the beauty in front of him and decide exactly where to go once they reached the mainland. There would be others around the dock at the end—fishermen, some coming from the small town near the area—but his eyes would be on the castle. He was quite sure that the man named Egan had operated from the MacKinnis Castle many years ago. He'd never seen him there since, but this was a new day.

"Over there, Meg. We'll hide the boat behind those bushes. I've done it often enough." There had been many times he thought he'd had the desire to chase after the fool, hopeful that coming to the same area would restore his memories, but it never had.

Until recently. For some odd reason, he'd remembered everything in a dream. He prayed that this would help them find Lia.

He hopped out when he was nearly onto the shallow beach, taking the front of the boat up over the sand. He held out his hand to Meg, though he feared she was angry enough to deny him. But she took his hand, and he tugged her close, giving her the most honest explanation he'd ever had. "Lass, being around you jumbles my mind more than anything else. You make me feel like a laddie hoping to get his first kiss. I apologize for muddling my words so. I never intended to insult you."

She stood in front of him, their gazes locked, and he lost track of his thoughts, so taken by her simple, exquisite beauty, by all the images she conjured in his mind that he had to tear himself away from. He dropped her hands so he could grab his weapon and hide the boat in the bushes, then led the way to the castle down the coastline to the MacKinnis stronghold, Kinlochaline Castle.

He'd visited with his mother many years ago after he'd been found on the shore, but out of respect for her, he'd never mentioned what had befallen him. He'd never told anyone exactly what had happened, mostly because he didn't remember all the details until years later. His sire had insisted, but he'd told him he didn't remember. At the time, he'd been telling the truth, but now he remembered, especially a man named Egan.

Lennox and Meg made their way around the coastline and headed to Kinlochaline. To his surprise, they met the clan chieftain, Angus MacKinnis, along the way, so he introduced Meg, then decided to be direct.

"Chief, forgive our intrusion. This is a friend of our clan, Meg. I met someone here many years ago, and I wondered if he was still part of your guardsmen. A man named Egan?"

"Egan?" Angus didn't try to hide his surprise, scratching his chin as his gaze narrowed. "I surely do recall him, but he's no longer with us. The fool decided to become involved in some unsavory practices, so I let him go. Probably over a decade ago, if my memory serves me correctly. Anything else I can help you with, MacVey? Care for a brief repast? You are always welcome."

"Many thanks, but I don't have time now. But if I may impose, could I borrow two horses? I promise to return them within a sennight."

"For certes. I know how difficult it is to get those horses across the sea. I think I owe you for the same kindness last autumn."

"Many thanks to you, Angus. Hope your wife is doing well."

"She is." Angus pointed to the rear of the castle. "Stables are in the area behind us. Isaac will assist you. He's been here a long time."

"Many thanks." Lennox set his hand at Meg's lower back, ushering her across the courtyard and toward the stables. He approached the building and a lad greeted him.

"My lord, may I be of assistance?"

"Aye, is Isaac available?"

A man came to the door of the stable and lifted his chin. "Och, MacVey. How have you been, Chief? And I see you have a pretty lass with you. How can I be of assistance?"

"This is Meg, Isaac. Would you find her a sweet mare and a nice stallion for me we can borrow for a day or two? Angus approved."

"Of course he would approve. You have to loan horses to your neighbors across the water. 'Tis the only way when you live on the sound. I've got two fine mounts for you who get along well, and I'll send a bag of food with you too."

Lennox had the urge to take Meg's hand, so he attempted, but asked, "Do you mind?"

"Nay," she said.

He led her inside to the back, away from the stable lads, so they could talk privately. "Isaac, I have a question for you. Do you recall a man named Egan?"

Isaac stopped and turned to face him. "The bastard Egan? The one who preyed on young boys just for coin? That one?" Isaac knew exactly who he was speaking of, something that was fresh in his mind.

"Aye. He's the one. Know you where he is? We have a missing lad nearby and I thought to look him up."

While Isaac saddled up the two horses, he carried on with his story. "He's a lying piece of... Your pardon, my lady. Egan's no good. Chief sent him away many years ago, but he's still doing his dirty deeds. I heard of it not long ago, half the year, mayhap. He stole a lad from Ardtornish Castle. And if you cannae find the no-good piece of... Sorry, my lady. If you cannae find him there, then go to Drimnin. You'll surely find him there."

"Isaac," Meg said. "You have not seen a golden-haired lass in green anywhere, have you? She's missing and we must find her."

"Nay, and I would notice if a lass such as that were about. No lassies around here."

"Many thanks, Isaac," Lennox said. "We'll see

if we can find out anything more about him in Ardtornish or Drimnin."

Isaac picked up an empty canvas bag and tossed it on the floor, stomping on it. "'Tis what I'll do to the fool if I ever find him again. Someone needs to put a sword through his twisted soul. Too many people turn their heads. Not me. I told the master soon as I saw what he was doing."

Isaac hadn't been here when Lennox was, or he probably would have prevented Lennox's abduction. This was not the time to think on what could have been. It happened, he remembered, and now it was time to find a wee lass before Egan was able to sell her.

Once the horses were ready, Isaac offered Meg a fur. "For your lap, my lady. A gift from me. The nights are cool, as you know. Godspeed to you both. Find the lying bastard."

They headed out, found the main path, and Lennox led the way toward Ardtornish Castle, near a thriving village. He hoped to find an inn, a good place to question the local villagers and find out if anyone knew anything about Egan or Lia.

They traveled inland through high sun and into the middle of the afternoon when they approached the outer edges of the village.

Aeoineadh Mor was a lovely village, situated not far from Loch Arienes, settled in a fine valley between the mountains of the Highlands. They found the inn and left the horses in the town stables so they could grab a bite to eat.

They had a lovely lunch—lamb pottage with

a small platter of fruit—but after questioning, no one had heard of Egan.

Lennox paid the innkeeper, bought some dried meat and cheese for their trip, then headed out. They were nearly mounted and ready to leave when a woman came running out of the inn. "Your pardon, but you are the ones looking for Egan?"

Lennox spun around and nodded at the woman who appeared to work in the kitchens. She latched onto his arm with a grip that told him how upset she was about the situation. "I couldn't let you go. Egan stole my son away nearly two years ago, but I'll never forget it. I've tried to have the sheriff take him away to gaol, but he always escapes." She stopped to gather herself, her breath coming out in small hitches.

"Know you where we can find him?" Meg asked.

"Drimnin. I swear that's where he does most of his work. Sells the bairns to work in Europe for the wealthy. I hate him. Please find him and rip out his heart."

Lennox nodded. "We'll do our best."

"Rip out his heart because that's exactly what he did to me. Find him."

## Chapter Twenty-Eight

*Connor*

---

"NORTHEAST, AYE?" CONNOR asked, looking to Alasdair, who nodded.

They ran into Alick a quarter hour later, and Alasdair updated his cousin on the situation. "I've got two score guards not far, Chief. I sent the other two score home. How many do you want to take with you?"

"Two men. Five of us will be enough. I don't want to be too obvious. I hope we're back by the end of the day, and if our mission is successful, you can head back to Grant land."

"Tora is well? And the others too?"

"Aye, wee Tora is tough like her mother. The two lads were more shook than either lass, but Tora told me she could see me nearby, so that calmed her." Connor shrugged. "If I must say, Astra was happier to see Tora than anyone else. She felt responsible because they rode the horse together." He knew how soft Astra's heart was, so he guessed she'd be returning to Grant land when he and Sela did. Wee Tora had the constitution of her mother and then some. He didn't understand his daughter's special talents, and now that his granddaughter demonstrated similar abilities, he understood it even less.

"Anything you wish for me to report back when I go, Chief?"

"I'm sure Sela will not allow me to return for at least a fortnight, but Alasdair I'll send back in a sennight unless we need him to stay. It shouldn't take us long to find these fools. We have plenty of men searching for them."

Alick nodded. "Godspeed with you. I'll not be far when you return."

They waited for the two men Alick chose to join their party, then headed out, explaining exactly what they were looking for.

Connor said, "Logan, you take the lead since you have the best tracker skills. Know you anything about this area from all your spy days?"

"Aye. I know of a kirk or two, but the one I'm thinking of is larger and has buildings behind it. Meg's description fit with what I recalled about it."

"What village?" Alasdair asked.

"Taynuilt. There's a chapel nearby, and it's about two-and-a-half days' travel by foot, so it would fit with their timeline."

"What about the cave? We could find it along the way. At least we'll know we're going in the right direction." Alasdair's gaze scanned the area. "Any passing knowledge about caves, Logan?"

"MacVey told me where it would be. Follow me."

They'd only been traveling for about an hour when Logan put up his hand. "Hold." He pointed off in the distance to a group approaching.

Connor pulled his horse abreast of Logan. "English? I think those soldiers are English. What the hell are they doing this far north of the border?"

As soon as the lead man of the English group caught sight of them, he waved to Logan, calling him over.

Logan approached but kept his distance. "What do you want? Are you not lost?"

The head of the small cavalry said, "I speak on behalf of Baron Neville de Wilton. We are searching for his betrothed who was stolen from her home. Have you seen a young lass held captive by anyone?"

"Nay. Go back to the Borderlands."

The man glared at him but turned his horse around and headed toward Oban.

"Who was that?" Alasdair asked. "I couldn't hear him."

Connor said, "I don't think I wish to hear your answer, Logan."

"I believe that was Meg's betrothed. Looking for a lass who was taken captive. Said she was the baron's betrothed. I hope they don't travel to Mull," Logan said, watching the group as they took their leave.

Connor said, "Naught like a score of Englishmen to convince MacVey to stake his claim." He grinned, and Logan snorted.

"Could be good if he went to Mull. I think we all know that MacVey will never let her go."

Alasdair said, "The baron's men are on the move. We need to make it back to Mull before they decide to head there. Let MacVey know he's coming for her. And let Meg know too. I wouldn't let her go with him. Arrogant bastard didn't even have the bollocks to speak himself. Made his second speak for him. I knew it was him hiding behind the others."

"Da would never have done so," Connor said. "He believed in leading his men wherever they went."

"That's why your sire has the reputation he has, and that fat arse couldn't even move his mount forward to speak with us." Logan spit off to the side. "Do you think he has anything to do with the bairns?"

Connor and Alasdair answered in unison. "Nay."

Connor continued, "He's only got one thing on his mind, and it's getting Meg with child. We have to warn Meg. Move along, Logan. Finish what we came for, then we'll deal with the baron and his men. If I need to send the rest of my guards after him, I'll do it before we cross the firth again."

The group headed northeast of Oban and found the cave without any problem.

Logan said, "It's exactly where MacVey told me it would be. I see evidence of bairns in the area, grass trampled in clumps. Bairns always move close together." Once they left, he added, "Remember, they were on foot. We should be there by the end of the day as long as we don't take many wrong turns."

"Agreed," Connor said.

They followed just off the main path, Logan tracking for heavily trampled grass and small broken branches about the height of the bairns. There hadn't been much rain since then, only drizzle, so he could still see where they'd traveled.

Just after high sun, the odor of a dead body reached them. Logan pointed to an area behind a group of trees. "There. The bastard is in there."

Connor dismounted and headed in that direction. Logan said, "I'll stay mounted. Check him up close to make sure he looks like Hairy."

Connor led the way, his nephew behind him, but neither were prepared for what they found. Connor hadn't seen anything like it before, the axe sticking straight up from the dead man's forehead. "Damn, but that lass can shoot an axe."

"She left it too," Alasdair said.

Connor snorted. "I couldn't hit a man like that if I practiced for two moons. What the hell? I'm impressed."

Alasdair chuckled. "MacVey better make her his soon. If he doesn't, someone else will be looking to take her as a wife. Any Highlander would steal a feisty lass like Meg for a bride. He better not let Broc get to know her."

They headed back to Logan, Alasdair explaining the best he could. "Axe planted right in the middle of a forehead, with long hair sticking up, down, and everywhere. And aye, I checked the ears. I'm quite sure he's Hairy Herbert."

Logan grinned. "Then we're headed in the right direction."

Connor took the reins of Logan's horse and led him to the right spot. "You have to see it for yourself. The lass has deadly aim."

Logan whistled when he saw the body. "She must have had another axe. MacVey said she nearly hit him with one."

Alasdair joined them. "MacVey got hit with a different kind, an arrow straight to his heart. My guess is he wants to make her his, but she's too unsettled to accept him. Emmalin was the same after all she'd been through."

Logan turned his horse and headed back toward the path. "I think MacVey will get exactly what he wants. My guess is he's been waiting for her. You both know how chieftains are. Won't settle for just a pretty face. Lasses would never guess that the way they fire an axe will get a husband faster than a pretty dress."

"Or how fast they can fire five arrows."

"Or the fact that they dare to stand toe to toe with a man and are not easily intimidated. Being as sickly as she was and still holding up the axe is a sign of a powerful constitution. Reminds me of Sela." Connor smiled at the memory of his wife when they'd first met in Inverness.

"And Emmalin."

"My Gwynie." Logan smiled. "When you find a lass with that kind of internal strength, you cannot let her go."

They moved on and made it to the chapel a short time later, where they dismounted and left their horses hidden. Logan nodded toward the church. "You wish to do the honors, Grant? She's your granddaughter. You have rights."

"I do," Connor said, moving to the rear entry of the main kirk, and nodding when he saw the outer buildings. Returning to the front he added, "Knock on the front door, Logan. Alasdair and I will go around back to catch him running."

Connor stood a horse length away from the door, his hand on the hilt of his sword. A few moments later, the door burst open and a man in robes flew out, looking over his shoulder at Logan behind him. He ran right into Alasdair.

"Going somewhere, Father?" Alasdair asked, holding the priest by the arm.

"Leave me be. I'm going to say my nightly prayers. How dare you stop a priest!"

"You aren't going anywhere, Father, until you tell me where the pirate is." Connor held his sword in front of him now, moving his arms to warm up his shoulders in case he had to defend himself. "Though I have my doubts that you are a real priest."

"The pirate?"

Logan came up behind him. "Look, you lying piece of shite. You are not a priest, you take coin for selling bairns, and unless you wish me to hang you on that tree by the bollocks, you'll tell us where the pirate is. The man with the patch over one eye who locked a group of bairns in that outbuilding over there. Shall I see how dirty it is? See any evidence of wee ones inside? They probably pished in a bucket that you haven't emptied yet. You do recall how you took innocent ones captive? We could lock you inside while we're looking."

"Nay, please, nay. He forces me. If I don't keep them for a night, he says he'll kill me and our cook. He has no respect for the collar at all. I don't want to do it. It's why I kept that lass to be nicer to the bairns, but they ran away. Herbert never returned, but Ellis said he'd be back."

"Does Ellis wear a patch over his eye?"

He nodded. "I don't know where he is."

The cook came out the back door and said, "I'll tell you where he is. He lives on the other side of the village, a small hut at the end of a lane by the blacksmith's shop."

Logan grabbed the man by the neck. "If not for that collar, I'd hang you on that tree for lying. These are bairns, you sick, twisted bastard."

He shoved him back, and the priest tripped over his own feet, landing face-first in the mud.

An hour later, the group located Ellis, but he claimed he knew nothing about what they spoke of. Connor tied him to his horse and made him run to see what had happened to his friend.

It wasn't long before they came upon the body behind the trees. Ellis shook his head. "Nay. I don't wish to see him again."

"You knew he was dead because you followed him. See how he looks now. Surely you recall your friend, Herbert?" Connor asked, shoving him forward toward the decaying body. "I think you should bury your friend."

"He's not my friend. I only knew him for one night."

"I don't believe you, but I'm not going to mince words. Do you recall the girl with the white hair that you held against her will? She's my granddaughter and I have two score men an hour away who are bored and would love to play hang and quarter with you."

Connor got off his horse and strode toward him. Ellis turned to escape but ran right into Alasdair's chest. Connor picked him up and tossed him over Alasdair's head, and he landed in a heap with a groan. Connor set his boot on Ellis's chest, the tip of his sword at his throat.

Ellis moaned, a wet stain appearing on his trews. "I didn't know. I swear. I thought they were orphans. We were going to give them a home."

"The chest or the throat? Make your choice because the next lie you tell will be your last. I promise you that."

"I didn't know. I didn't know. They don't tell us anything."

Connor grinned. "What do you recommend, Logan?"

"He only gets one chance. And if he doesn't tell us what we wish to know, I'll push your sword straight into his mouth until it comes out of the back of the fool's head. One chance, arsehole. If you tell us who else is involved, we'll not kill you and take you to the sheriff instead."

"I don't know."

"Sure, you do. You know who gives you the

coin," Connor said. He placed his sword against the man's belly and cut through his tunic. "Talk."

"I don't know."

Connor pressed, thinking of poor Tora and Magni and Lia and Rowan. "Last chance." He pierced Ellis's belly enough to make him bleed but not enough to do much damage.

"Egan! His name is Egan, and he was at Loch Aline, but then he moved to Drimnin."

Connor glanced back at Logan, who gave him a subtle nod, indicating he believed Ellis. "Bring him along. We'll send him with five men to the sheriff in Oban. We'll head back to talk with MacVey."

## Chapter Twenty-Nine

*Meg*

---

"How long will it take us to ride to Drimnin?"

Lennox leaned back, staring up at the gray sky. "Probably a full day's ride, but since we've lost half the day, we'll probably have to sleep under the stars. Are you up for it, lass? I swear on my honor I'll not hurt you or do anything I should not."

"I have no problem sleeping under the stars. I slept on the ground, in a cave, and in a locked dirty chamber with four bairns."

"And your preference?"

"I think the cave because it was raining." She took in the beauty of the landscape as they traveled, the greenery of the thick woodlands surrounding the path her favorite, though she could see the sea in the distance. "Lennox, may I ask you a question?"

"Of course," he said, moving his horse abreast of hers as they cantered along the path.

"Is my reputation ruined because we've been

seen alone? I don't know much about those types of rules, but I think I should learn." She glanced over at him in time to see the tension in his jawline.

"In usual circumstances, I would say aye. I didn't introduce you, so in the village, they probably assumed you were my wife. My guess is you have naught to worry about there. At MacKinnis Castle, I would say aye. Isaac is unlikely to say anything, but Angus took in that you were not my wife, because he knows I'm unmarried."

"You should have warned me before we left," she said, her lips pursed as she stared straight ahead.

"I tried to, though I'll admit not in the best way, but when I said you should not be rowing alone, it was intended as part of that thought. A single woman does not go anywhere alone, but with an older female escort or with her parents. I don't qualify as either. Now, I will say this—our rules are not as strict as in London, so you'll not be ostracized by anyone, but mostly because who will know? You do not live on Morvern, so no one will recognize you."

She considered his words, wondering exactly what she wished to do with her life, especially as it had changed so.

As if reading her mind, Lennox asked, "What do you wish to do with your life, Meg? What are your hopes and dreams?"

She thought of how she'd gone from a time of sheer happiness when her mother was alive, the days with her mother and sister the fondest memories she had, only to lose the most precious part of her family, and then several years later to lose her life's blood when Tamsin left. It certainly had felt as though she'd lost her only friend.

Her time with her father had been one of drudgery, the work hard with few rewards, and the hope of a different life impossible. There were no lads in the small village where they lived, only lasses.

But then the baron had come, promising to turn her life upside down in a day, and she'd run. She'd run as though ten boars had been chasing her. How lucky she was that nothing untoward had happened to her, but she'd had no idea of the possible harm that could have been lurking along the way.

She'd surely learned differently at the kirk. In a single day, she'd had a wee bit of hope at nearing the sea, then faced the grim reality of being taken prisoner to care for four bairns. The next day she'd turned sickly and eventually cast into the middle of an isle of so many clans and strangers that her head had spun from the first light until the last.

But much good had come from her adventures because what sprang from being among the Granthams and the MacVeys—of getting to know Magni, Lia, Rowan, and Tora—was the hope of a better life. Could it happen for her?

"I imagine you are confused by all your experiences. Have they changed your dreams at all?"

She cleared her throat, organizing her thoughts

before she spoke. "Aye. After leaving my sire's place, even though it was certainly a challenge, I have more hope than ever before. The hope of happiness in my life.

"When Tamsin and I were young, our mother made simple chores fun. We would see who could roll a pea across the table the fastest after shucking or see whose clothes would come out the cleanest. We would play tag in the village with the other lasses, but once we lost our mother, the fun left with her.

"I have hope now that someday I could marry someone who would respect me, then have bairns of our own, and still visit with my sister. I'm excited about the prospect of being an aunt to Alana, but I also recognize that I don't know enough about lads to know how to go about attracting one. But I surely hope that the baron does not come for me. I will not do anything with that man. I don't like feeling helpless." She paused then said, "Enough about me. Your turn, Lennox. What are your dreams?"

"Dreams? I can't say that I have any. Hopes, mayhap, but they seem to be dashing away as I grow older." He glanced over at her, something he did often, as if to check on her.

She didn't mind at all. He was an attractive man who she knew would protect her. Even though he had become stubborn and bossy, she still trusted him. She liked Lennox, and it wasn't the kind of like she had for her sister or for the bairns.

The way she felt about Lennox was completely different from anything she'd experienced before.

How she wished her sister were here, but she would find her once they found Lia.

Lennox continued, "My sire called me in when he was near death, and he made me promise to be responsible, to protect and take care of my mother and my siblings, the clan, and to marry and have heirs so that MacVey land stayed in MacVey hands. I guess my hopes are that I've made my sire proud for how I've run the clan. That someday I'll meet him again, and he'll tell me he's proud of me. But my mother feels I'm failing him, and she reminds me of it too often."

"How have you failed him? You have a beautiful home and fine clan members. I've met your brother and sister, and they are both happy."

"My mother constantly reminds me that I have one more obligation—to marry and have heirs. She thinks I'm ignoring that part of our legacy."

"May I be so bold as to ask how many summers you are?"

"Seven and twenty. And you, lass?"

"Seven and ten. So why have you not married? You are a chieftain. Are there not many lasses who would wish to marry you?"

He glanced over at her with a smirk, a devilish, lopsided smile that she liked. It was distinctly Lennox. "There are many who have asked, or should I say, their sires have proposed a betrothal."

"But?"

"They don't suit me." He took in the clouds changing overhead. "We're nearly at the coastline. You'll enjoy the view when we travel alongside it."

"And we turn that way?" she asked, pointing to the right.

"Aye, verra good. You like maps?"

"I do. I find them interesting and challenging. I hope to learn more so I always know which way to go. So if I were to leave your castle, I would know which way is Clan Rankin and Clan Grantham and Clan MacQuarie. How to get to the ferry. Am I being too simple for you?" she asked honestly. These were all new concepts to her after never having lived on an island.

"Not simple, Meg. Inquisitive. The sign of a strong mind."

She accepted that as a compliment so asked no more about it. "And your betrothed? What are you looking for?" This was sheer curiosity on her part because she had no idea what men valued in women, besides the baron's requirements—the ability to bear heirs. Though she had to admit that she still didn't understand exactly how that worked. How did one end up with a bairn in their belly? And how did it get out? She and Tamsin had guessed and giggled, talked to the other lasses in the village, but nothing had been confirmed. One lass who had raised two brothers had given them a vivid description of a lad's private parts, something that had made her wriggle her nose.

They reached the big bend in the path, heading down a line parallel to the shore, the sea breeze as sweet as anything. Meg tipped her head back to take in the sea air just in time to catch a huge bird flying overhead. "Look! What is it?"

"Och, that is a fine golden eagle. We have many

over Mull and Morvern. Puffins and warblers too. Otters, deer, pheasants. And I hope that on our way back, you might see some dolphins in the sound. They are frequent visitors."

"What's a dolphin?"

## Chapter Thirty

*Lennox*

Hellfire, but Meg was innocent in many ways. How could one have lived and never seen a dolphin? But then he thought on the fact that she had lived inland so was probably unfamiliar.

"There. Look into the sound. It's a distance away, but you can see what looks like a big fish coming out of the water, only to go back in. They're verra graceful creatures, swimming above and below the water as if they need to breathe as much as we do. And they can be verra fast, can keep up with any smaller boat if they like. They have a smile that makes them appear quite friendly. They're rarely alone, usually with several others, and they chatter like birds. If we had the time, I'd take you closer, but by the look of the clouds, I think we may have a downpour coming. There's a burn not far ahead, and I would bet a cave not far from it."

They traveled for a bit when she said, "You never answered my other question, Lennox."

He gave her a perplexed look, tipping his head. "I have forgotten. Ask again."

"What are you looking for in a wife? I don't know much about these things, so think of me kindly if I am being rude."

He thought for a moment, intermittently checking the cloud cover as they moved along at a steady pace. If he were being honest, he'd give her the simplest answer—someone like her. But he gave it careful consideration because it was important. "The obvious characteristics pop into my head. I would like someone kind and considerate, but I want my wife to be intelligent and thoughtful. I have issues with women who spend their time worrying about appearances and wanting more and more coin. Probably not something you have experienced, but anytime I was forced to go to the royal court with my sire, I was often offended by the women there, women who would push their breasts at me as if that makes them more attractive, or women bold enough to touch me where they shouldn't be touching. I could go on, but you have the idea."

Lennox shrugged as he led their horses down a different path next to a burn, the air taking a sudden cool shift. "She would have to understand the running of the clans, should be as good with numbers as I am. She should be able to read and write, yet so many women do not and don't care to learn. But most of all, I'm looking for a woman who would love me for who I am, not for what I am."

"I don't understand."

He thought about the best way to explain his meaning to someone as innocent as Meg. "Some women wish to marry me so they will have servants to wait on their every wish, or to live in a castle, order all their gowns to be made for them, not because they are interested in me, or care to hear my thoughts on issues. It's about the status of being a chieftain's wife." He nearly snorted. "Do you know that some men believe love is foolish? I don't. I wish to have a woman who takes hold of my heart and pulls on it. Every time I look at her."

Now Meg was totally confused. "Yet you didn't mention beauty."

"I don't care if she is beautiful." He stopped and rolled one hand back and forth. "I mean, she should be pleasing to the eyes, but others think I am foolish because I wish to marry a woman who incites a desire in me unlike any other. That with just a glance, I want her."

"I never would have expected that as an answer. My thanks for sharing." The puzzled expression on her face told him he'd confused her more, but he decided to let it go. He'd said enough on the subject.

Again, he thought, *A woman like you, Meg.* Every time he caught a glimpse of her, he had images of tasting her everywhere, of plunging into her until she screamed his name at the height of her pleasure, that she would cling to him as if he were the only man who existed. This one woman had incited so many carnal images that Lennox had a difficult time controlling his thoughts. He had an undeniable craving to watch her when she found her pleasure, to see that expression on her face caused by the pinnacle of pleasure coursing through her body.

To feel her innermost contractions squeeze him until he could take no more. Unlike most of the women he'd had who would lie there until he finished, no matter how he tried to incite passion in them.

He glanced over his shoulder in time to see the sky turn dark, about to unleash a fury on them. It was nearly dusk, they had dried meat and cheese and two skins of water, so they would be fine in the cave. They just had to get there and find a spot for their mounts before the sky dropped its worst on them.

Lennox approached the waterfall, expecting to find a cave behind it, and to their good fortune, he did, though it was small. Heavy woodland on one side of the cave would suit the animals. "I'll settle them if you grab the saddlebags and get them inside before they are drenched."

He helped Meg dismount and untied the two bags as the first drops of rain fell. He hooked the beasts to the bushes, then gave them each something to eat just before the sky let loose, and he raced to the opening of the cave.

The Highland gray clouds poured, unleashing a storm not uncommon to the Hebrides. He made it underneath cover with only getting a bit wet. Meg made her way around the small cave, he guessed to check for anything she didn't like.

He came up behind her. "Searching for cobwebs?"

"Nay," she said, turning back to him. "A nice flat surface to sleep on."

"Smart and practical. I think we are indeed here for the night. We should be at Drimnin by high sun on the morrow."

"Where will we look for Egan?"

"That I'm not worried about. Drimnin is small. A wee village with several fishermen's huts. One small chapel that isn't always occupied. They don't have horses, just boats because they live off the sea. If they need anything, they head to Tobermory. You'll see. You'll be able to see Rankin Castle, where Rowan lives, from the beach there."

"Why do people live there if it's so isolated?" she asked, pulling out the fur Isaac had given her and wrapping it around her shoulders.

"Because it's beautiful. They're verra happy people. They swim and fish and farm a bit. Raise their bairns. Build boats and go across for entertainment or any supplies they need. It's a simple life but a pleasant one, I think."

"And Egan would be there? That doesn't sound like the place for a man who would steal children."

"Aye, you are correct in that." Meg did have a quick mind. She questioned things that others would never consider. "He is probably inland, is my guess. They can put into the water in various places because the coast is level in areas. But his cottage will be isolated, somewhere no one will be able to see what he's up to. I would guess deep in the woods, a bit behind the village. It's quite a business when you're near water. Get the word out about what goods you have, set up a time for delivery or pickup, and you've got coin. The shameful part is he's selling bairns."

"For what?"

This was something he wasn't ready to discuss completely with the lass. She was too innocent. "As slaves to work. Wash clothes, dig gardens. They wanted me to carry stones to build a curtain wall. Those kinds of things, among others." That was as far as he would go. "I put some wrapped food from the inn in my bag. Are you hungry?"

They ate the dried meat and cheese as the rain continued, sitting on a boulder not far from the opening. The constant dripping at the front of the cave rang out even louder than the waterfall a short distance away. When the rain slowed, Lennox crept out into the dark to check on the horses, pleased to find them settled and mostly dry.

When he came back inside the cave, he was surprised to see Meg standing just behind the water, staring into the dark as if transfixed.

"Meg, are you hale?"

She nodded, swallowing hard, something he wondered about, but decided to let her speak when she was ready. Her mind churned with so many new thoughts that she must be struggling to work through them, but he didn't know what bothered her the most. He would give her whatever time she needed.

"I feel ignorant and foolish, Lennox. Do you

think that of me?" She turned to face him, her expression obscured in the dark.

Was she crying?

"Nay, I have never thought of you as ignorant and foolish, Meg. Innocent, perhaps. But not foolish. Why do you feel that way?"

"Because I know nothing about how the world works. I have never been to a royal court. Have no idea what that even means. I'm not sure I know who the king of England is. I don't even know what a dolphin is. How do I fix this?"

Lennox crossed his arms and said, "You don't need fixing, Meg. Mayhap you don't know some things, but I don't know how to sew a sweater or how to plant beans." He reached over and brushed a stray hair away from her face. "You are a quick learner, so ask questions, and I'll teach you whatever I can. I think you are near perfect the way you are. Strong, honest, compassionate, kind. There's naught wrong with you. Mayhap a bit stubborn, but then again, so am I." He smiled.

"Stubborn? Am I?"

"Aye, lass. You are, but that's not necessarily a bad thing."

She looked out at the rain again, thinking over what he'd said.

"Lennox, I feel that I should be in charge of my own destiny. Is that not true in your eyes? Because I'm a lass, does someone else have to tell me what to do all the time?"

This was a harsh reality for most women, though his mother would tell any woman she controlled her own destiny. But for the masses, the poor, the peasants in the village, the men controlled them completely. "In my eyes, you are on your own. You are a strong, independent woman who should make her own decisions about her life. You don't need to be controlled. I hope to see you connect with your sister, so she can also give you advice. Everyone needs someone to consult with when they're confused, especially when they're young." He didn't know where she was going with all this, but he was afraid to guess.

She took a deep breath and asked, "I would like to ask you to show me. I'm guessing it's not a conventional request, but I think somehow I'm different from most lasses you meet. I need to understand intimacy. Show me what goes on between a man and a woman, what it means to be intimate. Show me how bairns are made."

Lennox nearly choked, but he thought he held himself together quite well. He'd like nothing better than to make her his, but the lass was in a vulnerable state and had no idea what she was talking about.

At least, he guessed she was completely innocent.

"Your mother never discussed this with you?"

"Nay, she died over ten years ago. We were too young. Tamsin and I would try to discuss it based on the few things we heard from some of the neighborhood lasses, but we never understood it. They talked about the maidenhead. What exactly is a lass's maidenhead?"

Hellfire, but he was in for a long night.

## Chapter Thirty-One

*Meg*

---

"I'LL DO WHAT I can, but with words, Meg. Mostly because you don't understand the implications of your request. One step at a time." He cleared his throat, stared out at the rain, then turned back to her. "Your maidenhead is a small piece of skin that many consider a lass's greatest value. When a man and a woman engage in relations the first time, he will break through that skin, which causes her to lose her virginity. It is a belief by the church and by most men that a bride should come to her new husband with her maidenhead intact. If that skin is not intact, then they can request to annul the marriage, and the church will honor it. It's a barbaric practice, in my opinion. A woman's value shouldn't be placed on a piece of skin that cannot be seen."

"Can I see mine?"

He coughed again and said, "Nay. It is invisible, well hidden in your lady parts."

"Then how does anyone know if it's there?" More confused than ever, she had to persist, even though she could see the conversation was making Lennox uncomfortable.

"Because when it breaks, you will bleed. And that's all I'll say at this time. Tamsin will explain it to you, and if she doesn't, I'm sure my mother or sister would be happy to help."

"I accept that if I may ask one more question. So, you don't wish to take my maidenhead from me?"

Turning his body so his back was to the outside, Lennox tipped his head back so the water dripping in the opening drenched his face, then righted himself and swiped the excess water away, flinging it toward the rear of the cave. "I did not say that, Meg. Naught would please me more, but I will not take your value as a bride from you without a promise to marry me."

That confused her even more. "Even if I don't want it? If I understand you correctly, then the baron would not be interested in taking me as a bride if I did not have this piece of skin. So I wish to get rid of it."

"Even if you don't want it. It would not be the honorable thing to do, especially because I don't believe you truly understand what you're asking me to do. I'd insist on handfasting."

"Handfasting? I've never heard of that word. Would you explain, please?"

"Handfasting is something a couple does when it is impossible to find a kirk or a priest, especially in the Highlands, and we are in the Highlands here on Morvern. It's a matter of commitment, of committing to a year and a day with each other before parting. That the couple promises to stay together for at least that much time before breaking apart."

"But why? Why can we not have relations because we wish to?"

"For many reasons, but mostly because of bairns. In our case, suppose I took your maidenhead and planted my seed inside you, and you became with child. If you carry the child for nine moons and have a lad, that boy could not be my heir because he would be considered a bastard. He could not inherit MacVey land without a battle with someone."

Meg frowned. "There are too many rules for me to comprehend. It would not matter to a bairn."

"But if that lad became my heir and it was discovered he was a bastard, and I married someone other than you, had a son with that woman, the second son would be heir to the chieftain, not the firstborn. It would matter to the first son. I vowed to have no bairns outside of marriage, and I will stick to it."

"I don't understand it all."

He took her hand in his and said, "It is complicated. Now if you and I handfasted, which is a small ceremonial promise we make to each other, then if you had our bairn before the year was up, he would be my legal heir. And if we find we don't suit, then we can go our separate ways at the end of the year and a day. I'd keep the lad as my heir, and you would do as you wished."

"Hell nay, but that would never happen. My

bairn would stay with me." Lord above but she was more confused than ever.

"We'll discuss that if it ever happens." He gave her that lopsided grin again, one that made him look quite boyish, something he didn't share often if she were to guess. Then he added quite seriously, "But I'm pleased that you answered that way. It shows the devotion a mother should have toward their child."

"I'm sorry I made you uncomfortable, Lennox. And I am grateful for your honesty. Is there something you could do to show me without taking my maidenhead?"

Lennox ran a hand down his long hair in the back, wringing the water from the bottom of the locks that sat on his neck. The lass was certainly challenging him, but he thought of one thing. "I gave you a light kiss before. I would wager that you've never been truly kissed. Shall I teach you?"

"Probably not because it would not make me happy. I have been kissed before by the baron and it was disgusting. I don't want a slimy tongue in my mouth ever again. Stay away."

He chuckled, watching her. When she saw the teasing look on his face, she grew agitated.

"Lennox, this is not amusing for me."

"I know, and I am sorry. But I surely would like to see this baron of yours. I do hope I get to meet him someday."

That comment upset her more. And then he laughed again. This time she became so irritated she wished to shove him.

So she did.

Pushing his chest as hard as she could, she grumbled, "Stop laughing. I don't like people laughing at me. I lived alone for half of my life, so I don't know as much as others. It's not something that I think is funny."

The look in his eyes turned smoldering, something that said he liked her. It almost reminded her of the baron, but...

Lennox MacVey was nothing like the baron. Tears misted her gaze, but she fought them, refusing to let him see how he had upset her. *Forty-one, forty-two, forty-three...*

He took one hand and tugged her closer. "Lass, I'm not laughing at you. I find the way you're willing to stand up to me extremely alluring. Come closer. I wish to teach you something."

"What?"

"Closer." He tugged a bit more and she stepped toward him, his scent washing over her. Seawater and mint, that's what he smelled like. She was suddenly overcome by his closeness, his strength, how everything about him was all man, that he was hard everywhere—yet his touch was gentle.

There was nothing about Lennox MacVey that she understood, except that she liked him. He tugged her so close that she could see that smoldering look in his gaze, that the breadth of his shoulders overpowered her senses, heat emanating from every part of him. She could nearly look him in the eye, but not quite.

His gaze locked on hers and his aura overwhelmed her. Unable to control herself, she dropped her gaze and did the one thing she was powerless to stop. Her tongue shot out and licked the bead of water in the small crevice above his chin.

Lennox closed his eyes and let out a growl unlike any sound she'd ever heard. Waiting for his next move, she stared up at him until he opened his eyes again.

"You have no idea what you do to me, do you?"

"Nay, but…is it something good?"

In a voice two tones deeper than his usual, he said, "Oh, it is verra good."

She waited a wee bit more, noticing how her breathing had increased, something that happened when she was agitated, but then she noticed his breathing was faster than her own. She glanced up at his eyes, still locked on something over her head. She'd never been this close to a man either. His skin was a deep bronze from the sun, his beard scruffy since they'd been traveling. "Your beard grows quickly." She rubbed her cheek against his to see how scratchy it was, and he groaned again.

In a tightly controlled voice, he said, "I ask you to allow me to kiss you. You have never been kissed properly, and for someone as beautiful as you? That's a sin, in my eyes." His thumb brushed her cheek, and the other hand came up to sweep the stray hairs from her face as he leaned closer, the darkness of the night blocking out everything but him. He whispered, "You have a wee rash from my beard. Be careful. Your skin is too soft, much too fine."

He dipped his head toward hers, and she had the shocking urge to touch him all over. What would it feel like to be kissed by someone handsome and kind and bossy? *Sixty-one, sixty-two, sixty-three...*

"May I?" His blue eyes locked on hers, and he arched his brow.

She nodded, her hands reaching for his forearms, then sliding up to his powerful upper arms, just before his lips descended on hers. He kissed her tenderly and he tasted of mint leaves. He angled his mouth sideways, and his tongue teased her until she parted her lips, allowing him in, but just a wee bit. She didn't trust him, though she already knew this would be nothing like the baron's horrid kiss.

She stopped counting and sighed, giving in to him. Allowing him to do whatever he wished. He crushed her in his embrace and her arms moved around to his back, relishing the feel of his muscles in her hands as he moved.

His tongue ravished her, and she did the only thing she could think to do—she touched her tongue to his and he groaned, pulling her tighter, and she was lost. Lost in all that was Lennox—his strength, his taste, his power, his scent, the feel of his body against hers. She had the sudden urge to remove their clothes so she could feel his skin against hers.

Lennox awakened desires within her that she'd never had before. Her nipples tingled and her breath hitched, and the seam between her legs pressed against him, against something hard, something that confused her. Something that sent opposing feelings raging through her—the need to pull that hardness closer yet push it away.

She shoved at his chest and leaned against the cold stone wall, gasping, fighting to regulate her breathing. Her fingers went to her lips, surprised to feel them swollen.

"I'm sorry," he said in a ragged breath. "I went too far, lass. I shouldn't have."

She waited until her breathing calmed a bit, taking her time to study Lennox. He wasn't laughing now, his voice husky, his breathing more labored than her own. His hand ran down his face as his other hand went to his hips.

"I got carried away. You are too innocent. I'm sorry."

She whispered, "Don't be. I liked it." And she strode toward him, cupped his cheeks, and kissed him back, mimicking everything he'd done to her. Her heart soared as every part of her came alive. His hands came up to her breasts, rubbing her nipples through the fabric, and she arched toward him. He lifted her, wrapping her legs around him, then carrying her to the darkest corner of the cave.

He ended the kiss and said, "This has to end now or naught good will come of it, lass. Trust me. I'll get the plaids from my saddlebag." He set her down, grabbed the bag, and pulled out the extra plaids he always had, placing one on the floor and pointing. "Get comfortable. You'll sleep in my arms this night, or you'll become ill again."

"Lennox? Did I do something wrong?"

He stopped, reaching for her hand, kissing each fingertip. "Nay, Meg. Everything you did was right. But we are not married, and we have to find Lia."

"You won't take my maidenhead? Even if I wish to give it to you?" She took the fur that had fallen to the ground and settled on the plaid. "I would handfast with you."

"Nay. Don't get me wrong, naught would please me more. But it would be wrong to do so now."

Meg sighed and rolled over, facing the opening of the cave, the rain slowing but still rhythmic. She must have done something wrong.

He didn't want her.

## Chapter Thirty-Two

*Lennox*

---

GLAD TO BE on their way the next morn, Lennox considered how he'd left their relationship. He'd refused the offer of her maidenhead, something that his erect member had reminded him about several times in the middle of the night, her soft bottom often rubbing him in the wrong way.

He'd held strong, something he'd wished he'd failed at. He'd love naught more than to make Meg his, bury himself deep inside her while she cried out his name, her nails raking his shoulders as she crossed that threshold of exquisite pleasure.

But he would not do it without a promise of marriage or a handfasting, and there was a reason for his madness.

There was no doubt in his mind that once he had Meg, once would not be enough. If he were to wager, he'd never get enough of her. She was under his skin like the flavor of the finest wine or the scent of the sweetest flower in the garden.

Unfortunately, Meg needed a man with

patience because she was young and innocent, and he was not feeling patient at the moment. But he had no choice. She deserved nothing less than his best.

Today they would head to Drimnin and hope to find out more about the bastard Egan and his unscrupulous behaviors. If they were lucky, they would also find Lia safe and unharmed.

The path widened as they followed the coastline, and he pulled his horse abreast of Meg's. "What think you of Lia? What wee bit I know of her is unusual."

"In what way?"

"The way she speaks is a start, as though she were a wizened old healer, or some kind of odd witch. I've heard talk of the men looking for a faery. Think you she's a faery?"

Meg glanced over at him with a shrug of her shoulders. "Honestly, I don't know what to make of Lia. She told me things as if she'd met my sister. Told me Tamsin was in love with a chieftain and was verra happy, and this was before I told her I had a sister. Now I understand that she and Magni lived on MacQuarie land so she would know this, but Magni never considered making such a statement. How did she know Tamsin was my sister? And as I told you, she mentioned going to Loch Aline and that she would go alone. What young lass says such a thing? None of the other three had any interest in going anywhere alone."

"She is definitely a different soul, and while she appears delicate, she is far from it. I hope we find her, but I also believe she is far more capable of taking care of herself than the other three bairns."

"Lennox, may I tell you something without you thinking me daft?"

"Of course. Ever since the Granthams arrived, I've learned to open my mind to things that I've never known before. Like Tora and her mother being seers. I've heard of seers but never seen them in action. Now I'm starting to believe. I would love to hear your thoughts."

"I think Lia does things to draw people in a certain direction. I'm not sure exactly why I feel that way, but I think she wanted me to follow her to Loch Aline, mostly because I was the only person she shared her destination with at the time. Why tell me and not Magni? Or Connor? And that if I went, you would follow. And now she wishes us to go to Drimnin, to put a stop to this horrific business. She's leading us to certain places for a reason. If we find Egan and end his reign of terror, that would be wonderful for bairns, for parents like the poor cook we met, and for you. One trip could solve many problems. And if so, then she has some power I don't comprehend, but I'll respect it."

The village appeared over a small hill, and Lennox couldn't help but smile. He tipped his head toward the sea. "Is it not one of the most beautiful spots you've ever seen?" The rolling hills in the background, the serene bay, the carefully tended gardens and huts alongside fishing boats made the area appealing as any he'd ever seen. "Someday, when I'm old and decrepit, I wish to live here with my wife, watch the sunsets, fish for our dinner, swim in the warm water in summers."

"That sounds appealing to me too, Lennox, though I don't know how to swim. Do you truly swim in the sea? I've bathed in burns before but that frightens me a bit. But you swim in the sound, you said. Do you like it?"

He nodded. "Swimming will offer you a sense of calm unlike any other. I will teach you. What think you of the area? The village?"

"It is quite lovely. I see exactly what you mean. I'm surprised to see so many people milling about. What do you suggest we do?"

"Probably best for me to approach. I say we start on the beach where the two fishermen are pulling in their boat." He led the horses down the small incline until he hit the rocks, then dismounted, helping Meg dismount before he approached the men.

Meg immediately rinsed her fingers, cupping the water to splash her face.

"Greetings to ye. It's a fine morn. I've come from Dounarwyse Castle on Mull. Looking for a man named Egan."

Both men had long beards, their skin weathered and tanned from the sun. But their eyes took in everything about the two visitors.

"You're the chieftain, MacVey. I've seen you. What do you want with Egan?"

The two had a net of about six fish. "I see you have some mackerel. Do you get them often? And how big is the largest skate you've ever caught?"

One man grinned and his hands stretched out from his body, demonstrating the size of the skate he'd trapped. "Had to get him with my cousin's big boat. Could not have pulled him up with our small boat. But he was a big one. Delicious. My wife likes the pollack. We caught a fair-sized one this morn."

Lennox peeked into their net. "He's a beauty." Then he set his hands on his hips and said, "I've a score to settle with Egan. You related to him?"

"To that bastard? Nay. Wish he'd disappear. Gives our parts a bad name. I'll help you in any way I can to get rid of him. I don't like him or the way he conducts himself." The man pursed his lips and pointed beyond their village. "He don't belong here. We sent him off."

"Do you know where he lives now?"

"Deep in the woods," the other man said. "You'll need more than you, unless she's good with a bow. There's four of 'em. None that are big, but all nasty. They threaten us at times, so we mind our own business. Tried the sheriff once, but Egan knows when to hide and how to disappear."

"Horses?"

"Only one that I seen. They travel back and forth between the hut in the woods and a spot on the coast on the far side of Drimnin. You'll see it. There's a small hut there too. An old couple lives inside, but they're no trouble. He controls them."

"My thanks to you." He handed each a coin, knowing they could use it in Tobermory.

"Protect your wife, Chief. He likes 'em young. Uses 'em and sells 'em." He kept his voice down out of respect for Meg, but Lennox was sure she'd heard every word.

He turned to depart, but then spun back around. "Have you seen a golden-haired lass of about five summers in the area?"

"Chief, if there were a lass of five around here alone, he'd have her. I don't trust him at all." Then the man spit into the bay. "We'd be in yer debt if you got rid of him."

Lennox moved over to help Meg off the rocks and led her back to their horses, helping her mount. Once he climbed up, he nodded to the two men and headed down the path.

One called out to him, "Take the path between the two large oaks, marked with two rocks."

A few moments later, he led Meg toward the forest, stopping as soon as he saw the hut deep in the woods. "Lass, do you have your axe?"

"Aye," she said.

"Keep it handy. There are four of them, as I'm sure you heard. If you can take one out with your axe, I'll take the other three. Have you a dagger?"

She shook her head. "I've only used one for cooking."

"I have two, so you may have one since I plan to use my sword. I will not have any mercy for the fools." He reached into his saddlebag and pulled out a sheathed dagger then made sure it was clean before handing it to her. "Aim for the neck. If you stab an arm or a leg, you'll only pish them off enough to hit harder. You have to go for the neck, the inner side of the wrist, or deep into the flesh of the inner thigh."

She nodded, paling a bit, but she sat up strong.

Lennox knew he'd been foolish to come across without a guard, but the lass had gone out of the keep so fast, he'd not had the time to yell for any to follow. And he certainly hadn't expected to be all the way into Drimnin with Meg. His expectation was to travel to Loch Aline and back home again. That was two days ago.

He prayed he hadn't made a huge lapse in judgment, but Lia was close. He could feel it.

Dismounting, he helped Meg down and led the horses into a small copse to keep them hidden, hanging their reins on the bushes. He took Meg's hand and then crept around the hut, coming in from one side to listen for voices, scan for any activity.

There was a burn not far away and the rippling sound of a waterfall in the distance. It wouldn't be surprising if bairns were kept in the cottage. Water would be needed to keep them alive and clean.

He heard nothing, and Meg shook her head to let him know she didn't hear anything either. Moving over to the hut, he held his ear to the door, then opened it. The windows had fur coverings, so the place was dark, but quiet. He moved over and lifted one fur to light up the chamber, only to find it was a one-chamber hut, rows and rows of small pallets on the floor—pallets the size of bairns.

But they were all empty. There was no one inside.

They were about to go around back when four

men rushed them from the opposite side, tearing out of the forest, two going toward Lennox and two toward Meg.

Lennox had his sword unsheathed at about the same time Meg pulled out her axe. She threw it and caught the man square in the chest, dropping him to the ground instantly.

Lennox swung his sword, surprised to find one of his attackers bearing a strong weapon while the other held a small English sword. He took the one with the smaller weapon down quickly, but the other man was much beefier. He'd have to be on target to finish him off.

Meg screamed and ran away from him, her attacker in hot pursuit.

"Meg, your dagger!"

# Chapter Thirty-Three

*Meg*

---

MEG HAD THROWN her axe at one of her attackers as hard as she could. It landed in the man's chest, and he crumpled to the ground. But now all she had left was a small dagger.

She did the obvious, screaming and running, something she hated to do, but she didn't have the confidence to use the knife on him.

Lennox's voice caught her. "Your dagger!"

She tugged it out of the sack tied to her belt, glancing over at Lennox to see if he'd be able to help her. He killed one quickly, but the second one was tougher with a larger weapon.

"Fight, Meg! I'll be there soon."

She held her dagger out against the brute, but he grinned, lunging for her. She didn't see any weapon other than the man's fists, but they could do plenty of damage.

"You think you'll hurt me with that small knife, lassie? Try to get close enough because I'll get my hands on you then." He chuckled, an evil-sounding laugh that went right up her neck, making her hairs stand on end.

He jumped toward her, but she kicked at his waist and his hand caught her foot, tossing her onto her back. She hit the ground hard, but she still had her weapon. He grabbed for her, so she attempted to embed her dagger in his neck as Lennox had told her, but she missed, the blade landing in his shoulder instead.

"Bitch! You'll pay for that one."

Blood sprayed all over, but she had a moment when he pulled the dagger out, so she did the only thing she could think of—going back for the dead man and her axe. Lurching toward him, she landed on his legs and tried to pull herself up to his chest, but her adversary grabbed her feet, his hands scrabbling up her legs.

"My, but are you not a fine one. I have a baron looking for a wife. He'll pay good coin for you, so I'll not kill you, but I must sample you myself first."

"Egan, if you touch her, I'll kill you," Lennox shouted as he parried with the tallest man.

"How do you know my name?" Egan paused for a moment to stare at Lennox, then a grin crossed his face. "I remember you. The one I put in the cellars. I'm about to have a taste of your lady friend."

She kicked Egan in the face before she finally grabbed the axe, though she couldn't dislodge it from the dead man's chest. Tears blurred her vision as Egan's hand rubbed on her bottom, so she kicked and screamed again, pulling herself up enough to get leverage to remove the buried axe, but it wouldn't budge.

"You're mine now, lassie." Egan winked at her, and she punched him in the face, but his fist was far more powerful than her own. Her head snapped down against the dead man from the blow.

The weight of Egan lifted from her in one swift move as Lennox tossed him aside with a roar, then held the tip of his sword at his throat. "Why, Egan?"

"Why? For coin. Why else would I do it?"

"Why me?"

Egan chuckled, so smug that Meg thought Lennox would kill him just from the confident laughter. He didn't answer quickly enough, so Lennox pressed harder. Blood dripped down Egan's neck, his laughter ending quickly.

"Why me?" Lennox's tone dropped to nearly a whisper.

"Why you? Because I saw you at the festival, and you gave me that look, the look that says you were better than me. I knew you were a chieftain's son, everything given to you, and you should have been grateful. Instead you were arrogant, so when my boss said he wished for a man to carry boulders, you were my first thought." Egan looked at Lennox, then spit off to the side. "Thought you'd drowned. Hoped you'd drowned."

Lennox stood back, pausing to rake his hand through his hair.

In that one pause, Egan bolted up and lunged

for Lennox's sword, but he was too slow. Lennox stabbed him in the chest, ending the battle.

Meg got up and ran straight to Lennox, launching herself into his arms where she clung to him, sobbing into his shoulder. So afraid after all she'd seen and heard, she refused to turn her head to look at their dead foes. "Are they all gone?"

"Aye. Hush now," he said, holding her tight. He lifted her into his arms, her legs now around his waist as she sobbed into his shoulder. "Hush, lass. I've got you, Meg. They'll not return."

When she was finally able to lift her head, her breath hitched so that she couldn't say a complete sentence, only one word: "Blood."

"I know. We're both covered in blood. That's why I'm taking you to the beach. We both have another tunic, so we'll change. Wash the blood from our faces. I have a sliver of soap in my saddlebag."

He carried her to their horses, then to the beach a distance away from any fishermen. "Be ready, the water will feel cool at first." He set her on her feet, but she couldn't let go of his arms, the horror of what she'd just seen and experienced so awful that she couldn't slow her pounding heart.

He pulled a plaid out of his saddlebag, pitching his dirty plaid to the side and removing his blood-soaked tunic. "Sorry, but my clothes have to go. I cannot get any more blood on you. If you wish to turn your head, then please do. I'll change quickly. I'll take you in the water in your chemise, and I'll keep my plaid on until I can duck under water."

She reached for her own tunic, ready to remove it, and he asked, "You have a chemise on?"

"Aye. This tunic. Off, off. I want it off. Please, Lennox." She peeled off her leggings so they would stay dry as they didn't have blood on them, then tugged the chemise down to cover her lady parts.

She stepped into the sea, allowing the cool liquid to cover her. "Lennox, do not let me go, please. I can't swim." While part of her wished to be embarrassed because she was only in her chemise, she trusted Lennox completely.

He followed her in, holding his plaid up until he was covered by the water, then tossed his garment back onto the beach.

"I'll never let you go, lass. I promise." Lennox took the soap and a linen square and washed her from head to toe, so soft and gentle that her tears ended, and all she could think of was Lennox.

How they belonged together. How she was finally beginning to understand what all the lasses talked about into the dead of night, about loving a man. She was falling in love with Lennox MacVey. She'd never felt the same for any other person the way she felt for him.

When he finished, she took the soap from him and said, "My turn."

She washed his chest and then his face, neck, and his arms, swirling the water around to rinse the blood away. When she finished, he said,

"Come. We're going deeper. Hold my hand and I promise not to let you go."

"It's cool!" she said as she followed him out, the water nearly up to her shoulders.

"Tip your head back so you can wash your hair."

She did, but grabbed on to him as soon as she felt herself ready to drop.

"You won't fall. I have you."

She giggled and slipped enough so her face got wet. "It's salty."

"It is. Not a loch but part of the ocean, and the salt helps keep you buoyant."

"What?" She had no idea what he spoke of since her only experience with swimming was the small burn and waterfall near their home. She'd bathed there many times, but in summer she washed her hair under the waterfall's stream.

"I'll show you, but you'll have to trust me."

"All right."

Turning her around, he tugged her against him, her back to his chest, then wrapped his arm around her waist. "Promise me you won't struggle and you'll float with me."

"I'll try."

"Relax and you'll feel it. And if we are truly calm in the water, the dolphins will appear. Taskill and I used to do it all the time. Ready?" He arranged her in front of him, then fell back into the water, lifting his legs to propel her up. She squealed a bit, but then settled. "Look at the sky and put your arms out."

It took them a bit, but before long she was

floating next to him, his torso still partway under hers, his hand still on her waist. "Naught is more calming than swimming. And if we are verra quiet, you'll hear the dolphins talking to each other."

She did her best to keep still, and within a few minutes, she heard an odd chatter. Shocked by it, she waited, turning her head to glance over at Lennox, who pointed off to his right.

"Dolphins," he whispered.

So stunned, she set her feet down, pleased that she could touch still, and watched the graceful creatures in the water, gliding in and out of the surface. Lennox stood in front of her and she set her chin on his shoulder, watching the show in front of them. He glanced back and asked, "Lovely, is it not?"

"Lennox," she whispered. "I'm enchanted. Totally enchanted." Her hands wrapped around his waist, anchoring herself. It was so peaceful and serene, she didn't know what to say. She would remember this moment forever.

"Meg, your touch is affecting me in ways that tell me it's time to get out. The sun is going down, and we should go back to the cave and sleep. We'll find Lia on the morrow."

"I'm tired and chilling a bit."

He helped her out of the water and used his clean plaid to dry her a bit. "I'll turn my back and you get dressed."

She did as he suggested, removing her chemise and donning the tunic and her leggings. Then she joined him at the horse, where he lifted her onto his mount and climbed up behind her. They said nothing on the ride back to the cave. The sounds of the water lapping against the coastline was the most beautiful music she'd ever heard.

When they made it back to the cave, they dismounted and she reached for him, tugging him closer. "My thanks to you for showing me all you did. It was the most wonderful experience." She rubbed his arm.

His lips descended on hers and she was lost. Kissing Lennox was so luscious. He tasted like the mint leaves he chewed, and she loved being wrapped in his arms, his body pushed against her skin, inciting waves of tingling everywhere. She parted her lips and his tongue delved inside, dueling with hers until her breathing quickened, her body suddenly on fire.

How did it happen so quickly? He ended the kiss and her hand reached for his chest.

Lennox closed his eyes and stilled her hand, holding it inside his own. "Meg, your touch is too much for me. You have to tell me now or end this. Will you handfast with me for a year and a day? Once you touch me, I don't think I'll be able to stop. You've tested me since the day we met, and frankly, lass, I'm losing the battle."

She stared up at him, her green eyes locking on his, still misting with tears. "I love you, Lennox. Aye, I will handfast with you."

Lennox began the Gaelic chant he'd used on others in his clan, entwining his hand with hers as they pledged themselves to each other for a year and a day. He carried her into the back of the cave, whispering sweet words in her ear as he explained all that was about to happen.

She brought his lips down to hers, kissing him hard, teasing him with her tongue, and saying, "Just finish this. I wish to know all there is for us, but no more words, Lennox. Please."

Lennox made sweet love to her, and Meg learned more about life in those few moments than she had in her seven and ten years. Life could be wonderful.

She had hope that all would be well soon.

## Chapter Thirty-Four

*Thane*

---

THANE RODE WITH Artan and one other guard, Magni in the saddle in front of him. "Do you think Lia is back yet? I surely hope she is. I miss my sister."

"This is a meeting of the patrols, so I'm sure someone knows something." They approached Dounarwyse Castle on MacVey land, the place chosen as the center of the groups. As soon as they arrived, horse hooves could be heard coming a short distance down the path.

Magni squirmed to peek around Thane's shoulders as they entered through the gates and headed to the stable. "Who is it?"

"I would guess the Granthams. Dyna, Derric, Eli, or Alaric. It sounds as though they are coming from that direction." Thane moved to set Magni down once he was close to the stable. "Artan, you will stay out here with the guards. Ask questions. You may hear different answers from what I hear inside."

Magni let out a whoop of excitement as soon

as he saw his friends. "Tora. I'm here. Sandor and Sylvi, we can all play together." The lad loved nothing more than playing with others. He enjoyed playing with Tamsin's daughter Alana, but she was a wee bit young for Magni, though he was very patient with the toddler.

Dyna let Tora down and with a yell said, "You will only play in the courtyard near the keep. No wandering outside."

Thane understood exactly what she meant. After watching Lia and Magni stolen right in front of his eyes, he wasn't willing to give them much freedom. In fact, they hadn't been back to the beach since that awful day.

The group chatted in the courtyard before Sloan arrived with Rowan and his brother Rinaldo. Rowan jumped down quickly and joined the group of friends playing some form of tag.

Thane spoke quietly to Dyna. "Any word on Lia?"

"Nay, but I don't think Lennox is here. Rut and Taskill are greeting us. And I don't see Meg either. My father and Uncle Logan will be here shortly with Eli and Alaric."

Once everyone had arrived and all the groups had gathered, they went inside, bringing the bairns with them, though the young ones were not happy about it. Except Magni.

Magni wished to hear about Lia, so he would not leave Thane's side.

Rut laid out trays of berries and cheese for everyone while the serving lasses brought wine and ale, goat's milk for the bairns. Sloan moved over to Eva and said, "My, but you are looking lovely today, Eva."

Eva nearly snorted but said, "I look the same as I do every day, Sloan, except I have more worry lines on my face from my brother."

Sloan took the hint and moved away while Thane hid his smile.

Once the serving lasses were done, Rut stepped up and said, "I will lead the meeting because Lennox and Meg have not returned from their search yet."

This shocked Thane that Meg was with Lennox, and without a chaperone, apparently, but it was not his choice. He didn't think Tamsin would approve, but he'd find out soon enough.

Rut was peppered with questions, so she raised her hands and said, "Please allow me to explain what I know. Apparently, Lia told Meg that she had to go to Loch Aline just before everyone boarded the ship to return to Mull, so Meg wished to go since it is right across the sound from us. Lennox went with her because he knew someone of questionable character at Kinlochaline Castle, owned by Clan MacKinnis. I expected them back promptly, but they've been gone for two days now."

"Who is the questionable character?" Dyna asked.

To their surprise, Tora ran over to her mother, rested her hands on her mother's bent knees, and said, "Egan. The chief is going after Egan."

Then Tora ran back to her playmates. Dyna whipped her head around to stare at her father.

"Why does she see things I don't?" She shook her head and then turned back to the group. "Rut, do you know Egan?"

"I've heard the name. An unsavory character, for certes. But let's move on. I'd like to start with Sloan and see what he learned on his patrol. Then we'll go on to Thane, and finally to Connor Grant and Logan Ramsay."

Sloan stood and explained what areas he searched, then said, "Neil MacClane had three men he'd just hired as guards that he overheard bragging about making a large sum of coin. When questioned, he found that they'd taken part in Magni and Lia's kidnapping along with Rowan's. He banned them from his clan and from the isle."

"Did they say who paid them?" Logan asked.

"No names. Someone from Ardnamurchan."

"The mainland?" Thane asked. He wasn't as familiar with the area as others.

"Aye, west of Morvern," Connor replied before standing to explain about their patrol. "I'll go next. We found Herbert and Ellis, the pirate."

Rowan ran over to listen, standing next to Magni who stood so close to Logan that the old man finally found him a stool. "Are they coming for us again, Grandda?" Magni asked, staring up at his newly appointed grandfather. "Is Pirate Man on his way for us?"

"Nay, dead men can't steal you away, grandson." Logan took a swig of his wine. "But I would like to say that Meg has good aim with her axe. Did you see that man when he attacked, lads?"

Rowan said, "Nay, not when he attacked. Meg

made us stay behind some boulders, but I peeked when I had to pish later."

Magni giggled and said, "I pished on Hairy's hand. He was dead so he couldn't get me then. He was mean."

"She hit him in the middle of the forehead. Must have dropped him like a rock," Logan said, his approval apparent to everyone.

Rut said, "Thane, have you learned anything?"

"Nay, we turned up naught. But I don't have the best tracking skills. I'm still learning."

Rut asked, "Does anyone have any other information? I think we could be missing something."

Connor said, "Since Meg isn't here, I'll tell you what else we learned. The baron is looking for her. It hasn't occurred to him to look on the isle, but he seems persistent. I don't know if Logan's talk with him will dissuade him or not."

"How many men?" Thane asked.

"Two score. Naught we can't handle with our eyes closed. I'd gladly send a score to protect your clan until we take care of this situation. We brought another score to Duart after seeing the baron. Just let me know, MacQuarie," Connor said.

"I will accept. Obviously, if the baron learns she could be here, he may consider where her sister is. Her father probably informed the baron that he'd married the older sister to someone else. My thanks to you for the extra guards." Thane nodded, then asked, "Naught about Lia anywhere? No one has heard about the lass? No more faery talk?"

All the guests shook their heads. Magni's lower lip quivered, but he didn't let the tears out.

"Did I forget anything? Does anyone have any other comments, thoughts about strategies, ideas on where to go next?" Rut paced in a small circle.

Tora came barreling over to the group, stopping in front of Thane. "You must go to Drimnin." She had everyone's attention.

"Drimnin? Where is that?" His gaze traveled from one person to the next, looking for an explanation. "Why?" Thane had never heard of the place. Why would he need to go? He had no special knowledge of where Lia could be found.

Tora said, "Because Lia wants you to. Lennox and Meg are there now." Then she skipped back to her play spot.

Thane looked to the others. "Where is Drimnin?"

Sloan said, "Follow me back to my land. Drimnin is straight across the water from us. It's a small fishing village, low population. I don't know why Lennox would be there."

Tora ran back and said, "Because Egan is there. And Lia."

Thane stood up, took the last sip of his ale, then said, "Magni, we're headed to Drimnin. Lia said so."

Magni burst into tears as he chased out the door ahead of Thane, but then he ran back to hug Logan before taking his leave. "I love you, Grandda. We're going for Lia."

## Chapter Thirty-Five

*Meg*

LENNOX WAS SOUND asleep. She studied him while he slept, a light snore coming from his parted lips, his arm resting across her waist.

She liked sleeping in his arms. He was warmer than any blanket or fur.

Sneaking out the best she could, she managed to get away without waking him, making her way to the knoll where she could look out over the sound, listening to the hoots of an owl while she thought of all that had happened.

She'd lost her value as a bride, and she didn't care one bit. She'd also handfasted with a man she loved. That was a bit more intimidating, not because it was Lennox, but because he was the chieftain of his clan. What would her duties be as the chieftain's wife?

At this point, she was too afraid to ask.

Lennox stirred and called out to her. "Everything all right, sweet Meg?"

"I'm fine," she said as he came up next to her

and wrapped his arm around her waist, pulling her closer. "It's a wee bit chilly, aye?"

She leaned into him, resting her head on his shoulder, and said, "I had no idea."

"You found your pleasure after your pain. I'm sorry it hurt." He kissed her, a soft kiss that was simple but oh so sweet.

She laughed. "That pain was nothing. It was worth it for what came after. May I ask you a couple of questions?"

"Aye."

"So, this is how babies are made? Every time?"

"Aye and nay. It doesn't make a baby every time, just when it's the right time for the female. The cycle of your courses."

"This is why people marry? This part of a couple's relationship?"

"Aye. You are inquisitive. I like that about you. Shows an intelligent mind."

"How often do married couples do it?"

He shrugged. "I can't answer that. I've not been married, and most couples don't speak on it. I would guess several times a fortnight? What do you think?"

"More than that would suit me."

He kissed her cheek with a chuckle. "You know what the rule of the land is. Doing that made you mine."

She turned to look at him, perplexed. "Why do men get the power to make all the decisions?"

"I can't answer that. But we did talk about this. You recall that we handfasted, aye?"

"I do. I'm just curious about practices. I have

few memories of my parents together, so I'm confused about how a marriage works. About what happens every day for you and for your wife. Or do you make decisions for both of us?"

"Since we handfasted, I consider us husband and wife for a year and a day. Of course, I would be willing to discuss anything with you. Allow you to make decisions about some things, and other things for me."

"You would allow me to question some of your decisions?"

"Of course. Any decision that would affect you or our family would be up for discussion, although because I am chieftain and you are mistress of the castle, it would be wise to keep those discussions private." He kissed her forehead. "I am pleased that we handfasted. You are mine for a year and a day."

"Part of me likes the sound of that and part of me doesn't."

He wrapped his arms around her and whispered, "What part of you doesn't like the idea of being mine?"

"The part that makes me sound like I'm a possession instead of a person."

Hell, but this lass was going to push his understanding of everything. She did have a point. "I understand that."

"Mayhap you'll be mine," she said with a grin.

"I'm absolutely happy with that. And someday marriage, I hope."

She smiled, a twinge in her chest making her

happy, but she stepped back and stared at her feet. "I don't think I'm ready for marriage yet."

"We'll talk again after we find Lia."

She turned back to don her clothing. "After all, I just stopped hating you back at Loch Aline."

# Chapter Thirty-Six

*Thane*

Thane discussed the situation thoroughly with Sloan before he, Artan, and Magni climbed into the boat. They had no way to get their horses across, so they would be on foot. They left the guards behind because the boat was small.

Once they landed on the beach, two fishermen greeted them. "You looking for the MacVey chieftain?"

So surprised, he paused for a moment but then quickly replied, "Aye, if you please. You've met him?"

"Aye, they went after Egan. We just returned from burying that bastard's body for him. We said we'd gladly put him in the ground. MacVey and his missus headed to the small hut down the coast, around the bend that way."

Magni, who had been hopping from one foot to the other, finally stopped when he could speak. "Did they have a yellow-haired lass with them? Her name is Lia. She would be about this high…"

Thane smiled and set his hand on the lad's head. Magni's questioning mannerisms reminded Thane of his dear sister Mora. Magni stopped and adjusted his question. "Have you seen a wee lass?"

"Nay. They were looking for her too."

"Go that way." The other man pointed, so Thane nodded to Magni.

"Come. We'll find Lennox and see what he knows."

No one mentioned the comment about the chief and his missus, but it surely had caught him. Anxious to meet Meg, Thane couldn't help but wonder if Meg and Lennox had married along the way. They'd been gone for at least two days, so it was certainly possible, though he'd keep his thoughts to himself with Magni listening. A marriage would shock Tamsin more than anything else he could tell her, if he were to guess.

He hoped to propose to Tamsin soon. In fact, he'd planned on doing it the day the bairns had been stolen, but their abduction surely changed everything. He'd never been as happy as he was with Tamsin in his life. But he also loved having Magni, Lia, and Alana in his life too. The trio had brightened up their keep unlike any other.

Their clan was growing, and in the best ways. Now he had to find Lia and bring her home.

They trudged down the beach, Magni pointing out the wildlife around them—otters, eagles, dolphins, seals, puffins. The area was as beautiful as Mull.

They finally made their way around a bend full of rocks, and Magni let out a squeal. Ahead of them standing in the middle of a sandy portion of the beach was Lia, looking like an angel. The sun peeked out through the clouds, sending rays that surrounded her in such a light show that Thane was frozen.

Artan mumbled, "I've naught seen anything like it. What is she, Thane?"

"She's my sister!" Magni took off toward Lia, giggling with joy as he wrapped his arms around her. Up on the coastline stood Lennox and Meg, both grinning from ear to ear. Thane waved but greeted Lia first.

"Lia, you are hale? You've not been harmed?"

"Surely not, Chief. I was hoping you would come along. I have someone I would like you to meet."

Magni babbled on. "You look exactly the same. Where did you go? Why didn't you take me with you? Why didn't you come to Mull first, then leave?"

Lia turned to her brother, hugged him tight, then said, "Magni, I'd be pleased to answer all your questions after I show Thane what he needs to see. Will you wait for me, please?"

Magni stared up at Thane with a perplexed expression, but he didn't question Lia, instead saying, "Aye, I can wait. May I go with him? And with you?"

Lia said, "Would you mind waiting here with Lennox and Meg?"

Lennox and Meg joined them, both looking as though they'd come from battle, but smiling.

Lennox said, "Good to see you, Thane."

Magni hugged Meg and then stared up at her. "You look different. Did someone hit you?"

"Aye, Magni, but I'm fine now. We did have a wee battle with some evil men, but they'll not be bothering either of you again."

"Are they the ones who stole us away?"

"Aye. They paid men to steal you. Never again. Come, we have some dried meat for you to munch on. I don't know why Lia wishes to take Thane aside, but we'll let her have her way. We're just glad to see you two together again," Meg said, ruffling his dark curls.

"I am hungry," Magni said, flying up the incline to the horses, the others following.

That left Thane with Lia. "What is it, Lia?"

She took his hand and said, "Come with me. It is difficult for me to explain, but I see the world as needing fixing in some ways that it can't seem to fix on its own. It would be easier if I could do things myself, but I cannot. I can only lead people to certain areas, the same way I led you here through Tora. That's where I come in. To help where I can. What I wish you to see is in the small hut. I'll go in with you."

Thane decided to go along with her and not pepper her with more questions. He had no idea what it was about, but if she had already been inside, whoever was within the hut had not hurt her. But then again, better to be safe. "Do I need my weapon, Lia?"

She laughed and waved her hand. "Nay, they are older. They'll not fight you, I promise."

Thane ducked as he followed Lia inside the

door of the small thatched-roof cottage. There were two candles inside the small chamber with two windows uncovered for light. An old woman sat at the table, an old man behind her with his hand on her shoulder. They were both gray-haired and of slight frames, but he didn't recognize either of them.

As soon as he stepped inside, the woman began to cry, her sobs as quiet as any he'd ever heard. He glanced up at the man behind her and stopped. Something familiar about him.

"Thane?" the man uttered, the one word catching on his tongue. "Is it truly you, son?"

Son?

Lia pulled him closer and did her best to push his large frame into a chair. "I think you should sit for a wee bit, Thane. This is Thane, the chieftain of Clan MacQuarie on the Isle of Mull."

"And Brian? Mora? My wee lassie?" the woman asked, her cheeks flooded with tears.

The man said, "Give him a moment, Myra. We've shocked the lad."

Myra? Then Thane's gaze locked on the man's face.

He stood, knocking the chair backward with a thud. "Da?"

The man nodded, dipping his head as tears misted his gaze. "It is truly you, Thane. You've grown into a fine man, son."

"Da? Mama?" Standing before the man, Thane's knees nearly buckled at all the familiar signs. The scar under the elder man's left eye, the clarity in his gaze, the look of pride nearly undoing him.

Thane's mother pushed away from the table and stood, his father holding her arm to make sure she was steady. "Careful, Myra. Our son is a tall man."

"Thane, my wee laddie." She fell against him, hugging him tight as she cried, her head just barely coming up to his shoulders.

Lia said, "You see, they were stolen away just as you were, Thane. Egan and his men knocked them out and brought them here to take care of the bairns. He brought you to Raghnall Garvie to sell you to a royal prince in the Mideast, but their ship sank on the way. You know the rest of the story with the Garvies. I've explained to them how you were left on Mull alone, and how you raised Mora and Brian until you met Artan and started Clan MacQuarie."

He hugged his father and the three cried together until his mother pushed away. "Mora and Brian? They are well? We can see them? Will you bring them to meet us?"

"Nay, Mama. You are both coming with me. Home. You're coming home to live with me in our castle."

"Castle?" The two looked at each other, the shock on their faces clear.

"Aye, and I'll tell you all about Brian and Mora along the way. But they don't remember either of you. Please don't be disappointed, but they will love you with all their hearts."

"Egan? He's gone, Lia?" Myra asked. "Thane, your father tried to escape many times, but they always found him and beat him."

"Once they whipped your mother." His father's age showed, his head now dipped as he shook it. "I couldn't risk that happening again, so we stayed."

Lia touched Myra's hands and said, "That is all in the past now. You have three bairns waiting to get to know you. Egan is gone forever. Shall we move along?" Lia led them out the door and stopped in front of Lennox and Meg. "My mission here is done. We shall go for now."

Lia made introductions to Lennox, Meg, Magni, and Artan, but then brought them in the opposite direction.

Thane said, "Meg, you look exactly like your sister. She is more than anxious to see you again."

Meg wrung her hands. "I cannot wait to see dear Tamsin again. She is well?"

"Aye, and Alana is anxious to meet you too."

Lia said, "Please follow me. One more thing before we take our leave."

Lennox said, "Lia, you're going in the wrong direction. We're heading back to Mull."

"Be patient for a few more moments, if you please."

She continued to walk, this small lass of power, until she rounded another bend in the coastline, then led them up a knoll to look over the water.

"There," she said, pointing across the sea.

"That's the western section of Ardnamurchan," Lennox explained. "Several villages are there. Which one are you pointing out?"

"Kilchoan. See the castle? It sits on the

Ardnamurchan coastline. It will be our next challenge."

Thane asked, "In what way, Lia?"

"It's known as Mingary Castle in Kilchoan. Near Lochaber."

"Why are you showing us this?" Meg asked.

"Mingary is the base for the sea kings. It's known as the gateway for overlords and privateers. And some of them are not nice."

A cold wind blew across the bay and Thane shivered, his gaze traveling to Lennox's, seeing the same concern in his eyes that coursed through him. Were there more bairns at Mingary?

What the hell would happen next?

Thane wouldn't focus on that. He couldn't.

It was time to bring his parents home to Mora and Brian. And Meg home to Tamsin.

And Lia was finally reunited with her brother.

These were happy times. He'd not focus on the rest for now.

## Chapter Thirty-Seven

*Meg*

---

As they rowed back across the sound after returning the horses, so many thoughts swirled in Meg's mind that she couldn't decide what to say first. She loved Lennox, but had she made a mistake handfasting with him? It wasn't Lennox that worried her, it was his status. Peering up at the majestic castle they were approaching, she had no idea what she would do as wife to the chieftain of such a large clan. She needn't have worried about what to say because Lennox started everything for her.

"Meg, stay with me. Marry me. We can make it official."

"Nay, I cannot yet."

"Why? I've waited for you all my life. You're a part of me now."

"Because I have to find Tamsin. Please be patient. I must find my sister first." And herself. She had to find out exactly who she was and what she wanted. Mull, Ulva, Oban, Drimnin. She'd been more places in a fortnight than she had in her life. Her head spun with all that had taken place over such a short time. More places, more castles, more people.

They landed on the coast, and the two got out, their conversation uncomfortable but something necessary. They returned the boat to the boathouse and gathered their belongings, then faced each other.

"Why, Meg? Stay here. I'm sure Tamsin will visit, but we can wait a fortnight or a moon to marry if you like. Get to know each other better." He stepped toward her and attempted to pull her in close, but she wouldn't allow it.

"Lennox, I know we handfasted and I accept it, and do love you with all my heart, but I'm confused. Overwhelmed? In due time, I will return to stay with you and take my rightful place here as your wife, but now, more than anything, I need to see my sister. And I'd like to spend some time alone with her. We need to talk, get to know each other again. I promise that I will come back."

"I will remember that, though I'm happy to give you whatever time you need to be alone with her right here at our castle. I don't need to listen to your conversations. Bring her here."

Stepping back, she said, "You don't understand. Without my sister, I am no one. All my life, she is the only one who cared about me, who cared *for* me, who cared if I lived or died. I'm nobody without her."

"You just saved four bairns from a life of drudgery and pain. I'd say you are someone, Meg."

She whirled away from him. "I'm leaving,

Lennox. I need to go. I'm sorry. Tamsin has a daughter who she cannot leave. It's too difficult for me to explain what I feel deep inside, but I must see my sister on my own."

"Wait," he called out. "A sennight, please?"

Spinning back to face him, she said, "Nay. I'm going now because I have to. And I'm not changing my mind because some man told me I should. This is not about you, but about me. I know that having spent your entire life as a chieftain or the heir to a chieftain, you've been given your way in most things. Been waited on. Had people cheer you on. Have been the one to order others around and never been refused. Been thanked for things you have done. I've had none of that. I cannot explain..."

She tugged her hair behind her head, trying to restore her plait. "Lennox, I don't know who I am. What we've had, it's been wonderful. You are wonderful, but I must find my sister. She was the only positive thing in my life before I met you. Don't you see? I need to process all that has happened. Not be defined by who my husband is or what clan I'm in. I was just set free from a life of hard work. I need to understand myself, and as much as I love you, you don't know me well enough to help me with that, but Tamsin does."

Lennox's shocked expression hit her in the gut, but it was time someone told him. Even though she loved him, she wasn't going to give up her life for a spoiled chieftain.

She stepped closer and cupped his cheek. "You have given me so much, opened my heart to so much. Please, I beg you, allow me this without arguing. It does not mean I do not love you. I do. But I love Tamsin too. I need her help in sorting my life out. I feel lost, overwhelmed." She kissed his lips, but the tension emanated from him. "Remember that there is ten summers' difference in our ages. You have seen so much more than me."

"I'm not spoiled," he ground out, his jaw ticking. "I'm a hardworking, responsible chieftain whose leadership takes care of many people in our village."

"Of course you do, but allow me to explain what I mean. My mother died when I was seven summers, and ever since then, I'd get up before dawn, make porridge for my father, then prepare a sack of food for him to take on his journey wherever he was going. The rest of my day I might plant seeds, pull weeds, sew the holes in our clothing, wash the clothing, clean the floors, the pans, the dishes. Make our own gowns. Peel vegetables to soak in a pot. Chop vegetables. Skin and cut up rabbits and squirrels. Have you ever done any of those things, Lennox? Any of them?"

He closed his eyes and shook his head. "Wait, I've skinned animals. My sire forced me to do it when I was young."

She smiled and squeezed his arm. Her voice turned low as she leaned in. "And when my sire returned home, he would check everything and decide which of us deserved a swat, a fist, or the paddle. Which was your father's preferred method?"

He barely shook his head, but enough for her to know that he'd gotten her message. But she still wasn't finished.

"Then he married my sister off, so all the chores were mine alone. Alone. All the time Tamsin was gone, I was alone, and I missed her. Every. Single. Moment of every day. Then my father chose a husband for me who was more than twice my age and spent his time drooling whenever he looked at me. He never asked me my opinion. Never asked if I was ready to marry. Never asked if I liked the man. Instead, my father chose him, told me the day before I was to marry, and the last comment was the worst. My father made him promise to work me hard. Why? What did I ever do to anger my father to treat me so? I don't know.

"If that's how I lived my life, how can I ever be good at the job of a chieftain's wife? I have no idea what to do each day. How could I handle the chores? Handle the staff? Know what needs to be done on a daily basis?"

"I'm not worried about that because you are intelligent and caring. Those are the two only requirements in my eyes. And if you wish to run away somewhere, know that I'll run away with you, Meg."

"You'd do that for me?" Tears sprang to her eyes at the thought that this man would do anything she asked. It was indeed proof that he had deep feelings for her.

"I would. I love you with every part of my

being. I would rather live as a pauper with you than live in a castle without you."

She nearly cried over that because it was such a powerful statement, another reason to love Lennox MacVey. "I will think of you and that comment every night before I close my eyes." Perhaps she'd told him too much. It didn't matter. Her feelings were difficult to explain, but she needed Tamsin to help her sort her life out. On how to be a wife, how to love a man, how to be a mistress of a castle, how to believe in herself. "I don't even comprehend how the world works. Only the small one I was in, and I hated it. I wish to find a life of happiness, but I think I need my sister to help me work through it. Please don't take this as rejection, but postponement." She reached for him and placed her head on his shoulder. "I love you, Lennox, but this is something I must do."

He nodded, the click in his jaw bothering her again, but he was holding her, not pushing her away. "I will wait for you, lass. Thank you for explaining, and I do understand better, but please don't make me wait forever. I'll support whatever you choose to do now."

"I must find my sister. I have to follow my heart because I have nothing else to follow." She stepped closer and stood on her tiptoes, kissing his lips. "I do love you. It will always be you, Lennox MacVey. You've shown me gentleness, joy, and happiness. Those three things I've had to learn again because I lost them for so many years. Now I must determine if I deserve those things. Tell your mother I appreciate all she did for me."

"Ah, lass," he whispered, pulling her close to kiss her forehead. "You deserve so much more. But I love you, so I have no choice."

Confused by his last comment, she held his hand and tipped her head.

"I have to let you go. You've taught me more about strength and the capacity to love than anyone I know. You have it deep inside. You just don't know it. Go see your sister, but promise me that if you need anything, you will send for me."

"I will. My thanks for all your gifts."

He gave her that lopsided grin she loved so.

"Lennox, I think I have more to give, so I'll save it all for you."

Lennox said, "I will escort you to MacQuarie land. Please do not try to deny me this. I'll keep my distance, but I'll not sleep unless I know you've arrived safely. After all that has taken place, I must know you are safe. Once I rest my horse, I promise to return. And I would love to meet your sister and your niece."

"You mean our niece?" She made her way up to the back of the castle. "I will accept that. Stay for a brief repast and then return. I need to be alone, be with my sister."

She didn't understand the quandary in her heart—she needed to step away from him for a bit, yet she loved him.

What the hell was wrong with her?

# Chapter Thirty-Eight

*Lennox*

---

LENNOX HAD NEVER felt so powerless in his life. Here she was, the woman he'd waited for, a woman he admired and enjoyed more than any other, and he was allowing her to walk away from him.

A woman he loved, a woman he'd handfasted with, the one he wished to marry and bring their bairns into the world, raise them—and she was leaving him.

About an hour after they'd returned from their journey, Meg crossed under the gates, four other guards in front of her while he followed. Just under the portcullis, he heard a voice from above. He turned to see his mother hurrying down the stairs.

"Mother? What is it?"

She approached his mount, patting his calf, speaking in such a tone so no one else would hear. "Lennox, she'll be worth the wait. She loves you. She will return."

He hoped she was correct.

They said little along the way to Clan MacQuarie, Lennox's ears alert for any attack, though he hoped they'd caught all the criminals guilty of kidnapping. He didn't need to run into any fool who'd attempt bride-stealing.

When they had traveled an hour, Meg fell back to ride abreast of him. "Lennox, could we talk, please?"

"Aye. What is it you'd like to discuss?"

She cleared her throat, her anxiousness obvious to him, so he gave her the time she needed to organize her thoughts. "What would my duties be as your wife?"

He thought for a moment, then answered with the explanation he thought she was looking for. "Working with our cook to make sure we have enough food in our cellar stores and planning the menu. Usually, we feed the entire village once a sennight, and we feed our guards two meals a day. They go home for the evening meal.

"Overseeing the maids, taking care of the bedchambers for guests. Most of it is handling the help, answering questions. You're fortunate in that the current mistress of the castle, my mother, is still living with us and would be happy to teach you. My mother likes to teach some to read and write, but that would be entirely up to you. I don't know if I am able to tell you everything she does. She could answer best. You also would have Eva to assist you."

"Not you?"

"Of course, I would help wherever I can, but

I don't keep track of stores and menus. That is all my mother and my sister's concern. A head housekeeper oversees all the maids, just as Cook oversees the serving lasses. I handle the coin, and I would love to have you participate in running that part of the castle. Keeping the clan with enough food for winter and being able to buy what we don't have. That takes much planning and adjusting."

He watched her take in this information and sort through it in her mind. Absolutely confident that she would excel at the job, he didn't wish to be overly enthusiastic as she worked through everything. She blushed and turned to him.

"What is it? You are my wife, Meg. Ask me anything you wish."

"Could I ask you if you have been in love before? I don't wish to pry, but I wonder if you have, if she lives in the clan?"

Lennox nearly smiled because her question spoke of sheer jealousy, something he told himself didn't really matter. But it did to her.

"I'll be as honest as I can. I thought myself to be in love twice. Once was the first lass who ever lay in my bed, and I will tell you that my sire came to me and told me the strumpet was to leave and never come back." He had to chuckle at the memory. "He gave me a warning about bringing such women into our home. That it was an insult to my mother."

"Such women?"

Lennox was suddenly caught by the truth of his wife's innocence and wondered exactly how to explain this to her. "Women who are paid for their services."

She tipped her head, still confused.

"Have you heard of prostitutes?"

She shook her head.

"There have always been women who will provide intimate services to men for a coin. Even in Biblical times. Men's needs are usually stronger than women's, so they will pay for such services if they are not married." Then he thought a bit more. "And sometimes even if they are married. They decide they want someone different."

"You would do that?"

"Nay! I was just saying…" Hellfire, how was he to get out of this? "Some do not marry for love. If one does not have feelings for one's partner, they are not interested in sharing the bed except to bear children."

She still looked confused, but he said, "Meg, this is a question better directed to your sister." This conversation was helping him understand why Meg was so persistent about having alone time with Tamsin. Her statement about her ignorance didn't begin to explain her innocence. It wasn't just about dolphins, but much, much more. "Your sister was married to someone she did not like. I think she can explain it better than I can."

Apparently accepting of this, she nodded, but then asked, "And the other woman you loved?"

"The other woman was a beautiful lass from the Highlands who visited once, and I admit that I was attracted to her. Her father spoke to my father about a betrothal, and I accepted it. It made my mother verra happy until the woman came for a second visit and tried to give my mother orders. That did not set well with her, but we didn't suit either."

"But you thought you loved her?"

"I thought I could love her. Since you are my wife, I will be completely honest with you. She warmed my bed quickly, but that was the only way she wished it to happen. Quickly. She was not a virgin. Every visit was considered a bargaining event. How many gowns could she get? She'd love two new pairs of boots or mayhap four. Would I take her to court so she could have her wedding dress tailored from special fabric and the finest thread in the world?"

He paused for a moment, trying to come up with a way to explain what he thought of his betrothed after one moon of visits. "Shallow. She was an extremely shallow woman. I can't even call her a lass because everything she did was well planned, well executed." She was exactly the opposite of Meg.

As they mounted the next hill, Lennox sighed.

"What's wrong?" Meg asked.

"Naught. Once we reach the other side of this hill, our journey is nearly done. I guess I'm missing you by my side already. But keep your eye on the horizon. You'll see Loch Tuath and MacQuarie Castle. We'll approach from the front. I wish for you to see the full view. It is a lovely castle."

Lennox cursed to himself. Their time was nearly over.

What the hell would he say to her to convince her of his love? That they belonged together for eternity?

He had no idea.

# Chapter Thirty-Nine

*Meg*

---

AS SOON AS the castle came into view, her belly did those somersaults she hated so. Flip-flop, flip-flop. Where was her sister? Would she be happy to see Meg? *Thirty-one, thirty-two, thirty-three, thirty-four...* Her fingers ticked away against her leg.

They traveled down the path toward the water, Lennox pointing toward the fishing vessels. It was such a beautiful sight that it nearly made Meg cry, but she held the tears in because she didn't want to blur her vision. She couldn't wait to see Tamsin.

They rounded the bend and approached the gates. Lennox moved in front of her but took her hand to keep her horse close to him. "Lennox MacVey for your chieftain Thane. He's expecting us."

The gates opened, and Meg could hear Magni's shouts of excitement and Lia's giggles. She feared she would fall off her horse because she was so unsteady, glad that Lennox held her hand.

They crossed the bridge, went under the portcullis, and Meg searched the area for her sister but didn't see her.

Lennox dismounted and helped Meg down, and she lost her composure. "What if she's forgotten me, Lennox? Or what if she doesn't wish to see me? Mayhap she's so happy she won't want me around. Mayhap I'll be a bother to her."

She gripped his forearms, but he kissed her forehead and said, "You are the most wonderful, giving person I've ever met, Meg. Of course, your sister will wish to see you."

A squeal rent the air, cutting through all the other voices because she knew it so well.

"Tamsin!" Meg turned away from Lennox and caught sight of her sister, running to her. "Tamsin. Is it truly you?"

The next thing she knew, she was hugging her sister, both young women crying and stepping back to look at each other and then crying some more. Tamsin dropped her sister's hands and took the hand of a lass behind her. "Alana, this is your aunt Meg. You may call her Auntie Meg."

"Gweetings, Aunnie Meg."

"She's beautiful, Tamsin. She looks just like you. I cannot wait to get to play with you, Alana." She bent down and kissed the top of Alana's head.

Tamsin handed Alana to another lass, then took Meg's hand. "Come, I must greet the man who saved my sister and brought her to me."

Meg couldn't stop smiling as they approached Lennox, her tears flowing freely no matter how much she tried to swipe them away. Tamsin held her hand and marched up to Lennox. "I owe you my thanks, Chief MacVey, for bringing my sister to the Isle of Mull and to me now. I appreciate all you've done for her. Please come inside. Our evening meal is about to be served, and I would be honored if you would join us."

Thane came up behind Tamsin and said, "You've met my betrothed, MacVey?"

"Betrothed? Congratulations to both of you," Lennox said, clasping Thane's shoulder.

Magni shouted, "He proposed last eve, and she said she'd marry him. We're going to have a wedding."

It would have been the perfect time to introduce Lennox as her husband, but the words didn't come. Instead, Meg buried her face in his chest and sobbed tears of joy.

Thane said, "Time to go inside for a glass of wine. Let Tamsin and Meg get reacquainted. It's been more than two years, and my sister Mora is anxious to meet you, Meg."

The group proceeded into the great hall, Meg with one arm around Lennox's waist and the opposite holding on to her sister's hand.

Once inside, a beautiful young lass rushed over to her. Tamsin said, "This is Thane's sister Mora. His brother Brian is behind her."

Mora gushed, "I've been waiting to meet you, Meg. I have so many questions. How did you have the courage to escape the locked chamber? And how did you know that man was following you? And where did you learn to throw an axe? Would you mind teaching me sometime?"

Thane's hands came over Mora's shoulders, and he turned his sister around to their parents. Mora said, "Oh, and this is my mother and father, but you know them already. Can you believe we've found them after all these years? I was so surprised when Thane came home and told us he'd found our parents. And all this time we thought someone else was our mother, which couldn't be because my real mother is the sweetest woman in all the land, and I adore her."

Myra took her daughter's hand and said, "Mora, why don't we allow Meg to have a seat in front of the hearth? She's had a long journey."

"I'm sorry, Mama. I didn't mean—"

"Hush, lass. You were fine." Her father patted her shoulder. "I'm sure Meg enjoyed hearing your thoughts."

"I did. It's a pleasure meeting you, Mora."

Finally able to stop her tears, Meg looked to Tamsin who said, "Come, I'll show you to your chamber so you can change into something that isn't covered in dust from your journey."

Thane said, "Join me in an ale, MacVey?"

Lennox glanced at her and asked, "Do you want your bag, Meg?"

Magni shouted, "I'll get it for you, Meg!" Out he flew, the door banging behind him.

Tamsin led Meg up the stairs, chattering along the way, this and that about the castle. Once inside the chamber, Meg looked around and said, "This is beautiful, Tamsin." She touched the needlework of a cushion in the chair by the hearth. "This is your work. I would know it anywhere."

"It is." She gave Meg an odd look.

Meg fell into the chair. "Tell me. Just tell me one thing, Tamsin, and the rest can wait. Are you happy to be betrothed to Thane? Do you wish to spend all your time with him, share his bed?" She stared up at her sister, holding her breath. "Can marriage be a wonderful thing?"

Tamsin sat and took Meg's hands in hers. "Aye. I love Thane with all my heart. He is a wonderful man, and he will be a good father to Alana. I know the difference because the man our father betrothed me to was horrid. Raghnall was evil. He beat me and tried to kill me. If not for Thane, I would not be here now. So aye, I am verra pleased that he asked me to marry him. I've never been happier, especially with you here now. I have so much to tell you, but it can wait until the morrow." She helped Meg change into one of her gowns, then gave her another sisterly hug.

"I'm so happy for you." Meg didn't know what else to say, exhaustion suddenly overwhelming her. She stood and moved to the bed. "Would you mind if I took a wee rest, Tamsin?"

"Go ahead. I'll awaken you when our meal is ready. You must be exhausted. I've heard of all you've done. Magni and Lia have not stopped talking about your adventures. You've been to Oban and Drimnin and Loch Aline and even more. You've traveled farther than I have, sister, and I've been here for two years. You definitely deserve a rest."

Meg removed her boots and reclined on her side, closing her eyes for a moment. She fell fast asleep.

## Chapter Forty

*Lennox*

———∽∽———

LENNOX WAITED FOR Tamsin to come down the staircase. He was still in shock that Meg had fallen asleep and not joined them for the evening meal.

Then Lia said, "We should not forget all that poor Meg has been through. Promised in marriage to a man she didn't approve of, running away, finding four bairns who needed her help, putting an axe in a man who chased us, getting sick with the fever, waking up in a strange place with strange people, climbing in a boat to come look for me at Loch Aline, only to find herself in Drimnin and caught in a horrific battle. Have I recalled it accurately, Chief MacVey? I think she is deserving of a long rest."

Leave it to a child to simplify everything and make perfect sense. "You are correct, Lia. My thanks to you for reminding us of all she's been through."

Magni said, "I wish I'd seen the battle, but we were too late. How long did it last? Was she hiding while you fought off the fools, Chief? Did she use her axe again?"

Lennox hid his smile. "She did indeed use her axe. Meg is incredibly accurate with her weapon." He hadn't given that a thought until Magni had mentioned their battle again. Lennox had been in many, but not Meg.

"And that Egan. I'm glad I never met him. Pirate Man and Hairy were bad enough."

Lia came over and whispered in his ear. "Fear not, she does love you. Besides the battle think on the fact that she killed her first when she was fighting a fever. And then she killed another with you."

Lennox stared at Lia, the wisdom that was forthcoming from her lips so unusual he didn't know how to react. Except that she was always correct.

But his last part was on wee Lia. He'd never told her that Meg had killed anyone.

Yet she knew.

---

Lennox didn't sleep well, memories of their night together too fresh in his mind. Unsettled that he had finally fallen in love and she wasn't lying next to him, he was as uncertain about what steps to take next.

He didn't know what to do. And when Meg wasn't in the great hall in the morning, he had the worst feeling. Was she glad to be rid of him?

More confused than ever, he spoke briefly with

Tamsin, telling her exactly how he felt, then took his leave. He'd have to wait to hear from Meg.

On the way back, he decided to visit with the Granthams before heading to his castle. He found the four Grant cousins sparring in the lists, something he enjoyed watching—Alasdair with Alick, Alaric against Broc.

When they finally finished, he couldn't help but ask the most obvious question. "Are you all named with the first letter *A*? Other than Broc, it seems your names are similar. Why?"

Alaric laughed. "My three cousins were born on the same night, the first grandchildren of Alexander Grant. They agreed that whichever bairn was born first got to use his name, but they were all born at the same exact time."

"Exactly?"

Alasdair said, "Close enough to call it the same. I think Aunt Jennie and Aunt Brenna may have planned it ahead so Grandsire, their brother Alex, wouldn't know. Apparently, our parents argued about it so much that he wouldn't settle the argument as to who was the firstborn."

Alick added, "So we were all given names similar to Alexander—Alasdair, Alick, and Elshander. Alaric was a name chosen by Uncle Jamie to be like Alex as well."

Broc took a bow. "And then there is me."

Alasdair said, "Join us for the midday meal and an ale, MacVey?"

"Gladly. I'll follow you in." He led his horse to the stable, admiring all the warhorses inside the building.

Once in the hall, Dyna joined them. The bairns played off to the side with Sela and Gwyneth chatting near them. "Sorry, I cannot seem to let them play outside without constant supervision. Tell me you caught some of the fools, Lennox."

Lennox gave her a short explanation, including finding Thane's parents.

"Truly? After all these years? How the hell did that happen? How did you know?" Dyna asked.

"Lia. She brought us to the cottage near the water where his parents were kept to take care of any bairns brought in by Egan."

"Did you kill the bastards who controlled that situation?"

"Aye. All taken care of with many thanks from the local villagers in Drimnin."

The door opened, and Logan entered with Connor. "MacVey, that you?"

"Aye."

"Update?" Logan asked as he grabbed an ale for himself and handed one to Connor before taking a seat.

Lennox filled them in on what they'd found.

"Meg is with her sister on MacQuarie land?"

"Aye."

Logan said, "Fair warning. The baron is at Oban, asking questions. I suspect he'll find his way here in a day or two."

Lennox cursed. "Meg does not need any more trouble at the moment. She has enough to deal with." Hellfire, but that evil bastard was going to come for her. He feared it would happen, but what did he know of English barons? Something inside him stirred, his heartbeat increasing at the thought of that fool getting his hands on her. He couldn't lose her.

He would *not* lose her. But he wasn't sure exactly how to handle this situation.

"She just found her sister," Logan said. "Shouldn't she be celebrating right now?"

Dyna grinned, her eyes bright as if she truly could tell what he was thinking. "You handfasted with Meg, Lennox. True?"

"True. I thought she'd never leave my side, but she insisted on some time alone with her sister. After all she's been through, I couldn't argue with her. As soon as she settled in her sister's chamber, she fell fast asleep."

Eli approached and said, "Spit and slime, after all the poor lass has been through, I don't blame her."

Logan stared up at his granddaughter. "Besides getting captured and putting an axe in someone's head, what else has she been through?"

Eli gave an unladylike snort. "Besides the ugly troll she killed while she was with the fever, then she had to fight off four men in Drimnin. Or were you not listening, Grandsire? She put another axe into a man's chest when she was but a day away from being delirious with fever."

Dyna cut in, "The lass has not been trained in battle like we have. She's only used her axe on animals before. I'll never forget my first kill."

Eli chuckled. "After my first kill in battle, Alaric had to come and get me. I was screaming in the middle of hundreds of dead bodies in Skaithmuir."

"You killed more than one, granddaughter, so I was told."

"Doesn't matter. I'm telling you it was difficult for her." She crossed her arms and glared at her grandfather. "Are you that old that you don't recall your first one?"

Logan snorted. "I'll agree she's seen some challenges of late. And now the baron is on his way. Guess you have somewhere to go, MacVey."

What the hell was he to do now? Run back or leave her be until she was ready?

"Can you give me some advice about this, if you please? I spent some time in Europe, but I have no idea how to handle an English baron. Other than putting my sword through his heart, I don't know what else to do to stop him. That would be the best way, but then I'd find myself in gaol."

Connor said, "Nay, King Robert supports his people, especially his nobles. He especially hates it when they come this far across the border to attack people. If he threatens you or her, put your sword through him. You have the right."

"I hope it doesn't come to that. Do they believe in handfasting? She's mine and you know what that means. Will he?"

Alasdair thought for a moment, then said, "I dealt with a few characters before I married Emmalin. The English are stubborn fools. He'll not like it if he thinks you bested him. And if he does get her, if even for a short time, he'll make her pay for her believed shortcomings."

Lennox ran his hand down his face, then got

up to pace. He didn't like this situation, though he wasn't surprised by it. It had taken him a long time to find the woman he wished to spend the rest of his life with, and Meg was the only one for him. He'd not give her up, but how much blood needed to be spilled?

Logan said, "If I were you, I'd go drag her arse back to your castle where you can protect her."

Dyna swatted his arm. "Drag her back? What the hell, Logan?"

"You know what I mean."

"Well, I'm going to disagree with you. Right now, she needs her sister. She's lived through a fortnight of sheer terror. Tamsin is the calm she needs right now. Lennox, you must let her go. She'll come back to you." Dyna gave an emphatic nod to accentuate her point.

"And if the baron gets to her first?" Logan asked.

Dyna chuckled. "Meg can take care of herself. And besides, Lennox will find out as we will, and we'll all be there to support her. And to stop the baron if he's too persistent."

"When are we leaving?" Logan asked.

"I'm leaving now," Lennox said. "I'll go back to gather my guards, then we're headed to MacQuarie land."

"I would leave soon and keep your eyes open. They're likely to come by boat," Logan said.

Tora ran over and asked, "When are you leaving, Mama?"

Dyna gave her daughter a puzzled look. "To go where, Tora?"

"To save Meg from the bad man. You have to."

"Soon," she replied, crossing her arms and staring at her daughter, who ran back to play with her toys.

Lennox said, "I'm on my way." He sat for one moment to gather his thoughts, see if he had any other questions. He knew the value of being prepared.

Dyna said, "So, based on my daughter, I'm changing my advice. Go now, Lennox. We'll follow."

Tora hurried over and whispered in Lennox's ear. "Mama is right. We're all going."

# Chapter Forty-One

*Meg*

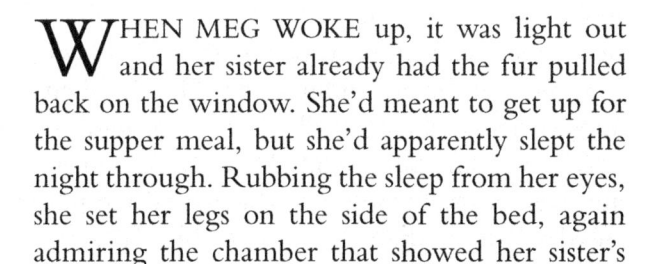

---

WHEN MEG WOKE up, it was light out and her sister already had the fur pulled back on the window. She'd meant to get up for the supper meal, but she'd apparently slept the night through. Rubbing the sleep from her eyes, she set her legs on the side of the bed, again admiring the chamber that showed her sister's touches, then got up to peer out the window.

Her chamber faced the sea. It was the loveliest view she'd ever seen. The sun shone bright across the water now dotted with fishing boats. The sparkle of the sun's reflection across the waves danced and shimmered as though the faeries frolicked upon the water.

"It is quite a view. Do you not agree?"

Meg whirled around to see her sister strolling toward her with a tray of fruit and a fresh loaf of bread. "Tamsin, that smells wonderful. You are cooking?"

"I am, and I'm enjoying it. Alana helps me and we assist Thane's cook, Agnes. She's a lovely woman. But enough about me. I wish to hear all about you, dear sister. I brought a warm cup of vegetable broth for you. Please sit and chat with me. I can't wait to hear about your adventures."

Meg gave Tamsin a brief accounting of all that had happened since she'd escaped their father's home—the kirk, finding the bairns, Lennox saving her, her illness, and the last trek across Morvern.

Tamsin said, "I've heard most of that from the others. Tell me about Da and the baron."

Meg scowled, not wishing to think on it, but if she was to share it with anyone, it would be her sister. "Tamsin, he was disgusting. Old with gray hair and a protruding belly. He kissed me and I wished to vomit. All he spoke of with me was giving him bairns. Lads. He only wanted lads and right away. Da never told me anything until the day before when I met the baron. He was to return for me the next day. I had no choice but to run away."

"The baron paid Papa for you, did he not?"

"Aye. I know not how much. Did that happen with Raghnall? And what happened to him?"

Tamsin took her turn and explained everything that had occurred with her husband. Meg had no idea that poor Tamsin's life had been so difficult. The beatings, the near-death experiences, the cruelty by her husband and his mother.

"And Thane saved you every time."

"He did. With help from Clan Grantham. I'd probably be dead by now if not for Thane and Eli. I adore him."

"And the marriage bed? Please explain it all to me. You know Mama told us naught."

"How much do you know, Meg? I heard rumblings about you and Lennox MacVey."

Her eyes misted, but she held in the tears. "We handfasted. And I think I love him, but I'm so confused. I don't understand everything about the intimacy or what I would do as his wife. I feel like I've walked from one world into another that is nothing like the first."

"You have. Things on the Isle of Mull are lovely compared to our lives with Da. I mean, with Mama we were happy because we were young, but Eli and Dyna took the time to explain to me how cruel the world can be when it comes to women. They don't accept it, and I don't either. Not anymore. But I had to learn to love myself first before I could let Thane in.

"After all the days of being told I was lazy and unsightly and ignorant, it took a while to realize that I had value as a woman. That a man did want me to be his wife, a man who respected me and asked my opinion about things. Thane is amazing. When you hear all the details about his life, you'll understand, but I learn something new from him every day. I adore him so much that it scares me."

Meg asked, "Scares you? Please explain because that's how I feel. I love Lennox, but I'm so scared, yet I'm not sure what I'm afraid of. Does that make sense? What if I do things wrong and he decides he doesn't want me in a year and a day?"

Tamsin got up and pulled Meg to her feet. "Aye, it does. If you are like me, then you fear that one day you will wake up and it will all be gone. That your husband will disappear and you'll be back in a horrible situation with cruel men around you. That you are in a dream that will be replaced by nightmares. I've had nightmares for a long time about Raghnall and his men. It's only recently that the nightmares have finally begun to dissipate."

And Meg was crying again. "That is it. I can't believe that a chieftain wants me, that I am capable of running his castle, that he'll not get sick of me and go for another. I don't know how to get rid of these thoughts. Help me, Tamsin. I don't wish to lose Lennox. I love him. I didn't think I understood exactly what love was, but now I do."

"You've been through some difficulties in a short period. Give yourself the time to relax. I know how Da worked you, but you don't have to cut vegetables and wash his clothing right now. And as for Lennox? Sometimes you must have faith. Lennox MacVey is a good man. He hasn't hit you, has he?"

"Nay. He would never hurt me."

"I didn't think he would, but I had to ask. If you love him, then trust that you will build a wonderful life together. It won't be easy, but together, the two of you will get through the most difficult situations. Working through problems with someone you love and who loves you in return is far better than any day with a cruel man. Whether either of us likes to admit it, many times, Da was cruel. Not always, but he was never happy after he lost Mama."

"I'm so glad I found you again, Tamsin. I think I'd like to get dressed and see Lennox."

"I'm glad to have found you again, dearest sister, but I'm afraid Lennox took his leave at dawn. I pulled him aside and spoke with him privately. He gave me a brief explanation of all you'd been through and told me how strong his feelings are for you. I do believe him, Meg. He asked for your hand in marriage and of course, I accepted. But he let me know that he will come back whenever you are ready. That he knows you have been through an ordeal and that you must sort through everything. He said it was difficult to let you go, but that he had to because he loves you."

Meg cried. "He didn't say goodbye. I feel awful. I should have seen him off after all he's done for me."

Tamsin set her hand on Meg's arm. "He's in love with you. Do not worry. Spend a few days with me, and we'll send a message that you are ready to return to him. He said he would wait for you, though it was difficult for him to leave you."

Meg nodded to her sister and squeezed her hand. Everything Tamsin said made perfect sense.

Then why did her heart ache so?

## Chapter Forty-Two

*Meg*

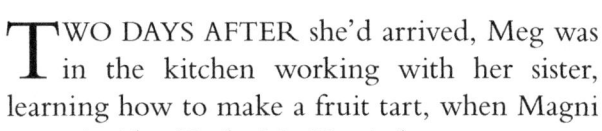

---

TWO DAYS AFTER she'd arrived, Meg was in the kitchen working with her sister, learning how to make a fruit tart, when Magni came inside. "Lady MacVey is here to see you, Meg. She's by the hearth."

Startled, Meg said a quick prayer that Lennox was hale. She had to hope that nothing had happened to him. After washing and drying her hands, she turned to Tamsin. "Do I look fine? No flour on me anywhere?"

"You look beautiful. I'll be there in a few moments to join you. I'd be pleased to meet Rut. I've heard much about her."

Meg hurried into the hall, glad to see it was nearly empty so they could speak privately. "Good day to you, my lady. I hope there is naught wrong at your castle. Lennox is hale?"

Rut waved her hand and said, "All is well. Fear not, Meg. Don't you look lovely today, my dear."

"My thanks. May I get you a goblet of wine or anything else?"

"I'd love a bit of wine."

Meg gathered two goblets and handed one to Rut, also handing her a fur for her lap because of the chill in the hall. She decided not to say anything, that Rut would let her know the reason for the visit.

And she was correct.

"My dear, I hope you haven't decided to stay here with your sister. You would surely be close enough to visit from Dounarwyse Castle. We'd love to have you back where you belong."

*Eight, nine, ten...* Her fingers began to tick away the numbers, something she hadn't done in a while. Thinking carefully before she spoke, she needn't have worried because Rut had more to say.

"Oh, lass. Forgive me. I know you handfasted, and Lennox misses you terribly. When will you be returning? I'd be happy to hand over some of the duties to you as soon as you arrive."

"But I don't know how to do any of the duties..." *Fifteen, sixteen...*

"Of course you do. Any simpleton could do the job."

Meg could feel the blush deepening on her face. "I've never lived in a castle, my lady. I'm afraid I won't know what to do at all."

Rut let out a small gasp. "Forgive me. Of course I knew that." She stared at Meg for a long time, then said, "You listen to me, young lady."

Meg wished to yell for her sister to come help her. What was she to do now when the woman was about to holler at her for being a terrible wife to Lennox? Her hands kneaded in her lap, twisting the fabric in and out. *Sixty, seventy...* Lordy, the woman had her counting by tens.

"Lennox has been a patient man. He has waited for you to come into his life for a verra long time. Countless women have thrown themselves at his feet and he's ignored all of them. Then you step into his life, and he falls in love with you so hard and so fast."

"Forgive me..." Her tears were coming, and she wasn't going to be able to stop them.

"Just a moment. I'm not finished. You may have your say soon enough." Rut straightened the folds in her skirt. "My son adores you, and I can see why. You have more backbone, more compassion, more wit, more intelligence than any other woman he's met, and I'll not allow you to walk away. You're a beautiful girl who has a strong moral character, one who battles for those who are weaker." Rut paused to pull a linen square from the fold of her skirt to dab her eyes. "Now, I know you were taken ill, you were forced to travel across half of Scotland, and you even had to battle fools to find Lia, so I understand you needed a rest. You are tough and sweet, yet kind. One who will always stand up for her beliefs and not allow a man to put her asunder.

"One who has the strength of character to run his castle well, to stand by his side, to carry his sons and daughters in her womb and raise them properly. You are everything he's ever wanted in a wife. He just didn't know it until he met you."

Rut stood and looked down at Meg. "Now,

when are you going to come home to him? He's heartsick without you by his side."

Meg's tears erupted and she stood, threw her arms around Rut, and hugged her. "Soon, verra soon. Will you promise to help me, my lady?"

"Rut. Call me Rut. Eva and I will both help you. And your sister." She waved her hand over toward the kitchen door where Tamsin stood with a wide smile on her face. "Surely she will come to visit. You may share holidays. She will not be far."

Meg wiped her tears and said, "I love Lennox. I've been exhausted."

"I can attest to that, my lady. My sister has been exhausted, sleeping half the days away. I'm Tamsin."

"Good day to you, Tamsin. I met you, but you were unconscious at the time. What a beautiful lass you are."

Meg said, "I'd like to send a message home with you to Lennox, if you don't mind."

"Of course not. I'll head back first thing on the morrow. Take your time." Then she cupped Meg's cheeks in her hands and kissed her forehead. "Lass, I've been waiting for you as long as Lennox has. Fear not, you will fit in well with our clan and our wee family. Welcome to Clan MacVey."

Tamsin said, "Come, Rut. I'll show you to your chamber."

Meg went to find her writing utensils.

It was time to go home to her husband.

She entered her chamber, searching for what she needed to pen a short note to Lennox. Her heart ached for him in a way she didn't understand. A knock sounded at the door.

"Enter, if you please."

Turning around, she was surprised to find Lia there.

"Greetings, my lady. I'm so happy to see you are completely healed now."

"I am? I guess I am, Lia. I still feel tired."

"You are going to send a note to someone?"

"Aye, to Lennox." She sat down, her implements now set on the table.

"I'm glad. You know you and Lennox have two hearts, but you are meant to be one on the same journey. The two of you are one of the reasons I came to the Isle of Mull."

"But I thought you were Magni's sister?"

"I told Magni to say that because it is an acceptable explanation to all, but I know you can understand my existence. My purpose is to guide you in the right direction, which was to the bairns and then to Lennox. So, I am here to give you that final push."

"You came for me? Truly? As a faery?"

"You were part of my instructions. Some people are dealt more than they deserve in this life, so we are sent to change things. To redirect destiny. We cannot do it for you, only guide you. My goal was to help many—you and Lennox, and your sister and Thane, his siblings, their parents, and Magni. Such a group who are all in the same area. So unusual for us to see."

Meg was so overcome with emotion that she couldn't speak.

"Angels send you pushes too, but some evil forces are too powerful to overcome. So, you will return to Lennox? His heart belongs with yours."

"Aye, I love him. But will you go back? I don't want to lose you, Lia. And if you go, Magni will be devastated."

"No, I am not finished yet. I have another wee one I must protect. He is not here yet, but he's on his way. And you are correct. Magni still needs me, and I am happy to fulfill that need for a short while longer."

Still speechless, Meg stared at Lia who sat with her hands folded demurely in her lap. Within seconds, a green aura surrounded her, as if to convince Meg that she was indeed something special.

"Oh my, Lia. The aura is impressive."

"I have to stop it most times, but I thought you might enjoy it." She stood, the aura disappearing. "Now, you need to appear out front. You're needed there but trust me that the angels will take care of everything for you. And you can put the note aside. Lennox is on his way."

Magni burst in the door. "The baron is here for you, Meg. Don't go out. Hide. Thane is arguing for you, says he'll send him away, but you cannot leave us." He ran over and wrapped his arms around Meg's waist. "You saved us."

Lia said, "Calm down, Magni. I'm sure Thane can handle everything, and if he cannot, I'll tell you a wee secret. But only if you promise not to scream out there. Thane will handle everything until the others arrive."

"I promise. I promise. What's the secret?" Wide-eyed, he hopped from one foot to the other and back again. "Lia, tell me, please. The baron has at least a score of men out there coming for Meg. Who are the others? When are they going to get here? Meg can't leave me. I'll cry."

Lia leaned forward. "There are many men coming."

"More men for the baron? How many more?"

"Nay, not the baron's men. Lennox and the MacVey guards and your grandfather are all coming with the Grant guards."

"Grandsire Logan! I love him." Magni whirled and ran out the door, yelling behind him. "Come on, Meg! You too, Lia."

Meg looked to Lia, gave the wee lass a hug, then asked, "Lennox is on his way?"

Lia nodded, taking her by the hand and leading her outside.

Meg followed her down the steps and met Tamsin and Rut at the door. Tamsin said, "Meg, please do not go out there. Those men remind me of Raghnall. I can't lose you again."

She turned to her sister and said, "I must go. I refuse to go with that man, so fear not. I have faith that this will put an end to the baron's threats. I will not marry him." Then she looked to Rut and squeezed her hands. "I have a husband whom I love dearly. I belong with Lennox." Then she squared her shoulders and headed out the door of the keep toward the gates.

Rut and Tamsin followed, Rut wearing a wide grin. "She's the one for him, Tamsin. I'm telling you that. She's lovely in that blue gown. The baron will drool over her." She grinned and squeezed Tamsin's arm. "Naught like a wee bit of jealousy to force my son to be decisive."

Meg stopped in the courtyard, a short distance from the gates, watching as the two men bantered about her life, making decisions for her as if she were but a bairn in her mother's arms. She strode over to the bridge, but Thane waved her back.

Tamsin tugged on her sleeve. "Meg, don't go. If you get close enough, he'll have his men grab you, throw you in the boat. Men can be horrid that way."

"Nay, Tamsin. This is my life, and he doesn't have the right to decide for me. I don't want him and won't marry him."

She was not a child. Why did they not understand that? Tears misted her gaze, but she fought them back, thinking of the one person she loved with all her heart.

Lennox MacVey.

Now that she'd stepped away from him, she knew his value. Knew she loved him. Knew he was the only man she'd ever allow in her life. Why had she left him? If he were here, surely he could find a way to get rid of this derelict.

She had to believe that Lia told the truth and Lennox was on his way. Until he arrived to offer her assistance, she would stand tall as a woman who would make her own decisions. Marry whom she wished, live where she chose. No old man was going to order her around.

The baron shouted to her, "Margret, you will

come here right now. I paid for you, and you belong to me. I will have my men carry you here if you do not do as I tell you to do immediately."

Tamsin gasped, whispering to her sister. "I never liked that name Margret. You're a Meg."

His men continued to walk across the beach, exiting their boats with their paltry weapons, forming a semicircle behind the baron.

"I'm not going to marry you, my lord," she said in as loud a voice as she could.

She could almost hear the man grit his teeth. "Your opinion does not matter. You will bear me the heirs I was promised if I have to lock you in a chamber until you've given me the three lads pledged to me."

"I did not promise you anything. I will not marry you." She took two steps forward and lifted her chin. "I've already committed myself to another."

"Then that will be annulled. The one who owns you made me an oath, and I expect it to be honored. Just stop talking, Margret. Your words have no bearing on this conversation. This is between men. Your job is to follow instructions."

She didn't know what else to say, but the baron's attention wavered, turning to the side as a group of horses came down the path.

Lennox approached, a line of guards behind him, quite regal in their green plaids, looking far more impressive than the unsightly baron standing in front of her. Could Lennox discourage the baron?

"Who the hell are you?" the baron bellowed.

"I'm Meg's protector. Chieftain of Clan MacVey, the name is Lennox."

"I will be her protector as her husband," the baron growled.

Lennox laughed and said, "She'll never be yours. She handfasted with me. Meg does not wish to marry you. I heard her tell you so twice."

Meg's heart swelled listening to the man she loved defend her. Would the baron listen?

"Handfasting," the baron said, spitting off to the side. "A practice used by savages that won't stand up in the English courts. You're a bigger fool than she is, whoever you are. You Scots do not intimidate me." He made a motion for his men to cross over to the other side of the moat. "Bring her to me."

Lennox moved his horse in front of the bridge, and Thane joined him. Their two horses were wide enough to keep anyone from crossing.

Meg's hands began to sweat because she wished this to be over, and she surely did not want anyone hurt because of her. But she would not go with the baron. The way his eyes raked over her body made her feel dirty, unsavory. *Eighty-one, eighty-two, eighty-three...* Her fingers ticked away, but her sister reached over to still her. Meg glanced at Tamsin, so beautiful and strong, a testament to how much a woman could bear. Her sister was an inspiration.

Lennox's men surrounded the baron's men, though he was so pompous, it didn't seem to faze him. "Do as you wish. I'm not leaving without her."

"I'll return your coin, but she's not going with you. She's much too intelligent for you." Lennox dismounted, his hand now on his weapon's hilt.

The baron laughed, throwing his head back. "You have not seen her with her hands in the dirt pulling weeds like I have. She's a woman, and women's brains are smaller than men's. Everyone knows that."

Lennox's sword came unsheathed so quickly that Meg jumped. "That is my wife you are insulting."

"You know nothing of her. She's half daft and will service me well. I have my king's writ giving her to me. Hand her over or my men will attack, killing anyone who tries to stop me. Margret, get yourself over here. Do as I say or pay the price for your insubordination to your master."

Lennox moved closer until the point of his sword was at the baron's throat. "You will apologize for insulting her. Meg, not Margret, is the most intelligent and caring woman I have ever met. She has an uncanny understanding of how to deal with bairns and warriors alike. You are not worthy of eating the crumbs that fall from her bread."

The baron said, "Bertram, get my betrothed so we can be on our way."

The thunder of horse hooves echoed from both sides of MacQuarie Castle, and Lennox let his sword fall from the baron's neck. A sea of red plaids surrounded the baron and his men, a sea that kept coming and coming, a few blue plaids mixed in.

Alasdair and Alaric led the charge of guards. Alasdair said, "I believe you were told to leave MacQuarie land, and we're here to escort you."

The baron glared at the man, then headed across the bridge, pushing everyone out of his way. "I'll get the fool myself."

He shoved at Lennox's horse, an act that caused his beast to dance. As Lennox was forced to calm his horse first, the daft fool was able to get past him, but once Lennox had the beast settled, he chased after him and grabbed the baron from behind, throwing him to the ground. He set his foot on the man's chest and placed his sword at his throat. "You will not touch my wife."

"Fine. You may have her. She's just another whore to me." He glared at Meg, his fists clenching by his side.

Lennox stepped back, making sure Meg was still behind him, when he allowed the man to his feet, though it was a trial. Once the baron finally made it to standing, his face was reddened and swollen, but he said nothing. He turned and headed toward the beach, and the group broke apart.

As soon as Lennox turned toward Meg, he caught the lying bastard out of the corner of his eyes. The baron whirled and ran straight for Meg, a dagger held high enough to strike her heart.

Lennox swung his sword and cut off the man's hand.

"You fool! Look what you've done!" The baron held up his arm, then grabbed the end in a futile attempt to stem the flow of blood. "Help me,

Bertram!" His scream echoed across the area as he fell to his knees in agony.

A man appeared at de Wilton's side, removing his coat to wrap around the baron's bleeding stump, but it was too late. He'd lost too much blood, enough for him to crumple to the ground. Bertram barked orders at two other men who came along to lift him and carry him back to his galley.

Meg heard one soldier ask another, "Shouldn't we attack since he attempted to kill the baron?"

"Apparently, you haven't noticed the number of warriors and warhorses around us. If you'd like to commit suicide, then please do attack, but not until I can get away, fool."

The English cavalry returned to their boats, and when Lennox was certain it was safe, he turned around, his gaze scanning the area just as a lovely figure flew across the bridge. Meg launched herself at Lennox and buried her face in his shoulder, clinging to him. The baron was gone forever, if she were to guess. "I'm so glad you came. I was penning you a note to come for me just before the baron arrived." She tipped her head back to look at him. "I've missed you so much. You are the other half of my heart, Lennox MacVey. We belong together."

Lennox dropped his weapon and wrapped his arms around Meg, taking in her sweet scent, then kissed her. "I love you, Meg. Come home with me, please. Marry me. Make it official with the church?"

"Aye," she said, grinning from ear to ear. "Naught would make me happier."

She swore she heard someone clapping behind them again.

## Chapter Forty-Three

*Meg*

---

THE DAY HAD finally arrived, and Meg couldn't possibly be any happier. The forecasted rain was going to hold off until the evening. She'd made a point to ask Lia about the weather. The sweet girl had smiled at her and said, "Of course, we will see that your wedding day is as wonderful as you all deserve. This is a day for many of you, not just you and Lennox, but Thane and Tamsin and his parents. And I'll tell you a wee secret. Magni has been counting the days because he's so excited."

Meg finished dressing and went to her sister's chamber to help her do her hair. Knocking on the door, she hid the wrapped gift inside the fold of her gown. When she entered, Tamsin gasped. "Oh, lassie, you are so beautiful. You will be the most beautiful one there, by far."

"Except for you. I have something for you that I nearly forgot." She held the twine-wrapped package out to Tamsin.

"What is it? I have no guesses at all."

Tamsin sat on the bed, unwrapping it carefully until the bracelet nearly fell out.

"Do you remember it?" Meg asked, fiddling with her fingers, but not counting. Something she worked on frequently.

"I do. Oh, Meg. I do recall when I made these bracelets for us. I loved the blue yarn. You still have yours? I think I have mine too." Tamsin moved over to a chest and rummaged through it. "It's here! I found it. Shall we wear them?"

"Aye. We should. And we nearly match. The green MacVey plaid is lovely too. It reminds me of a forest in spring, the blue thread is the same shade as the sky and the bracelets." Tamsin teared up. "I couldn't have asked for a better ending for the two of us. I'm sorry Mama isn't here to enjoy our weddings."

Lia opened the door and held it for a moment, but no one entered.

"Lia, is everything all right?"

Lia wiggled her nose and said, "All is fine. Do you lasses believe in heaven? You do, surely?"

The sisters nodded in unison. Meg looked at Lia, "Why do you ask?"

"No reason."

Meg didn't believe Lia. After learning the truth about her, she guessed she had a reason for asking, but she had no idea what it could be.

Tamsin said, "I do believe in heaven, and I think Mama is watching over us right now, and she is more than happy."

A waft of berry blew past Meg, and she breathed

in the scent, then gasped, looking at her sister. "Tamsin, it's her. Do you smell it?"

Tamsin turned to face Meg and said, "Oh my, it is Mama. How could that be?" Tamsin teared up, and the two turned to look at Lia, her face smug.

"Lia?" Tamsin asked. "What do you know of this?"

Lia whispered, "I know not what you mean. But it's a lovely day, is it not?"

Tamsin wiped her tears and said, "It is the loveliest day of all. I hope our mama is here, but I hope she hasn't seen all we've gone through because of Papa's choices."

Lia whispered, "I would wager she is proud of all you both have become." Then she giggled.

A knock sounded, and the door flew open with a bang. "Sorry. I didn't mean to do that." Magni stood there, flushed and upset about something.

"Magni? Is something wrong?" Meg asked, sitting on the bed and tugging him in front of her. "I love how you arranged your plaids."

"Do you think my adopted grandsire will be angry with me? Eli suggested this and helped me sew it this way." The lad wore the Ramsay plaid on the top over his shoulder and the MacQuarie plaid wrapped around his hips.

"I think Logan will love it," Meg said. "Do not worry, Magni."

"But if he gets mad, he might not adopt me." He had the famous Magni scowl they'd all come to recognize, his lower lip jutting out and his eyebrows nearly touching in the middle.

Lia gave him a side hug and said, "Logan does

not do things to hurt bairns. He loves bairns more than most."

Magni looked at Lia and asked, "How would you know that, Lia? Sometimes…" He glanced at Meg and Tamsin, then said, "Never mind."

"Where's my grandson?" A booming voice carried up the staircase, and Magni jumped, a wide smile filling his face.

"Grandsire! He's here. I have to go." And the lad was gone in an instant.

Lia said, "Come along, ladies. The men are waiting for us."

Meg followed everyone down the stairs, where they found Rut waiting for them. "Ladies, you look lovely. Here, I have small floral arrangements for you. These are for your hair, and these smaller ones attach to your wrists."

"Rut, many thanks to you," Meg said, admiring the green and purple flowers.

Rut said, "I hope you are not upset that we decided to have the wedding here. I needed Douglas to see Lennox married."

Tamsin said, "I don't mind. You have a larger courtyard than we do to handle guests. And your castle is more central for our friends from Duart Castle and Clan Rankin to attend. We are all excited for this celebration."

The door opened, and Meg's gaze caught her husband-to-be standing in his full-dress plaid. He wore a white léine with his forest-green plaid over it, his sword sheathed to his side. She was about to approach him when a force flew across the floor to stop in front of Lennox and Thane.

"Look what my grandsire brought me. I have a léine just like you, Thane. And I have new boots too. I look just like a chieftain, do I not, Grandsire? Meg! Look at me."

The lad spun around, his words bubbling out as fast as he could say them. Lia said, "Magni, you are as handsome as anyone here."

Tamsin went to Thane's side, so Meg joined Lennox, who leaned over and whispered in her ear, "I do prefer you with naught on, but you look quite regal in that dress, Meg. You are as gorgeous as ever." He kissed her neck, and she giggled like a lassie.

Rut said, "Lennox, you are as handsome as your sire was when he was young." His mother teared up, but then she stopped to say, "What I like best is how happy you are. I've waited a long time to see it. I thank you for finding him, Meg."

Logan came out and bellowed, "Move on. Everyone is waiting for you!"

The group proceeded out, Magni stepping up next to his grandfather. "Which one? Do I ride with you, Grandda? You'll not give me away now that I have another grandsire, will you?"

Logan pointed to one of the warhorses. "We're leading and nay, I'll not give you away. All bairns need two grandsires. Grandparents stand by their grandbairns, through the worst or the best. Now climb up there, lad."

Thane strode over to Midnight Star, one of the Grant warhorses that Connor had loaned them for the processional. "Finally, and with Tamsin near me. The best day ever."

Lennox led Meg over to her horse, and it wasn't until he lifted her on his mount that she was able to look about them, a semicircle of small ponies with Tora, Rowan, Sylvi, Alana, and Lia leading the processional behind Logan and Magni, who reminded everyone at least five times, "I'm first!" Then Logan arched a brow at him and Magni grinned. "We're first."

They led the group across the courtyard, through the gates, and onto the nearby meadow where the guests waited, seas of different plaids brightening the area. Once they made it to the priest, Lennox helped Meg down and held her hand.

"Not so tight, Lennox."

"Sorry. I just wanted to make sure you were not going to slip away. You have that habit, lass."

"Never. I'll be by your side forever."

Lennox wiped a tear from his eye.

## Chapter Forty-Four

*Lennox*

---

LENNOX LAY BESIDE his wife in the middle of the night, taking in her long lashes, the few freckles on her nose, her slender fingers wrapped in his hand.

Hell, but he'd never expected this.

She opened her eyes, a heavy-lidded gaze, and smiled. "What are you thinking?"

He played with her fingers, shaking his head. "That I never thought it possible."

She frowned, arching a brow at him.

"I never thought it possible to love someone as much, as thoroughly, as I love you. I want you by my side when I awaken in the morning, and in the same spot next to me at night. You took me by surprise, as subtle as a bolt of lightning in a night sky. And it's not just for the sexual parts either. I love discussing things with you because you give me insight I've never had before." He leaned over and kissed her lips as tenderly as he could. "I am forever grateful that you have accepted me as your husband."

"And I am excited to see what our life together will bring us, Lennox. I look forward to every day we have together. I pray we are blessed with many bairns and much happiness."

He heard an odd sound, and Meg lifted her head as though she'd heard it too. "What is it, Lennox?"

"It's my mother. She climbs up to the parapets on many nights. She thinks my father can hear her when she's closer to heaven."

"Go talk with her. Make sure she doesn't fall on those steps."

Lennox said, "She's done it enough times that I'm sure she won't fall."

"But go speak with her. She probably missed your father more today than any other day."

"You don't mind?"

"Nay. I'll close my eyes for a bit. You did wear me out, husband."

"Um, I think you wore me out, Meg." He gave her bottom a soft caress before getting out of bed and donning his plaid, folding it quickly. "I won't be long."

He headed down the passageway and up the stairs to the parapets, opening the door to find his mother seated on her stool. "Mama, you are hale?"

"More than hale, Lennox. It was a lovely day, a lovely ceremony, and you have a beautiful bride. You chose well."

"I did. I needed to find her on my own."

"You probably wouldn't have found her if I hadn't given you that nudge."

Lennox rolled his eyes. He knew the nudge had nothing to do with his finding Meg, but if she wished to think so, he'd allow it. "Anytime I find a lass protecting four bairns with an axe over her head, she'd have my attention, Mother."

"Oh, I suppose you are right. I am just pleased it has finally happened."

"Were you talking with Da?"

She gave him an exasperated look. "You know I do."

"But you don't need his help for me anymore, do you?"

"Of course not."

"Then what brings you here?"

His mother tipped her head back, crossed her arms, and looked at the stars overhead. "I was just discussing my next endeavor."

"Your next endeavor? Or should I ask *who* your next endeavor is?"

"I've just made up my mind. Taskill isn't done with his flirting yet. It's your sister. I have to find a husband for Eva."

"Good for you." He leaned over and kissed his mother's cheek. "Then I'll leave you to discuss it with Da."

Lennox couldn't wait to tell his sister about that statement.

Or perhaps he wouldn't tell her at all.

# EPILOGUE

*End of summer, a few weeks later*

A LOUD CHEER ERUPTED as soon as Maitland and Maeve made their way off the boat, followed by applause that put a smile on both of their faces. The day was still warm, though the cool breeze let them know that autumn was near. Maitland wore a tight plaid wrapped around him, a wee bald head peeking out of the top that he kept his hand on quite often.

Dyna and Derric led the row of horses to Duart Castle, not a sound from the wee laddie wrapped up tight against his father's broad chest. Dyna said, "I cannot wait to hold him, Derric. I haven't held a wee bairn in a while. It's so exciting to have a newly born babe with us. Eli!" she shouted to the rider behind her. "Your turn next."

Eli let out an unladylike snort. "Spit and slime, not likely!"

Once back at the castle, the group crowded into the great hall, with everyone anxious to get their first peek at Maitland and Maeve's son. They'd married late in life and were so excited with this bairn, probably their only child.

The hall filled with clan members and visitors while Grant and Menzie guards surrounded the castle, chaos reigning with the chatter of voices, giggling children running about, and two proud parents, neither one allowing their gazes to travel away from their son for long. Once everyone was inside, Maitland let out a whistle. His son, still strapped to his chest, now faced everyone, his wide eyes taking in everything with a fist in his mouth. Just over two moons old, he was as happy as any baby Dyna had ever seen.

But she knew this baby was special. She'd seen it in her dreams, told her husband, and felt it to her bones. Decades ago, a woman had come to her in her dreams and told her she was to be the protector of her grandfather, Alexander Grant. The day he'd passed on, he visited her early and thanked her for watching over him.

He'd known all along.

She'd been informed a while ago by the same woman that she had a new assignment, the newborn son of Maitland and Maeve.

"What's his name?" Connor asked. "Before we can go home, Sela and I have to know."

Maitland moved to the dais with their son, Maeve holding one hand and looking as proud and happy as ever.

"Name! We need a name," Alasdair said, waving his hands to everyone to shush them. "Come on, Chief. Tell us."

The group began to chant, "Name, name, name, name...!"

Maitland waited until everyone quieted, and Maeve leaned against him, wiping the happy tears from her face. "Do you wish to tell them, Maeve?"

His wife had always been shy, and things hadn't changed. She shook her head and said, "You. Your voice is stronger. You tell them." Since she was an adopted daughter of Alex and Maddie Grant, she'd always been more reserved and lived at home until she'd married Maitland almost a year ago.

"Everyone, meet our son, Alexander Drew Menzie Grantham."

Dyna whispered, "Alexander Grantham. Oh my. Another one."

Her father moved over next to her and asked, "What do you think?"

"I love it. It's perfect." How she hoped Grandsire was listening. Surely, he was.

"I can't wait to tell everyone when we go home," her father whispered.

Tora ran over and tugged on her grandfather's plaid. "Uppie, Gwandpapa."

Dyna's father lifted Tora up and tossed her into the air twice, a fit of giggles bubbling from her belly. "Now what is it you wish to tell me before we go?"

Tora placed her hand on his cheek and brought her face close, looking at her mother and then back at her grandfather. Then she whispered, "You canna go home, Gwandpapa. Don't tell."

She started to shove against her grandfather's chest to get down, but her mother stopped her. "Why can't he go, Tora?"

Tora pointed to the baby. "Don't tell Maitland."

---

It was nearly the end of the day and Magni was tired. The hall was full of good cheer and happiness. They'd come with Thane and Tamsin to welcome Maitland back and to meet his wife and son. There had been laughter and food and storytelling all day, but Magni was exhausted.

Where was his sister?

He looked around for Lia but couldn't find her anywhere. He began to panic, but then glanced around the hall full of chieftains and warriors. No one would have dared to come in here to steal her away. Logan Ramsay was near the hearth and the giant Connor Grant was seated not far away, Sandor bouncing on his knee. Alasdair and Alick guarded the door and no one would dare argue with those two big brutes.

Nay, Lia was here somewhere. He'd noticed how much she'd enjoyed the new bairn, but he had gone into the tower with his mother. Magni snuck over to the door of the tower and peeked inside. Sure enough, Lia sat in a chair next to the basket the wee bairn slept in.

He tiptoed in because Maeve was sound asleep on the bed, a blanket wrapped over her. He crept next to Lia and said, "Come, Lia. I think we're leaving."

Lia shook her head.

"Aye, Thane said we were leaving soon."

Lia waved him close, then reached for Magni's hand and said, "I know you won't like my answer, Magni, but please remember that I love you dearly." She let out a deep sigh and said, "My place is here for a while."

"At Duart Castle?"

"Aye and nay. Not necessarily."

He tipped his head because he didn't understand her answer. He would argue with her, but he didn't wish to awaken the lady or the babe. "Where, then?"

"By Alexander's side. It's where I belong for now. Thane needs you at home, but I'll stay here to help with the wee one for a short while. Think of me as Lady Maeve's helper. I'm Alexander's nanny."

"But you're only five, Lia." He scratched his head, still trying to understand. "You cannot be a nanny." He knew Lia was special, but watching over a wee bairn seemed more than a wee lass could handle. Even a faery lass.

"But I'm six summers now, Magni." She patted his shoulder and said, "Come visit me in a sennight. I'll be right here."

---

Down in the tavern in Craignure, not far from the ferry, sat two unsavory characters, both chugging down as much ale as they could. They'd received a new assignment, but they had to wait a few more days yet.

"So, those are the ones?"

"Aye. They're here. We just have to wait for final instructions. They'll tell us exactly when and how."

"The bairn and the golden-haired one, true?"

"Aye. And the mother too."

He grinned and said, "And then we're off to Kilchoan."

---

Connor paced at the water's edge beneath Duart Castle after everyone had gone home, the moonlight reflecting off the water. "I don't like this one bit, Logan. I wanted to go home, but I can't ignore my granddaughter. What the hell did she mean telling me I can't go?"

Logan crossed his arms and said, "Quit your pacing, Grant. We'll handle it."

"But if anything happens to that lad, Maitland and Maeve…it will kill them both. We have to protect them."

"And we will. Look, we know what the job is. We can handle it. Stop fretting so. Just because he's your sire's namesake doesn't mean this is going to be anything unusual or something we can't handle."

"Nay?" Connor asked, his fists on his hips. "Then tell me why that odd golden-haired lass of only six summers refuses to leave that baby's side? That unsettles me more than Tora."

"Grant, she's a faery, I tell you, and she's protecting the lad. That comforts me a bit. It should comfort you too. She'll turn anyone who bothers him into stone or ash or something."

Connor sighed and looked up at the moon. "I told Sela we couldn't leave yet, but I didn't tell her why."

"Gwynie knows. She senses it in Dyna too. She gave me my orders."

Connor grinned. "And what are your orders?"

"My wife told me I couldn't leave that bairn's side. That if anything happened to that lad, I'd have to drag her across God's land to find the fool who stole him away so she could be the one to put a dagger in the bastard's heart. Or mayhap she said bollocks. I forget."

"Sounds like neither of us is leaving, Ramsay."

Logan pointed to the sky. "Did you see that?"

Connor tipped his head back. "Aye. Two of them."

"Two shooting stars. I've never seen that in my lifetime."

"Me neither. What the hell does it mean?"

"I have an odd feeling…"

"Dyna used to tell me it was Grandmama talking with Grandsire whenever she saw a shooting star."

"Ohhh…" Logan trailed off. "That's both of them. Alex and Maddie are talking to you."

"Saying what?"

Logan shivered. "That you're staying."

*THE END*

*http://www.keiramontclair.com*

DEAR READER,
Thanks for reading Book 2 in the Clans of Mull, a five book series planned at present.

Next up in the third book will be Eva MacVey and Sloan Rankin. I can't wait!

Happy reading,

*Keira Montclair*
*http://www.keiramontclair.com*

# NOVELS BY KEIRA MONTCLAIR

## **CLANS OF MULL**
THE PLIGHT OF A SCOTTISH LASS
THE BURDEN OF A SCOTTISH CHIEFTAIN

## **HIGHLAND HUNTERS**
THE SCOT'S CONFLICT
THE SCOT'S TRAITOR
THE SCOT'S PROTECTOR
THE SCOT'S VOW
THE SCOT'S DESTINY
THE SCOT'S WARNING
THE SCOT'S RECKONING
THE SCOT'S LEGACY

## **HIGHLAND SWORDS**
THE SCOT'S BETRAYAL
THE SCOT'S SPY
THE SCOT'S PURSUIT
THE SCOT'S QUEST
THE SCOT'S DECEPTION
THE SCOT'S ANGEL

## **HIGHLAND HEALERS**
THE CURSE OF BLACK ISLE
THE WITCH OF BLACK ISLE
THE SCOURGE OF BLACK ISLE

THE GHOSTS OF BLACK ISLE
THE GIFT OF BLACK ISLE

**THE BAND OF COUSINS**
HIGHLAND VENGEANCE
HIGHLAND ABDUCTION
HIGHLAND RETRIBUTION
HIGHLAND LIES
HIGHLAND FORTITUDE
HIGHLAND RESILIENCE
HIGHLAND DEVOTION
HIGHLAND BRAWN
HIGHLAND YULETIDE MAGIC

**THE HIGHLAND CLAN**
LOKI-Book One
TORRIAN-Book Two
LILY-Book Three
JAKE-Book Four
ASHLYN-Book Five
MOLLY-Book Six
JAMIE AND GRACIE-Book Seven
SORCHA-Book Eight
KYLA-Book Nine
BETHIA-Book Ten
LOKI'S CHRISTMAS STORY-Book Eleven
ELIZABETH-Book Twelve

**THE CLAN GRANT SERIES**
#1- RESCUED BY A HIGHLANDER-
Alex and Maddie
#2- HEALING A HIGHLANDER'S HEART-
Brenna and Quade

#3- LOVE LETTERS FROM LARGS-
Brodie and Celestina
#4-JOURNEY TO THE HIGHLANDS-
Robbie and Caralyn
#5-HIGHLAND SPARKS-
Logan and Gwyneth
#6-MY DESPERATE HIGHLANDER-
Micheil and Diana
#7-THE BRIGHTEST STAR IN THE HIGHLANDS-
Jennie and Aedan
#8- HIGHLAND HARMONY-
Avelina and Drew
#9-YULETIDE ANGELS

## **THE SOULMATE CHRONICLES TRILOGY**
#1 TRUSTING A HIGHLANDER
#2 TRUSTING A SCOT
#3 TRUSTING A CHIEFTAIN

## **STAND-ALONE BOOKS**
ESCAPE TO THE HIGHLANDS
THE BANISHED HIGHLANDER
REFORMING THE DUKE-REGENCY
WOLF AND THE WILD SCOTS
FALLING FOR THE CHIEFTAIN-
3RD in a collaborative trilogy
HIGHLAND SECRETS -
3rd in a collaborative trilogy

## THE SUMMERHILL SERIES- CONTEMPORARY ROMANCE
#1-ONE SUMMERHILL DAY
#2-A FRESH START FOR TWO
#3-THREE REASONS TO LOVE

# ABOUT THE AUTHOR

KEIRA MONTCLAIR IS the pen name of an author who lives in South Carolina with her husband. She loves to write fast-paced, emotional romance, especially with children as secondary characters.

When she's not writing, she loves to spend time with her grandchildren. She's worked as a high school math teacher, a registered nurse, and an office manager. She loves ballet, mathematics, puzzles, learning anything new, and creating new characters for her readers to fall in love with.

She writes historical romantic suspense. Her best-selling series is a family saga that follows two medieval Scottish clans through four generations and now numbers over thirty books.

Contact her through her website:
keiramontclair.com.

Made in the USA
Columbia, SC
08 July 2025